JUSTICE IS SERVED

JUSTICE IS SERVED

Linda Sole

This first world edition published in Great Britain 2007 by
SEVERN HOUSE PUBLISHERS LTD of
9–15 High Street, Sutton, Surrey SM1 1DF.
This first world edition published in the USA 2008 by
SEVERN HOUSE PUBLISHERS INC of
595 Madison Avenue, New York, N.Y. 10022.
This first trade paperback edition published 2008 by
SEVERN HOUSE PUBLISHERS, London and New York.

British Library Cataloguing in Publication Data

Sole, Linda
  Justice is served
  1. Murder - Investigation - Fiction 2. Detective and
  mystery stories
  I. Title
  823.9'14[F]

  ISBN-13: 978-0-7278-6551-9   (cased)

All Severn House titles are printed on acid-free paper.

Typeset by Palimpsest Book Production Ltd.,
Grangemouth, Stirlingshire, Scotland.
Printed and bound in Great Britain by
MPG Books Ltd., Bodmin, Cornwall.

One

'That is ridiculous,' Miranda said into the mouthpiece of the telephone. She was standing in the small back parlour of her home in Mayfair, looking out at the garden, a shocked expression on her lovely face. Newly married to Lord Peter Bellingham, she was an acknowledged beauty and fast becoming one of the most admired women in all the best drawing rooms of London. 'I can't possibly raise that kind of money – and why should I?'

'Because otherwise your husband will receive a very interesting package through the post,' the male voice replied at the other end of the line. 'You haven't always behaved yourself, Miranda darling, and I have the photographs to prove it.'

'You wouldn't . . .' Miranda inhaled sharply, because the fear had lingered at the back of her mind, even though she had been promised faithfully that it would not happen. 'You can't have . . . they were destroyed. Giles swore to me that he had burned them.'

'He lied,' the voice said, menacing and sinister. 'Giles was always a liar, you knew that surely?'

'Yes but . . .' Miranda shuddered as she thought of what would happen if this man carried out his threat. 'Who are you – and why did Giles give the pictures to you?'

'He owed me and it was his way of paying a debt. I want five thousand by the end of the month. If I don't get it, your husband is going to discover that you're not quite what he thought you.'

'I told you, I don't have that sort of money.'

'The emeralds you were wearing at that charity bash the other night must be worth double or treble that.'

'But they are family heirlooms. I couldn't possibly—'

'Then find it some other way,' the harsh voice said. 'I shall be in touch again soon. If you don't want your husband to know the truth, find that money!'

Miranda hung up when the line went dead. She looked at her reflection in the mirror. Her hair was a silver blonde, her eyes deep violet-blue, her complexion a soft cream that owed nothing to Elizabeth Arden's preparations, though she did wear one of the latest shades of lipstick. Her figure was the perfect hourglass that many women aspired to, and she made the most of it by wearing haute couture gowns whenever possible. This particular morning she was wearing the skirt of a tailored suit by Beer, a crisp white blouse with a mandarin collar and her long pearls. Her shoes were black patent leather with an ankle strap and a sensible heel, because she had intended to go shopping in her favourite stores today. She visited either Harrods or Fortnum & Mason at least twice or three times a week, though most of her clothes were made for her, as were her shoes.

She looked what she was, the spoiled and pampered darling of an older man. Pouting at her own reflection, Miranda wrestled with the problem of finding what was for her the huge sum of £5,000. It was nothing to Peter, of course, but although generous with her allowance, he wouldn't just hand her a cheque for £5,000 without wanting to know what the money was for. He had settled £10,000 on her when they married, but it was tied up in bonds that gave her an extra income of her own, on top of the allowance Peter made her each quarter for her personal expenditure. Had she been less extravagant she might have had a few hundred pounds in her account that she could offer her blackmailer, but she had barely £50 and would have to run up bills until the end of the quarter.

Miranda was thoughtful as she went upstairs. Her jewels were kept in a safe in her bedroom, and she was mentally reviewing them and their likely value if she were to sell or offer them in settlement. The emeralds were out of the question, of course. Peter liked to see her wearing them and would ask if she didn't at least once a week. There was the diamond choker he had given her for her birthday just last month; that must be worth at least as much as the emeralds, but the same thing applied, as it did to almost all of her jewellery. Her husband had given most of it to her, and he would ask if she didn't wear something he liked.

She fingered the pearls, for they were the one thing of any

real value that Peter hadn't given her. They had been an eighteenth birthday present from her godmother. Amelia Beaufort had been extremely generous and Miranda hated to part with them, but apart from a brooch Giles had once given her when he was in funds, and a couple of rings that had been her mother's, there was nothing else. She knew that combined they would not bring in a fifth of what the menacing voice had demanded on her telephone.

'Damn him!' Miranda muttered, her pretty face dark with anger. 'And damn you, Giles! I'll get even with you for this, just see if I don't . . .'

She took off the pearls, touching them reverently as she laid them in their velvet box. It might be a good idea not to wear them so often, because Peter would notice if she suddenly stopped. She would put them away for the moment and if she were driven to it, she would take them to a discreet jeweller in Bond Street and ask for a valuation, casually asking what they might be worth if she wished to sell. She could say that they did not suit her and that she was thinking of buying something more modern, though in actual fact she liked them far more than the emeralds or the diamonds. However, she had little choice, because although Amelia might be offended if she didn't wear them when they met – which they would in few weeks, when they were staying together in the south of France – Miranda could always say the clasp needed mending.

It would be a sacrifice to part with them, but she couldn't think what else to do. Giles Henderson had given intimate photographs of her to a man she had never met, though over the past few days his voice had become oddly familiar. He had phoned her three times now, gradually working up to today's threat. If she knew who he was . . . wild thoughts of murder flitted through her mind. She was frowning as she went to the safe and took out several jewellery boxes, opening one to look at the emeralds. She just did not dare to sell them, because Peter would be furious if he found out. It seemed that she was trapped, though she wasn't going to sell the pearls just yet. She would have them valued, and then she would think about what to do next.

First of all, she was going to speak to Giles. If he would tell her who had the photographs, she might be able to think of a way to get them back. And if she couldn't . . . Miranda's red lips settled into a thin line. She wasn't the kind to roll over and play dead easily. Whoever this man was, he must have seen her at the charity affair she had attended recently; otherwise he would not have known that she was wearing the emeralds. She knew that photographers had been banned from the prestigious affair, and she was sure that her blackmailer must be someone who knew her. She might not have noticed him, but he was probably a hanger-on, someone who envied Miranda her lifestyle.

If she could just discover who he was . . . her thoughts were interrupted by her husband's voice calling her. He came into the room a moment later, just as she was putting her jewels away.

'Peter,' she said, smiling and going to kiss him on the cheek. He was nearly twenty years her senior, a little heavier than was strictly good for him, though still an attractive man. She knew that everyone thought she had married him for his money, which wasn't quite true. The money had drawn her to him in the first place, but then, to her own surprise, she had fallen in love with him. 'You are home early, darling. I was just about to go shopping.'

'Then I think I shall come with you,' he said and kissed her cheek. 'We've been married for nearly six months. It's time I gave you a little present.'

'You are so generous,' Miranda told him. She was tempted to ask for the £5,000 she needed, but it was too difficult to explain why she needed the money. 'But you don't have to keep giving me presents, darling. I love you.'

'I know you do,' he said, 'but that's one of the reasons I like to spoil you.'

Miranda felt a little trickle of ice at the nape of her neck. Supposing she couldn't find a way to get those photographs back? She would do anything rather than let Peter know that she had had a torrid affair with Giles Henderson. It would be so embarrassing for him to see those pictures of her. She had to discover who had them and get them back somehow!

She decided that she would telephone Giles the first opportunity she got.

*   *   *

'But, Miranda darling, you know I destroyed the negatives. You saw me do it,' Giles drawled, as he looked at his reflection in the mirror above the half-moon table that stood in his hallway. The table was early Sheraton and quite valuable, as were many of the things he had collected about him, but he had chosen it for its style. 'Why do you ask?'

He glanced at his shirt cuffs, admiring the pearl and gold cufflinks a certain grateful lady had recently given him. Older women were so much easier to satisfy, he always found, and less expensive than the beautiful variety, though there was a certain young woman he was pursuing at the moment. He smiled as he thought about her. Sarah Beaufort was refusing to cave in to his charm and that always brought out the hunter in him.

'What happened to the prints you made?'

Giles frowned as it got through to him that Miranda was very angry. He knew that he hadn't destroyed the prints, because he had anticipated that he might have a use for them one day. They were, he was quite sure, in the top drawer of his Georgian bureau.

'I am not sure,' he prevaricated. 'Why? Wherever they are, they are quite safe.'

'I'm being blackmailed,' Miranda snapped. 'Whoever he is, he says that you gave him the photographs to settle a debt. Tell me the truth, Giles – did you give them to one of your friends?'

'I promise you I didn't,' Giles said. 'Hold the line for a moment while I check if they are in the bureau.'

Giles laid the receiver down on the surface of his precious table and went through to the sitting room. He was thoughtful as he opened the top drawer. He had kept the prints for his own pleasure and for personal insurance, because Miranda knew things about him that he wouldn't want everyone to know. However, he would never have given them to someone who might use them to blackmail her. Why should he give away what might be useful to him?

Pulling the top drawer open, he glanced inside, expecting to see the small black folder into which he had placed the revealing photographs. A brief search told him that they were not there, and he frowned. He was fairly sure that he hadn't moved them, because he liked to keep things just so. He checked the next drawer and then left it open as he returned to the telephone.

'I can't find them at this moment,' he said. 'I thought I knew where they were, but I seem to have misplaced them.'

'If you're lying to me, Giles . . .'

'I promise you I'm not, my sweet,' Giles said hastily. 'I'll have a proper look for them and ring you back.'

'Just remember that I know things about you too, Giles!' Miranda said sharply. 'I want those photographs back so that I can destroy them myself.'

'I'll find them,' Giles soothed. 'Don't worry, darling, I am sure they can't have gone far.'

He was angry as he hung up, because he knew that he would be foolish to ignore Miranda's threats. She was a kitten with very sharp claws and she wouldn't hesitate to use them. He would have to find the damned things and give them to her.

He searched the second drawer to no effect, going through the third and fourth in quick succession. Where had they got to? Giles cursed several times as he tried to imagine where he might have put them.

He hadn't moved them. He was quite certain that they had been in the top drawer only a couple of weeks previously, which meant that someone must have taken them. Frowning, he made a mental review of his visitors over the past week or so.

'Damn him!' Giles muttered, suddenly realizing who must have taken the photographs. His expression hardened, because he'd suspected that someone had been through his things once before. He'd lost a silver cigarette case that he had been particularly fond of that time, but he'd told himself that he must have left it somewhere.

And then there was that other business. He was pretty sure he knew something about these jewel thefts that were going on all over the place. He had suspected it for a while, but if he went to the police it could reflect poorly on someone he cared for – however, this had gone beyond a joke.

Giles was thoughtful as he lifted the lid of an enamelled cigarette box, which he had bought from Asprey's when he was in funds. Using his gold lighter, he lit an Egyptian cigarette, inhaling deeply as he considered what to do next.

The photographs had obviously been stolen and Giles was pretty certain he knew who had them now, unlikely as it seemed, for the man was not someone he would have imagined to be a petty thief – or a blackmailer.

He might be able to retrieve them. He would make damned sure he did! His mouth settled into a grim line. They were his property and he wanted them back! However, he hadn't yet made up his mind what he would do with the photographs when he had them in his possession once more.

Miranda was angry and making threats, but Giles was feeling the pinch just now, because of a few unlucky bets at Newmarket. If he could get Miranda to pay him something for helping her, it would make things easier. He wouldn't be greedy: a couple of hundred would see him through for a while. Besides, someone else might pay more to keep his nasty little secret.

Giles smiled as he drew on his cigarette and blew a little smoke ring. Miranda hadn't mentioned how much had been demanded for the pictures, but he wouldn't make the mistake of asking too much. He would prefer that she remained his friend, because you never knew when you might need a friend.

First of all, he needed to get his property back. He was thoughtful as he went back into the hall and picked up the telephone. He would arrange a meeting for that afternoon. It had to be the afternoon, because he was planning to visit the theatre that evening. He hadn't missed one of Sarah's shows since he'd first seen her on the stage.

Sarah Beaufort read the postcard for a second time, smiling as she pictured her friend in Venice. Larch had been sending her messages every few weeks, just a few words scribbled on the back of a card, giving her news of his travels and his work. It seemed that he was painting far more than ever before and relishing the experience. His enthusiasm for travelling showed no sign of abating and he hadn't said a word about when he was coming home.

She gave a little sigh as she tucked the card into a corner of her dressing mirror. She missed Larch and she would find it strange without him if she went down to her grandmother's home in Beecham Thorny once the show ended. It had been great fun appearing on stage in London and she had really enjoyed herself, making a lot of new friends and gathering some admirers. She had only a small spot in the show, singing two solo numbers, but she was in the front row of the chorus now instead of the back. She supposed that she was making progress slowly. However, the show was closing after a successful run of six months, and so far she hadn't found anything else.

There was an advert for an audition for a summer show that she had cut out and left on her dressing table. She hunted for it amongst the clutter of bottles and trinkets that she needed for her stage make-up, finding it at last under a pot of vanishing cream. She was just deciding whether or not she wanted to try for another seaside show when the door of her dressing room opened and her friend Janey entered.

Janey was blonde, pretty and bubbly, a wonderful dancer who deserved more than the chorus work she had been given. She and Sarah had become good friends these past weeks, sharing their lodgings and their food to make the pitifully small wages they both received go a little further.

'I'm glad you're still here,' Janey said and grinned as she saw that there was another card tucked into the mahogany frame of Sarah's mirror. 'Has he written again? Where from this time?'

'Venice,' Sarah said and nodded as her friend looked at the card. 'You can read it if you like. It doesn't say anything that half the postmen in London haven't already read.'

Janey laughed and picked out the new card, turning it over to read what Larch Meadows had to say. She had thought it an awfully odd name at first, but Sarah said that it suited him, and when she'd seen a picture of Sarah's friend, she had agreed.

'He sounds like a lovely feller,' Janey said and grinned at her. 'Why don't you marry him and give up this lark?'

'Two reasons,' Sarah said with a husky chuckle. 'Firstly, Larch hasn't asked me, and secondly I'm enjoying myself at the moment. I want to make a success of this, prove that it wasn't just a foolish whim.'

'To your father?' Janey asked, understanding Sarah's feelings. Her own family had raised objections to her becoming a dancer and she knew that Mr Beaufort had been so against his daughter singing on stage that he had stopped her allowance. He had regretted it later and offered to make things right, but Sarah had refused his money. She had spent two days with him at Christmas, and Janey knew that things were sort of all right between them, though Sarah was determined to show him she could make her own way in life.

'Yes, I suppose so,' Sarah said in answer to her friend's question, 'but for my own satisfaction as well. Besides, Larch said he needed to get away somewhere to paint, because he felt his experience was too limited. He wasn't ready to hold an exhibition of his work, though I know there was quite a bit of interest.'

'He sounds smashing,' Janey said, because she thought his picture was dreamy and wished she were his friend. Those eyes! Just looking at him sent Janey into a spin. 'How long have you known him?'

'Oh, years,' Sarah replied. 'My grandmother and his parents know each other well. We were friends before the war, but when he came back he was different. I hardly saw him for ages, until last autumn . . .'

Sarah's thoughts drifted away. She and Larch might possibly have got together the previous year had it not been for those awful murders at Beecham Thorny. Sarah had been the one who discovered most of the clues, which led to the eventual arrest of the murderer. Then Larch had tried to shut her out of things, because he thought that it was getting too dangerous. When she'd gone off on her own and discovered the missing link, Larch had been angry. They had quarrelled and though they'd made it up later, Sarah believed the rift between them had helped Larch make his decision to go off on a painting tour.

'I wonder if he will be here this evening?'

Janey's voice broke into Sarah's thoughts. She frowned as she looked at her. 'Larch? Oh no, I am sure he is still abroad. He hasn't said anything about coming home – as far as I know, anyway.'

'I meant your admirer – Giles Henderson.'

'Oh, him,' Sarah said and pulled a face. 'No, I should think he has given up since I told him I wouldn't go to dinner with him last week. He hasn't been for the last three nights.'

'You've broken his heart,' Janey teased and laughed, because she thought it was unlikely. Giles Henderson was known to quite a few of the girls who worked in the theatre. Well dressed and attractive, with dark hair and blue eyes, he was not quite a gentleman, though he had attended Eton and his father had been an officer in the Guards. Giles, however, was a playboy and a gambler, sometimes splashing his money about as if he had come into a fortune, at other times stony broke and not above cadging a few pounds from one of the girls he took out. He was said to have broken a few hearts, but most of the girls liked him, because he could be fun and was always free with his money when he had some. Giles Henderson was one of those men it was fun to know, but foolish to love.

'I am sure I haven't,' Sarah responded immediately. 'I am glad he has decided to stop coming to the show. It made me uncomfortable knowing that he was out there watching me night after night.'

'He sent you some lovely flowers,' Janey reminded her. 'I wouldn't mind having an admirer like that, Sarah.'·

'You are welcome to him.' Sarah arched her brows. 'Just be careful. I wouldn't trust him, Janey.'

'Oh no, I wouldn't either,' her friend murmured wickedly. 'But I could just eat a gorgeous dinner at the Ritz. It would make a change from cheese on toast and cocoa.'

Sarah laughed at Janey's expression. If anything, Janey earned even less than she did, and unlike Sarah, she was always hungry.

'What are you going to do when the show ends?' Sarah asked. 'I'm not sure whether to audition for a seaside show or wait and see what else turns up.'

'Most of the places for dancers will be filled by now,' Janey said. 'I did an audition last month and they offered me a place in a revue at Blackpool, but I wasn't able to take it, because I thought we might run a bit longer.'

'I never expected the show to last this long,' Sarah told her. 'I've been invited to stay with—' She broke off as the door opened and another girl came in.

'Have you heard the news?' Esther asked. Like Janey, she was one of the hard-working, underpaid dancers. 'Everyone is talking about it – it is so horrible.'

'We haven't heard,' Janey said. 'Unless you mean the show closing in two weeks' time?'

'No, though that's bad enough,' Esther replied with a gloomy look. 'It's about Sarah's admirer – the one who came every night to watch her.'

'Do you mean Giles Henderson?' Sarah asked. She had an icy feeling at the nape of her neck, similar to something she'd felt the previous autumn when Morna Scaffrey had been strangled in Thorny Woods.

'Yes,' Esther said, sounding uncertain now. 'I hope you didn't like him too much, Sarah, only he has been murdered. Someone shot him in the head about three days ago – in his own flat they say . . .'

'Giles is dead?' Janey looked shocked, her face turning pale. 'That is so awful. Who would do such a thing? I can't believe it.'

'Do the police have any clues?' Sarah asked. 'I suppose a man like that has probably made enemies . . .' The other girls stared at her, clearly surprised that she had taken the news so calmly. 'Well, you have to think about these things. Ben says that most murderers are known to their victims.'

'Who is Ben?' Janey asked, staring at her.

'A friend of Larch's father,' Sarah said. 'He used to be an inspector at Scotland Yard, but he retired. I met him last year when he came down to help investigate several murders at Beecham Thorny.'

'You haven't told me any of this,' Janey said, a faint hint of accusation in her voice.

'I didn't particularly want to talk about it,' Sarah said and a little shudder ran through her, because it was only good luck that had kept her from becoming one of the victims. 'I was attacked twice myself and it was all rather unpleasant.'

'Oh, Sarah, how awful for you!'

Sarah shook her head. 'It's over now. The murderer is being confined in a secure hospital for the time being. She went into a catatonic state after they arrested her and Ben says that she will probably never stand trial.'

'Poor you,' Esther said. 'Now your admirer is dead – that's spooky. It's as if you're cursed or something . . .'

'Of course she isn't!' Janey cried, defending her friend fiercely.

'I don't think what happened to Giles Henderson has anything to do with me or the murders at Beecham Thorny,' Sarah said with a wry look. 'But it certainly isn't pleasant.'

'Someone said that the police may want to interview some of us,' Esther said. 'One or two of the girls had been out with him – but everyone knew it was you he really wanted.'

'It was a good thing that you didn't go out with him,' Janey said, looking at her friend. 'You might have been involved . . .'

'Perhaps,' Sarah said, 'but as it is, I hardly knew him . . . though I know someone who did . . .' She shook her head as the girls looked at her, because she rather thought she ought to keep what she knew to herself. 'Oh, nothing . . . I'm sorry for Giles. I didn't dislike him and he didn't deserve to be murdered. I just wasn't prepared to be another notch on his bedpost.'

'Sarah!' The other girls went into fits of laughter. 'The things you do say!'

Sarah smiled and stood up. 'I'm going home. I'm tired and I want a nice, long, hot bath.'

'Is something the matter?' Lady Meadows asked as she looked at her husband across the dining table that evening. 'You're very quiet, William.'

'Yes, my dear. I am sorry. There is something on my mind as it happens.'

'Do you want to talk about it?'

'Jack Henderson was on the phone earlier,' Sir William said and frowned. 'I told you about Giles, didn't I?' Lady Meadows shuddered and he nodded his agreement. 'Yes, bad business. I think he was a bit of a rogue by all accounts, but a likeable one. His father is devastated. He isn't happy with the police, because he thinks they are dragging their feet over this business. They seem to think it was a burglary gone wrong . . .'

'And Major Henderson doesn't?'

'No, not really. He went up to town as soon as he was informed, of course. Apparently, the flat had been ransacked but hardly anything was missing that he could see – just a rather nice enamelled cigarette box and some pieces of gold jewellery. He thought that strange, because there are some good antiques there, small pieces that any thief who knew their business would not be so careless as to leave behind . . .'

'Unless they were disturbed, perhaps?' Lady Meadows said and frowned. 'It does sound as if it might simply be a burglary gone wrong. Perhaps Giles surprised the thief and he shot him in a mad moment?'

'But why take a gun there if there was no intention to use it?'

'I don't know. I suppose it couldn't have been Giles's own gun?'

'You mean he discovered the thief and pulled a gun on him – and they struggled . . .' Sir William.frowned. 'That is always a possibility, of course. I don't have any idea what really happened. The police haven't released many details as yet, other than that he was shot three times . . .'

'It sounds as if whoever shot him was frightened.'

'Or angry,' Sir William said. 'Anyway, Jack Henderson asked me if I knew anyone who would investigate in a private capacity. Well of course I had to give him Ben's name – though I'm not sure he will thank me for it. I thought last year when he solved our little murders that he might have considered applying for a licence to take up the business for himself . . .'

'Become a private detective?' Lady Meadows wrinkled her nose. 'That's all to do with following people to gather proof about affairs and things, isn't it? I can't see Ben Marshall wanting to do something like that – can you?'

'No, perhaps not,' Sir William said. 'Not much of a job really, is it? It is a pity he retired when he did in my book. I am sure he must be bored sitting around all day with nothing much to do.'

'Yes, well, perhaps you are right,' Lady Meadows said. 'Though I believe he is quite interested in those prize cats of his.'

'He can always turn Jack down,' Sir William said. 'I suppose I had better give him a call, just to tell him what to expect.'

'Haven't you done that already?' his wife exclaimed. 'I think you should do it straight away, William. You really ought to have asked first, before you gave his name to Major Henderson.'

'I know, but Jack was in such a state . . .' Sir William

gave her an apologetic look. 'I think I had better do it right now . . .'

'Yes, my dear. I rather think you had,' his wife said. 'And then you had better get ready. We are supposed to be going out later this evening.'

Two

'She didn't deserve to win,' Ben Marshall said to his wife as he stopped the car in their front drive. 'I'm telling you, Cathy, that cat wasn't a patch on Bella. The head wasn't as it should be and one of her back legs was crooked.'

'I'm sure it couldn't have been,' Cathy Marshall said, smothering a sigh. 'I agree that Bella ought to have won, but that's the way it is . . . sometimes the best cat is overlooked.'

'It was because she is who she is,' Ben said, still feeling aggrieved as he reached into the back of his car. He carefully lifted out the cages in which two of his best Siamese cats were happily snoozing on soft blankets, impervious to the fact that they had won only the silver medals, when they ought by rights to have won the gold. 'The judge probably thought she wouldn't be invited to Lady Avery's next society bash if she gave her the silver – but I saw the look in her eyes and I know she thought Bella was the best cat in show.'

Cathy sighed deeply. It had been a long drive and Ben hadn't stopped complaining about the unfairness of the competitions in the cat world the whole journey. He was convinced that it was a hotbed of corruption and avarice and she was a little tired of hearing the same thing over and over again. It was a relief to hear the telephone ringing as she went into her house.

'Hello,' she said. 'Cathy Marshall speaking. How may I help you?'

'It is William here – William Meadows. Would it be possible to have a word with Ben by any chance?'

'It is nice to hear from you, Sir William,' Cathy said. 'We've been to a cat show and just got back. Ben is putting his cats away. Will you hold or shall I ask him to ring you back?'

'I'll hold, thank you.'

Cathy laid the earpiece down and went in search of her husband. It was a couple of minutes later that Ben came to answer.

'Meadows?' he said. 'Good to hear from you. Sorry to keep you waiting, but the cats come first. Everything all right? How is Larch and that girl of his?'

'I had a card from Larch a month ago. He shows no sign of finding himself a job and settling down – and Sarah is doing very well. We went up to see her in that show a couple of weeks back, took her out for dinner afterwards. She seems quite happy. Over that other business at any rate.'

'Good! That's what I wanted to know. I was sorry that she was attacked like that – she's a bright girl and brave too.'

'She certainly is,' Sir William agreed warmly. 'If Larch had any sense he would come home and marry her.' He hesitated, then, 'It's a bit awkward, old fellow. I may have landed you in some bother. I'm afraid I spoke out without checking with you first . . .'

'Sounds ominous,' Ben said but grinned. He had enjoyed his trip down to Beecham Thorny the previous year, and if he were honest he was getting bored with being at home all the time. 'Have you had another murder?'

'Not here,' Sir William said. 'But the son of an old friend of mine was murdered last week. Henderson was very distressed when he learned about it from the police. Giles lived in London, you see. Shot in the head three times while in his own flat. Jack Henderson thinks the police are missing the obvious and he asked if I knew anyone who might do a bit of investigation in a private capacity.'

'And you gave him my name – and telephone number?'

'Well, yes,' Sir William admitted. 'He's a decent sort, Ben – former Guards officer and good family. I think Giles was a bit of a playboy, though I didn't know him well. Saw him a couple of times in the past five years when he was visiting his father, you know the sort of thing – but people talk and I think my assessment is probably not far from the truth. Jack is in a bit of a state. Giles was all he had and he wants to know what happened to him. I thought you might be able to discover whether the police really think it was a burglary or whether they are working on some other theory . . .'

'Yes, I don't see why not,' Ben said, feeling pleased with

the idea. 'I could take a trip up to the Yard, see a few friends, and ask around. I could take Cathy with me. She might like to do some shopping while I'm busy and we could meet for dinner and go on to the theatre later. I should like to see Sarah's show.'

'So you don't mind that I gave him your number?' Sir William was relieved. 'I'll ask next time, though.'

'Yes, best to check with me,' Ben said. 'But I don't mind. I've been promising Cathy a holiday but we haven't managed it, though I've decided we'll go soon. She might want to get some new clothes before we go to France. It will make a change for us both to have a day in town.'

'Oh good,' Sir William said. 'Give Sarah a ring. She can probably fix tickets for you. The show is closing soon and I think they are like gold dust.'

'Why close it then?'

'Apparently, the theatre is booked for another show. I suppose they underestimated the success of this one. Don't understand these things, but Sarah said something of the sort.'

'Well, I expect she would know. I have a lot of time for that girl.'

'Yes, I rather like her myself. Hadn't taken much notice until last year, but I thought she handled that dreadful business brilliantly. No tears or tantrums; just got on with things. Exactly the qualities you need in a wife.'

'Yes ... er ... um ... sure you're right,' Ben said, slightly uncomfortable under the enquiring gaze of his wife. 'Well, I'll wait to hear from your friend then, William. I'll give you a ring when I know a bit more, keep you in touch.'

He replaced the receiver and looked at Cathy. 'How do you feel about a nice day out up the West End? We could have dinner at a decent hotel and visit the theatre ...'

'Just what are you up to, Ben Marshall?' Cathy asked, a gleam of humour in her eyes. She didn't often bother to go up to the West End, because they had plenty of shops in Romford, which was closer. However, it was ages since she'd done anything exciting and the idea appealed.

'Sir William has given my name to someone who wants me to investigate his son's murder,' Ben told her. 'I thought I would spend the morning seeing old friends at the Yard and finding out what I can. You can buy yourself some nice clothes and we'll meet for dinner, and then go to Sarah's show. You remember I told you how helpful she was last year?'

Cathy nodded and smiled. Anything to get him off the subject of pedigree cats and the corruption in the judging system at the various shows up and down the country!

'It sounds good to me,' she told him. 'I'll buy something smart and change for the evening. We could take a room for the night at a nice hotel and then we needn't travel back late. Make a real treat of it.'

'Good idea,' Ben agreed, surprising her. 'And next month we'll go to France like I promised you. I've been busy with Bella's kittens, but they've all gone now and it's time I gave you a bit of a treat.' He grinned at her and tapped the side of his nose. 'I know you have a lot to put up with sometimes, love. I do go on a bit – but that judge and Lady Avery have something going on between them, you mark my words.'

Miranda jumped as the telephone rang. She had been on edge lately, not knowing when he would ring again. He had said that he would get back to her soon, but he hadn't rung since before Giles was murdered – but that didn't mean he had given up blackmailing her.

She answered tentatively, her heart beating very fast. 'Miranda Bellingham speaking.'

'Oh, Miranda,' a female voice said. 'I was just ringing to see if we could meet for lunch one day this week? I wanted to make sure you were coming next month?'

'Lady Avery?' Miranda's heartbeat returned to normal. 'Yes, of course I should be happy to meet for lunch – and I am looking forward to staying with you at your villa.'

'Thank goodness,' Lady Pamela Avery said. 'It is so difficult to balance the numbers for something like that, and I wondered if you might not – in the circumstances.'

'I am not quite sure I understand you,' Miranda said, though she knew exactly what the older woman was hinting at. 'Peter has to go to New York. He will be away for ages, and he knows I hate hanging around waiting for him. He is quite happy for me to spend three weeks with you in the South of France.'

'Yes, well . . . Giles, you know. It was such a horrid thing to happen. I know you married Peter, but I thought . . . you and Giles were such friends last year . . .'

'Yes, we were,' Miranda said. 'But that was before I met Peter. I've hardly spoken to Giles for months. I don't know when I last saw him.' She knew to the exact minute when she had last been to Giles's flat, but that was something that she would never reveal to anyone.

'Oh, I know there was nothing going on between you,' Pamela Avery said and laughed. 'Giles has been hankering after a showgirl for months now. He went to the theatre almost every night – at least five times a week. If he hadn't needed to keep in touch with friends I think he would have gone every night. He told me it was the real thing at last, but that she wouldn't go out with him. I daresay it was the thrill of the chase – you know Giles.'

'Yes, and that doesn't sound like him,' Miranda replied with a frown. 'I know he might have had a fling with a girl like that – but not seriously. Giles always liked the best of every-thing. I can't see him marrying a common girl.'

'Oh, I've probably misled you,' Pamela said and laughed again, sounding a little false to Miranda's ears. 'She is perfectly respectable – at least she has good connections. Her grand-mother is Amelia Beaufort. As a matter of fact, I've invited her to stay next month. I don't know if she will come, because she is in that show. It has done very well I believe, but it ends soon.'

'Are you talking about Sarah?' Miranda was shocked. 'You are, aren't you? She is singing on stage in the West End and her father is furious about it. Amelia said he threatened to cut her off at one time, but has apparently relented now.'

'Yes, that's her,' Pamela said. 'I suppose you know her – Amelia is your godmother. I had forgotten that for the moment.'

'I know Sarah but not all that well,' Miranda said. 'We've met a couple of times at Amelia's house, but that's all – apart from weddings and christenings. We get on all right but I wouldn't say I know her.'

'Well, you might enjoy getting to know her when you're both staying with me,' Pamela said. 'That is if she comes, which she might not. I suppose she has to work for her living now. Tommy says I shouldn't have invited her. He thinks she might not go down well with some of the other guests, because she sings on stage, but I told him that he is a snob – which he is, of course.'

The Honourable Tommy Rowe was her brother. The grandson of an earl's younger son, with no prospects of inheriting the title, he was nevertheless accepted everywhere and considered an arbiter of good taste: he made a living writing about gardens and design in fashionable magazines. His own tastes were lavish, and he sailed close to the wind, sponging on his sister and others whenever possible. Miranda didn't like him much, but she couldn't tell his sister that so she simply laughed.

'When shall we meet for lunch?'

'What about tomorrow?' Pamela suggested. 'I shall be visiting my dressmaker in the morning and I could meet you at about twelve thirty – at the usual place?'

'The Savoy,' Miranda agreed. 'Yes, I should enjoy that, Pamela. I shall probably do some shopping myself.'

She looked thoughtful as she hung up. It was interesting to discover that Giles had been pursuing Sarah Beaufort without success. She knew her godmother's granddaughter rather better than she had made out to Pamela, but she preferred to play her cards close to her chest. She still had the threat of blackmail hanging over her – and there was the other thing. A picture of Giles staring up at her with dead eyes kept coming into her mind.

He had promised to ring her and let her know when he had found those damned photographs, but when he hadn't rung her for two days she had gone to his flat, letting herself in with the key he had given her a year ago. He had been lying there on the floor, the blood congealed into a dark mass about him. She had noticed that it looked as though the flat had been ransacked, but she hadn't dared to stop and search for her property. Miranda had just run out and left him there, so terrified that she had been sick soon afterwards, and she hadn't stopped trembling for hours.

Was his death something to do with those photographs? Miranda had an uneasy feeling that there might be some connection, though she couldn't be sure. He might have been murdered for a very different reason. Giles could have been mixing with dubious company. She knew that he had some disreputable secrets, and he wasn't always honest. He had once fenced a valuable diamond necklace for someone. She had found it in his coat pocket when looking for his lighter, and she'd guessed that it didn't belong to him when he became angry.

He had told her that he was selling it for someone, but Miranda suspected that it was stolen. She had accused him of it and he had denied it, but she'd known that he was lying, hiding something from her. He'd had plenty of money to spend only a few days later, and walked about looking like the cat that got the cream.

It was soon after this that she had met Peter and broken off her affair with Giles. She'd made him burn the negatives of those damned pictures of her posing in the nude, but he had said he couldn't find the prints. She wished that she had never been foolish enough to let him take them, but at the time she had been wild for him.

Maybe it had been Giles all the time, Miranda thought. She had been expecting a phone call every day but it hadn't come so perhaps it had been Giles on the phone threatening to send those pictures to her husband. She shrugged because whatever the truth it had given her breathing space.

In the meantime, she might telephone her godmother and ask Amelia for Sarah's number. If they were both going to be Pamela Avery's guests in France, it might be a good idea to make contact . . . and it was just possible that Sarah knew something about Giles that she didn't . . .

The telephone was ringing when Sarah came out of the bathroom that morning. She knew that Janey had gone out earlier and hurried to answer it.

'Sarah here,' she said, a little hoarsely.

'Ah, Sarah my dear,' her grandmother's voice came over the line. 'You sound breathless. I hope it is not inconvenient to talk now?'

'No, of course not, Gran darling,' Sarah said, patting her red-gold hair, which was still wet. 'I've just come from the bathroom and Janey is out so I rushed to answer. You know I always love to talk to you.'

'Thank you, my dear. I wanted to ask if you had made up your mind about the holiday?'

'I am still wondering if I ought to look for another job,'

Sarah said. 'I'll decide in a couple of days and let you know.'

'Lady Avery says she understands that you are busy, but she would like to know, Sarah. She needs to plan her guest list, you see.'

'I'll telephone her soon then. How are you, Gran?'

'Very well. I thought I might bring a friend up to see the show, perhaps on your last evening – if we can get tickets,' Amelia Beaufort said. 'I thought we might all go out to dinner afterwards – unless there is a party or something?'

'Yes, there may be a party backstage,' Sarah said. 'But you could come to that and then we could go out to dinner afterwards. I never stay long at these things, just to have a drink and say goodbye to everyone.'

'A party backstage? How exciting! I think Rosalind would be thrilled to meet you all. It was her idea to come up, because she says she loves to see a West End show and she was extremely interested in you, Sarah. She thinks that you must be talented.'

'That is very kind of her,' Sarah said, her greenish-blue eyes bright with mischief. 'But I'm not sure I know who you mean, Gran.'

'Oh no, you probably wouldn't,' Amelia said. 'Rosalind Darby is a widow, a little younger than I am, and she recently moved into Janet Bates's cottage. Janet's brother decided he didn't like living in the village after all, and he decided to rent it rather than sell.'

'Oh . . .' Sarah wrinkled her smooth brow. 'Does Mrs Darby know what happened there?'

'Yes, of course. Janet's brother was quite honest with her, but she said she didn't mind in the least. She asked if she could have her own furniture and Keith agreed, and it looks very different now. She has two large Afghan hounds and they bark their heads off when anyone approaches, though she says they are great daft lumps – but I think they make her feel safe.'

'Yes, I think it is a good idea to have the dogs. She is rather close to the woods in that cottage and they can be a bit creepy at times.'

'You never used to think that, Sarah. I remember you were always going there to pick wild flowers and play.'

'Yes, I know. It is because Morna Scaffrey was murdered there I suppose – but I expect I'm being silly. It is all over now.'

'Yes . . .' Amelia was silent for a moment. 'I spoke to Ronnie Miller's mother the other day. She told me that the doctors are very pleased with him at that . . . place . . . and they are saying that he may be allowed to come home. Just for a few days at first, to see how he gets on.'

'Yes, well, I always thought it was very unfair that he should have been sent away,' Sarah said. 'He had nothing to do with any of the murders, did he? It was unfair to say that he should be shut away for life when he hadn't done anything wrong. I am very pleased for Mrs Miller and Ronnie.'

'I'm not sure how she feels about it really,' Amelia said. 'I think he got into bad company for a while and started drinking – but of course that is all over now.'

'Ronnie may be a bit slow sometimes,' Sarah said, 'but he's just like an overgrown child and no danger to anyone. Anyway, I wanted to ask a favour of you, Gran . . .'

'Ask away then, my dearest. You know I am always ready to help you if I can.'

'I wondered if I could have a friend to stay for a couple of weeks? Janey hasn't found a new job yet and she doesn't have a lot of money to spare.'

'That's the girl you share a flat with, isn't it? Yes, of course, Sarah. She always sounds very pleasant when I telephone you and she answers. Bring her with you if you wish. You know I love young company about me.'

'Oh good, I shall ask her when she comes back this morning. I hadn't said anything because I wanted to ask first.'

'Unfortunately, it will be for just a couple of weeks,' Amelia said, 'because we shall be off then – at least I shall.'

'And Daddy wants me to visit him if I don't come with you,' Sarah said. 'But I probably shall. I know I can't invite Janey to come to France with us, Gran, but she couldn't afford to anyway. She has been looking for a job and if she gets one she will probably refuse to come at all.'

'Yes, well, just as she likes. Oh, one more thing, Sarah. Miranda rang me earlier. She asked for your number because she wants to arrange to meet you one day. I told her that you didn't have much free time, but she said she could fit in for a coffee or anything you liked.'

'Miranda? Oh, yes, of course. It's ages since we've spoken. I suppose I ought to have rung her before now, but I wasn't sure she would want to meet . . . since she married Lord Bellingham.'

'Miranda isn't a snob, Sarah. I thought it was nice of her to want to get in touch, because she will be staying with Pamela in France at the same time as we are.'

'Oh, I see . . . yes, it was nice of her,' Sarah agreed. 'Well, if she does ring I can meet for coffee, between rehearsals and the matinee show.'

'I expect you want to get off to rehearsals now?'

'Not this morning. We've all been given the morning off. I think some of the girls have booked for auditions.'

'You haven't?'

'I went for one last week but they said they would let me know. I have decided not to do a seaside show this year. I'm going to try for something in London again.'

'Oh well, you know best, my dear. Do you think we shall be able to get tickets for your last night?'

'Yes, of course. We all have a few to give away. I was going to ask if you knew anyone who would like mine. I shall look forward to seeing you, Gran.'

'Thank you, my love. Rosalind will be so pleased.'

Sarah smiled as her grandmother hung up. She was thoughtful as she went to get dressed. It might be a good idea to go shopping, buy a few new clothes. Her father had given her a small cheque for Christmas, which she had been keeping for emergencies, but if she was going to stay with Pamela Avery for a couple of weeks she would certainly need something new to wear.

Miranda was about to leave the house when the telephone rang. Mrs Wilson, her housekeeper, came into the hall to answer, but stopped as she saw her.

'I thought you had gone out, Lady Bellingham,' she said. 'Shall I leave it to you?'

'Yes, thank you,' Miranda said and picked up the receiver. 'Miranda speaking . . .'

'Did you think I had forgotten you?' The menacing voice

sent a shudder down her spine and for a moment she couldn't answer. 'I know what happened to Giles. You're in big trouble now. I want ten thousand pounds. You've got a week to find it.'

'What do you mean?' she demanded. 'I didn't kill Giles!'

'Try telling that to the police. You were there at his apartment and I've got letters as well as the photographs now. I wonder what your husband would pay to keep them out of the papers . . .'

'You can't do that!'

'You can buy them from me. I've told you my terms.'

'I don't have five thousand or even five hundred pounds at the moment. I can't pay you.'

'Sell the emeralds.'

'I can't do that, because they don't belong to me – they are heirlooms.'

'Get them copied then,' the voice said. 'Or tell your husband they've been stolen – but get the money.'

Miranda took a deep breath. 'I'll need more than a week. It would take a month at least to get them copied.'

'I'll give you three weeks. Surely a girl like you can think of a way to get some money. Your husband has plenty of it – but perhaps I'm dealing with the wrong person? Maybe I should go straight to him . . .'

'No! He wouldn't give you anything,' Miranda said, though she knew that Peter probably would pay to prevent her name being dragged through the mud. He might hate her for it, but he would pay to keep his wife's name from being splashed over the newspapers. 'I'll try to get some of the money but not ten thousand pounds.'

'You'd better start thinking, Miranda,' the voice said. 'I don't like being messed around. I'll ring you again soon.'

Miranda swayed slightly as the line went dead at the other end. She looked at her reflection in the gilt-framed mirror on the wall above the small Pembroke table, and replaced the telephone receiver. Her face looked white, terrified. She had begun to hope that her tormentor had decided to leave her in peace, but he had come back and his demands had become impossible.

She couldn't find £10,000. Even her pearls wouldn't fetch that much, though of course the emeralds ought to be worth more. What was she going to do? He had suggested that she have them copied, but she hadn't the first idea how to start. If she went to one of the respectable jewellers in London they would ask lots of questions, and she might find herself having to explain to Peter. Besides, he might want to have the emeralds valued for insurance at some future date and how would she explain then? It was impossible!

She had to think of something else. His veiled threat about the police and having some letters of hers was unsettling. She hadn't killed Giles, but she might have to prove it – and it would cause the very scandal that she was trying to prevent.

If only she had some clue as to the identity of her tormentor. Miranda went back upstairs to her bedroom and opened a gilt casket on her dressing table. A small, pearl-handled pistol lay inside, covered by some lace handkerchiefs. Her father had given it to her when she was fifteen, telling her that it might come in useful one day. He had taught her to shoot it, though she hadn't used it in years and wasn't sure she still could – but if she were desperate she might.

She wondered who had killed Giles. Could it possibly have been the man who was blackmailing her? If he had seen her leaving Giles's apartment that day, he must have been there himself. Was that when he'd found her letters – or was that just a lie to frighten her?

Miranda was very disturbed by his threats and the prospect of what might happen if she didn't produce the money the blackmailer was demanding. If she could just discover the name of her tormentor she would force him to return her property. If he refused she would kill him!

A thrill of horror ran through her at the thought. She looked at her reflection in the dressing mirror. She was just desperate enough to do it. Besides, if he had murdered Giles, he deserved it – didn't he?

She might find a clue to his identity at Giles's flat. When she'd fled in panic after seeing him lying there covered in blood, Miranda had felt that she would never wish to go there again, but now she thought that perhaps it might be worth the risk. Giles had an address book. If she found that, she might track down his killer by a process of elimination.

It was surely worth a try? She looked at herself in the dressing mirror, seeing the steely determination in her eyes, and knowing that she would do anything rather than see Peter hurt. She loved him and she enjoyed being his spoiled darling. If any of this came out, she would lose everything. Murder was a terrible thing, but she might be forced to it rather than give up her husband and all that entailed.

Three

'We'll meet this evening at the Cavendish,' Ben said as he kissed his wife's cheek and then saw her into a taxi. 'Have a good day, love, and buy lots of nice things for the holiday.'

'You might wish you hadn't said that,' Cathy chirped and laughed, because they both knew that she wouldn't go wild. Ben had never denied her anything, but she was always sensible. She would buy what she needed and no more.

Ben waved as the taxi drew off. He was thoughtful as he considered his day. He had rung a couple of his colleagues and he had a meeting arranged for lunch at the pub. He was quite sure that he would be given a true picture of the situation when he met Gareth Hughes, because they had always been honest with each other. But he needed to be able to interpret what he was told, and that meant he would prefer to see the murder scene for himself.

Ben had a key to Giles Henderson's apartment in his pocket. He fingered it thoughtfully as he left King's Cross and went over the busy road to the bus stops. He'd put Cathy in a taxi, but he preferred the bus himself. He enjoyed watching the people who came and went, and having a good clear view of the traffic. He rarely came into this section of the town these days, but it had once been a part of his everyday life.

Ben frowned as he dismissed the old memories. He had made his decision, and though there were times when he felt a little bored with his life, he didn't regret it. He had more time for Cathy, and she'd been very loyal and uncomplaining during the years when he was never home. However, he wasn't averse to taking private work now and then, and it might be sensible to apply for a licence. He couldn't rely on the goodwill of his ex-colleagues for ever.

He frowned as he reviewed his interview with Major

Henderson. He had delved beneath the man's stiff upper lip manner and seen the grieving father. Giles might have been a bit of a rogue – his father hadn't denied it – but he was the only family the old man had had, and the murder had knocked him for six.

'I know nothing will change what happened,' Major Henderson had told Ben, 'but I don't believe it was simply a robbery that went wrong, Mr Marshall. I just want the truth.'

'The truth sometimes hurts,' Ben replied. 'If I discover that Giles was mixed up in something unpleasant you might wish that you had let the police put it down to burglary.'

'Giles may have done things he ought not,' Major Henderson agreed. 'I would never say he was the perfect gentleman – but he wasn't evil. Whoever killed him deserves to be punished.'

'If I discover something that leads me to the killer, it will be down to the police from then on. I can't guarantee that they will take him to court – or a conviction if they do.'

'All I want is the truth. Without that, his death will haunt me until my dying day.'

'Right. I'll do what I can,' Ben said. 'Would you be willing to give me a key to his apartment? I should like to spend some time there alone, looking round, getting a feel for his life. The police will have been over it for clues, but they may not have been looking for the same things.'

'They told me it was all right for me to clear the apartment out if I wished,' Major Henderson said with a nod of understanding. 'But I haven't touched anything. I had a quick look but, tell you the truth, I couldn't face it.'

'Know how you must feel,' Ben said gruffly. 'It's a good thing you left it untouched. It may be just a small thing that gives me the clue to work on – but don't expect too much. I may not find anything.'

'I've heard good reports of you, Mr Marshall.'

'From Sir William?' Ben smiled as he nodded. 'I was able to clear up a bit of bother last year, but I had help – a great deal of the clues came through a young woman who knew the people involved. That is why I need Giles's address book, so that I can talk to a few of his friends – see who he had been meeting recently, and if he had been acting oddly.'

'What do you mean, oddly?'

'Was he worried, upset, angry . . . just an idea of whether someone was perhaps threatening him.'

'Giles was pretty easygoing on the surface,' Major Henderson said with a little frown, 'but he didn't frighten easily. I would think it might be the other way round.'

'You see, that is exactly the kind of thing I need to know,' Ben said. 'I'll have a look round and remove anything I think might help me – but I'll give them back to you once I've studied them, if that is all right with you?'

'Yes, of course. I shall be very grateful if you can find anything at all.' He cleared his throat. 'In the matter of payment . . .?'

'At the moment I'm not doing this as a job,' Ben said. 'Think of it as a favour for a friend. You can buy me a drink or lunch if you like.'

'That's very good of you,' Major Henderson said a little tentatively. 'I believe you are thinking of going to France for a holiday soon?'

'Yes, I am,' Ben said, a little surprised that he should know. 'Did my wife mention it?'

'You said something yourself when I phoned you to arrange this meeting,' Major Henderson replied. 'As it happens, I have the use of a small villa on the coast there. I shan't be using it myself this year, but I could arrange for you to have it if you wish?'

'Well, that is very kind of you,' Ben said. 'I had thought of booking a hotel, but I'll talk to Cathy and see what she says – and I'll let you know after I've been to the apartment.'

'Yes, well, just a suggestion, you know,' Major Henderson said gruffly. 'Very grateful for your help, Marshall.'

Ben brought his thoughts back to the present as the bus stopped close to the Kensington apartments he was making for. They were in what had once been a rather large house with a pavement fronting, but, he had been told, boasted a decent garden at the back. Giles had the garden apartment, and the floors above were let to tenants who used them only occasionally when in town on business. At the time of the murder, the top-floor tenant had been abroad and the middle-floor tenant had been at his home in Dorset. The whole property belonged to Major Henderson, though the rents had been paid to his son to augment his rather precarious income.

Ben looked up at the windows above; the blinds were still drawn so it seemed that no one was in residence. No help to be obtained there then, which was a pity. Neighbours usually had a lot to say about the people who lived near them, especially in a case like this – and of course they wouldn't have heard the shot either and in some cases timing was important.

He let himself into the apartment, struck immediately by the smell of a woman's perfume. It was so noticeable that he thought she must have been in the apartment quite recently – might even still be here.

'Hello?' he called. 'Is anyone here? I'm a friend of Major Henderson . . .'

Hearing a slight noise in the room at the far end of the hall, he strode swiftly towards it, seeing at once that the French windows were open. Someone had definitely been here a moment ago. He went to look out at the garden, which was large and had a summerhouse about halfway down. As he couldn't see anyone, he walked out through the French doors and down to the summerhouse, opening the door to look inside. There was no sign of anyone, and he returned to the house, because he could see that the garden was walled in and there was no escape here.

As he re-entered the house, he heard a door slam, and knew that he had been fooled. The French door had been left open to make him think the intruder had gone that way, but whoever it was had somehow evaded him and left by the front door. He quickly followed and looked out on to the street. He caught sight of a well-dressed woman disappearing around the corner and swore, knowing that by the time he locked up and followed it would be too late, because she would have disappeared into the crowds. He had fallen for a very neat trick!

Returning to the room at the back of the house, Ben closed and locked the French doors, looking round for the real route of her escape. He realized that there was another door, which led into the next room. Opening it, he discovered a bedroom and off that was a bathroom, which in turn led back into the hall. So whoever she was, she knew Giles well enough to plan her escape this way. Ben nodded grimly. The incident wasn't much help in itself, but it told him something.

The woman knew Giles well and she had come here because

he had something she desperately needed. The thing was, had she found it – and, if so, had she taken it with her?

Ben was thoughtful as he looked around him. It was obvious that the apartment had been searched, by the murderer and the police – and perhaps by the mystery woman. But had any of them found that clue? In Ben's experience there was nearly always something that was overlooked, something insignificant but of vital importance. He just had to find it!

The bedroom looked immaculate. He didn't think that anyone had made much of a search there so that was where he would begin. If he were lucky, he might find that address book or even a diary. Had Giles been the sort of man who would keep a diary, and if he had, where would he have hidden it?

Ben opened the wardrobe and looked at the suits hanging up, most of them with layers of tissue paper over the shoulders to keep them free of dust. On the rail beneath several pairs of handmade shoes were ranged, each of them neatly placed level with the next. The shelves were just as neat, shirts folded exactly, pullovers in a separate pile, cashmere and silk in different piles from the wool. The clothes were expensive and of good quality – gentlemen's clothes, Ben thought with a grimace. Giles had known exactly what he would need for various social affairs, and it was all there. But the manner of its storage told him something about Giles. He was almost obsessively neat.

He wouldn't leave anything important just lying around. It would be in its own special place. Ben sighed, because this was going to take a long time. He would search the bedroom now, but he would probably have to come back this afternoon to finish his task.

The telephone was ringing when Miranda entered the house. Mrs Wilson was about to answer it, and Miranda shook her head, indicating that she wasn't at home. She wasn't in the mood for talking to anyone just now. It had given her the fright of her life when she heard someone come into Giles's apartment. At first she had thought it might be *him* but then, when the voice called out, she had panicked, because she couldn't afford to get caught. She had opened the French doors, but gone into the bedroom, because she knew that there was no way out through the garden. She had rushed out into the hall immediately she heard someone in the next room, terrified that he would discover her. If he really was a friend of Giles's father, he would have demanded an explanation.

How could she explain that she had been there to look for Giles's address book? It was a black leather-covered journal and very stylish, with a silver clasp. She had expected it might be in the hall but it hadn't been there and she'd had to hunt for it for some minutes before she found it in the sitting room. She hadn't had time to look inside, so she'd slipped it into her bag and fled with it still there.

Did that make her a thief too? Miranda was feeling sick and ashamed inside. She was getting deeper and deeper into this thing, and it didn't feel very nice. She hadn't enjoyed searching Giles's apartment. They had cared for each other once, and she felt as if she had betrayed him by touching his things. She had wanted to see if she could find her letters, though there was nothing particularly revealing in them, except that she might have mentioned that she was longing to see Giles a couple of times. Peter wouldn't enjoy reading them, but the photos were the things that would really distress him; they were quite shocking.

Still feeling a little sick, Miranda sat on the edge of her bed and opened her bag. She took out the address book, staring at it for several minutes before attempting to open it. It made her feel like a voyeur and she wasn't sure that she wanted to go on with this just now. A person's address book was very personal, and she had no right to pry into Giles's affairs. And yet she had to do something, because she couldn't find £10,000 without disposing of the emeralds.

She opened the clasp, which was very stylish – like every-thing that Giles chose for himself. He had liked different things, something that added spice to his life, and perhaps it was his habit of collecting unusual people as well as things that had led to his death.

Knowing Giles, everyone would be listed correctly under their full names. She looked for herself first and discovered that she was listed twice, under her maiden name and her married name; that made her smile and she relaxed a little. Giles had always liked things in their right place.

As she flicked through the book, she began to notice that there was a code beside certain names, a letter combined with a cross or a minus sign. She had no idea what it meant, unless Giles was reminding himself of something. She found Lady Pamela Avery's name, frowning as she saw that it had the letter 'F' and two 'X' signs beside it. Now what did that mean? Just above it were two names she did not immediately recognize – Nancy and Harvey Ashton. Who were they? She had a feeling she might have met them at one of Pamela's charity affairs, but couldn't recall their faces.

Most of the names were known to her, because they had moved in similar circles until she married, and still shared some acquaintances, but there were a few that she didn't recognize. She ignored the females, because it was a man she was looking for, making a note of three men she didn't know. She was about to put the book aside when something made her turn back to a name she had looked at earlier.

Giles had written the name of Pamela Avery's brother, but there was something not quite right with the entry. She hadn't picked it up the first time, but looking at it now, she laughed. Giles had written 'The *Dis*honourable Tommy Rowe' and ended with an exclamation mark and the letter S. Now what did that represent?

Giles was always so meticulous about these things. He had done this deliberately, and looking more closely, she realized that the first three letters were added in slightly different ink, as if it had been done later. Perhaps recently?

'Tommy Rowe . . .' Miranda breathed. 'Tommy Rowe . . .'

She felt a tingling sensation at the base of her spine. It was possible that he might be her blackmailer. She didn't know him all that well, though they met now and then at society affairs. She had instinctively disliked him from the first, and perhaps she had made her feelings too plain, because he hardly spoke to her these days, giving her a cool nod whenever their paths crossed. She had thought that perhaps he was the kind of man who preferred men's company and she hadn't realized that Giles was on close terms with him. On the other hand, might it be that Giles had discovered he had reason to distrust Tommy?

She took up a pencil and drew a circle around the name, as if to isolate it from all the others. Giles had changed it for a reason. She thought that he was either very angry or in a mischievous mood when he made the alteration.

Miranda frowned as she slipped the address book into the top drawer of her dressing chest, hiding it under some lace underwear. The more she thought about it, the more certain she became that she had discovered the identity of her tormentor.

A little smile curved the corners of her mouth, because if it was the Dishonourable Tommy Rowe who was trying to blackmail her, it gave her a slight advantage. He would no doubt be staying with his sister at her villa in the South of France in a few weeks' time, and perhaps she could think of a way to get her property back without paying him a penny.

Sarah replaced the telephone receiver with a frown. She had an odd feeling that Mrs Wilson had lied to her, because there had been a slight hesitation before she said that Miranda was not at home. Oh well, she had tried to make contact, as she'd promised her grandmother, but if Miranda was too busy to talk there was nothing more she could do.

'Sarah . . .' Janey's voice was excited as she entered the flat at that moment, her pretty face glowing. 'I got the job! It's in Yarmouth for the summer season and I've been given a solo spot for my gypsy routine as well as the chorus.'

'That's good,' Sarah said, delighted for her friend. 'When do they want you to start rehearsals?'

'The end of next week,' Janey told her. 'It means I can come with you for a few days, if that's all right with your grandmother?'

'She will be delighted,' Sarah said and hugged her. 'You know that I'm going to France for a few weeks, and then I suppose I ought to spend a few days with my father – but after that I shall come down to Yarmouth and we'll meet up for supper afterwards.'

'Lovely.' Janey hugged her back. 'I wish you were coming too, Sarah. I shall miss sharing with you. We've had such fun these past months, haven't we?'

'Yes, we have,' Sarah agreed. Being with Janey and some of the other girls was a big part of the pleasure for Sarah. She thought that she would not have enjoyed the experience half as much if she hadn't made so many friends. She was almost regretting having said that she would go to France, though she had done so for her grandmother's sake. She didn't particularly like Pamela Avery's crowd, though it might be all right if Miranda was friendly. 'I am going to miss you too, Janey, and Esther and the others . . .'

'You will keep in touch, won't you?' Janey looked at her oddly. 'You're not giving up the stage – are you?'

'No, not if I can help it,' Sarah said. 'I shall do some more auditions when I come home from France I expect.' She wasn't quite sure what she wanted to do next. It was odd, but she hadn't had a card from Larch for more than two weeks, and that had left her feeling slightly unsettled, though she didn't know why.

Ben looked at his former colleague across the table as they sat in a corner of the smoky room. He was very much aware of the noise and the sharp smell of stale beer and grimaced, because he was used to better things these days. Cathy wouldn't be seen dead in a place like this, though he had frequented it often enough in the old days.

'I suppose there is no objection to my making a few enquiries about this murder? I'll keep you fully informed of anything that I think might lead you to the killer, Hughes.'

'As long as you do, I shan't blow the whistle on you. To tell you the truth, I've missed our talks, Ben. You've got a way of stripping away the dead wood that used to come in useful.' Gareth took a mouthful of his warm beer and grimaced as he swallowed. 'We've made enquiries about Mr Henderson. He seems to have been well liked – bit of a rogue where the ladies were concerned. You might call him a gigolo or something fancy like that if you were inclined . . .'

'You mean older women paid him for his services?' Ben was surprised. 'I hadn't imagined anything like that – bit sordid if it is true.'

'Probably more likely to have given him gifts,' Gareth said and winked. 'But what I mean is that he was popular with the ladies, and seems to have got on well with most people we spoke to concerning the crime. No one had a bad word to say about Giles Henderson.'

'That's a bit unusual in itself,' Ben said, slightly cynical. He poked at his pie and chips dubiously, rejecting it mentally in favour of the dinner he would have with Cathy that evening. 'If he was a bit of a gigolo, I would have expected someone to condemn him. How many people have you actually interviewed?'

'We spoke to his boss – he wrote a society column for one of those gossipy magazines. It's called *Society Today* or something close. Complete rubbish if you ask me. The owner is an odd chap, tiptoes around like a bleeding fairy. He is called David Barratt, lives in a flat over a shop. He gave us the name of a girl who did some typing for Henderson. Her name is Angela Cole, and she appears to have idolized him. She told us that he went to all the main society affairs of the year and knew everyone. She wrote out a list of people he had written about recently . . .' Gareth fished in his jacket pocket and brought out a small sheet of paper. 'I copied them down for you, though I'm pretty sure they won't be of much help. They wouldn't tell you anything important if they knew. One sniff of scandal and these people clam up for all they're worth.'

Ben scanned the list, picking out a name he knew. 'What did he write about Lady Pamela Avery?'

'Know her, do you?' Gareth frowned. 'Oh yes, I remember. I think she breeds the same kind of cats you do . . .' He nodded, his frown clearing. 'I am not sure. I think it may have been something about a stolen necklace of hers. Apparently, it was all a mix up and it was merely mislaid, not stolen after all.'

Ben put a finger to the side of his nose. The familiar itch made him suspect something wasn't ringing true here, but at the moment he couldn't see the wood for the trees. He slipped the list into his pocket. After he finished searching the apartment, he might try researching some of Giles's recent work. Perhaps he had overstepped the mark and trodden on someone's toes.

'Thanks, I'll do a bit of digging, see what I come up with.'

'We're putting it down to burglary for the moment, because we don't have any clues,' Gareth said. 'There was no weapon, no footprints in the garden, nothing to help us . . . no neighbours to report an argument. They were all away somewhere the whole week. Let me know if you come up with something I've missed. I've been catching it in the ear lately for not achieving a high enough clear-up rate, so I could do with some help.'

'What about girlfriends? Not the paying variety, but someone he might care about, share his secrets with?'

'He visited the theatre a lot. We interviewed some of the girls in that musical show that's closing down tomorrow night. What do they call it – *Songs and Laughter*? Something like that, anyway. Apparently, there was one girl he particularly liked, but she turned him down – wouldn't go out with him at all.'

'You'd better give me her name,' Ben said and took a notebook and pen from his pocket. 'She might be able to give me something – even if it is only the reason why she turned him down.'

'She told us she didn't dislike him, but didn't want to get involved with him, because she wasn't interested. Sarah Beaufort, that's her name . . .'

'He was pursuing Sarah? Good grief!' Ben was taken aback for a moment. 'No, she wouldn't have been interested. She already has someone in mind.'

'You sound as if you know her well?'

'Yes, I do. She helped me sort out that business at Beecham Thorny the other year. Actually, she worked it out sooner than I did. If she knows anything at all about Giles, it will probably be useful.'

'I quite liked her myself,' Gareth agreed. 'Pretty girl . . . nice. She didn't seem the sort to be singing in a show like that somehow.'

'Her father almost disowned her for going on stage,' Ben said with a grin, 'but I think he is coming round to her point of view now. She's got a smashing voice, though I feel pretty sure she will give it up to get married before too long.'

'Much better for a girl like that,' Gareth said. 'She doesn't want to get mixed up with Henderson's sort.'

'You don't think much of him then?'

Gareth pulled a face. 'I'm not sure. I've got a feeling there might be more to this than meets the eye, but the super didn't want me to waste time on it. We've had a spate of jewel thefts recently and he's got some important people breathing down his neck demanding results. One of the robberies happened to a friend of his – member of the Rotary Club . . .'

'Ah,' Ben said, understanding why the murder was being shoved under the carpet for the moment. 'Like that, is it?'

'You should know,' Gareth said ruefully. 'It was the reason you resigned. If I could afford it I should do what you've done and get out, though I'm not sure what I would do all day. What do you do?'

Ben wrinkled his brow. Contrary to what most people imagined, his time was usually spoken for, though he had no objection to doing a spot of detection now and then for friends and friends of friends.

'Well, there's the cats, and Cathy likes visiting gardens – and we've got quite a big one ourselves. Cathy wants to redesign it, and I shall probably give her a hand with that. We're going away for a couple of weeks soon . . .'

'You had a bit of a legacy, didn't you?'

'My father left me his house and a few bob,' Ben agreed. 'I suppose I've been lucky – but you could get out if you wanted, Gareth.'

'And do what?'

'Set up a private detective agency or become a security guard.'

'Following cheating husbands or sitting in a van with a box full of money delivering to banks?' Gareth frowned. 'It doesn't exactly appeal. I suppose I shall plod on until I get my pension.'

After that, the talk moved on to colleagues they had both known who had either retired or been thrust into a desk job. It was nearly three when Ben left the pub and caught a bus back to Kensington. He was thoughtful as he let himself back into Giles's apartment. Major Henderson was right in assuming that the police had settled for the murder being down to a burglary gone wrong – at least that was the official word, though he was certain that the case would be kept on a slow burner just in case. Gareth Hughes was too good a copper to let it go until he was satisfied.

The smell of perfume had almost gone now. Any hope that the woman might have returned to the apartment faded, but it had been a forlorn hope at best. She wouldn't have fled the way she had unless she was frightened that she might get caught. After what Gareth had told him about Giles being a bit of a gigolo, that wasn't surprising. She had probably been looking for something that could be embarrassing if it came to the attention of the police.

And yet Ben had got the impression that she was quite

young. Her perfume was a young woman's scent, and the
dress he had caught a glimpse of as she turned the corner had
looked very smart and expensive. Cathy could probably have
told him where it was bought if she'd been here, because
although she didn't buy that many clothes, she took the magazines regularly.

It could have been Sarah, of course. It was the kind of thing
she might have done had she been involved with Giles, because
she would have been determined to discover who had killed
him, but Ben was pretty certain she hadn't been. Besides, it
wasn't her sort of perfume. Ben recalled that she had worn something light and flowery, while this had been spicy, exotic . . .
expensive again.

He had searched the bedroom without success earlier, and
he had made a start on the sitting room, but there were still
a few places to look. The bureau hadn't yielded anything so
far, though it wasn't as neat as the wardrobe in the bedroom,
which meant it had been searched before. He thought that he
would look in the little pigeonholes at the top next, just in
case he came across something of interest. Gareth had given
him several clues, though Ben didn't think that his colleague
was aware of it. Nothing was of any real significance but there
was enough to give him somewhere to start, even if he found
nothing here.

He took everything from the little compartments inside the
fall of the bureau. Most of the papers were unpaid bills for
wine, extravagant food and clothes, and a couple of betting
slips. Giles had extremely expensive tastes and must have
lived way beyond the income he got from his property and
writing that gossip column – and he must have got the money
infrequently, because he had clipped the paid bills together,
all of them settled on the same day. It looked as if he was in
need of funds or waiting for some to arrive.

Ben put the unpaid bills to one side, because Major
Henderson might want to settle them if he was aware of his
son's debts. At the back of one of the pigeonholes Ben saw
something that sparkled. He put his hand right in the compart-
ment to bring the object out and discovered that it was a single
earring, possibly a diamond with a pearl drop. There seemed
to be only one, even though he searched for its pair, and then,
as he was about to move on, he saw a little wooden lever at

the back of the pigeonhole and pressed it. The secret drawer
had been cleverly hidden behind a curved pelmet at the top
of the little drawers, and Ben wouldn't have thought of looking
for it if he hadn't seen the earring. As he picked up the small
leather-covered book lying inside the drawer, he had a feeling
that he had found the clue he was looking for. However, his
smile of satisfaction faded as he opened it and saw that the
pages were covered in fine writing in what was clearly a code.

He turned the pages, noting that the same series of numbers
and letters were repeated every so often, but they meant
absolutely nothing to him. Ben swore beneath his breath. He
knew that the notebook probably contained invaluable information about Giles and the people he had known, but was
little help at this moment.

He slipped it into his pocket, because he knew of people
who could break most codes given time. He would take it
with him and look more thoroughly later, but he was just
about done here. He glanced at his watch. He might just have
time to speak to the man Gareth had called a 'bleeding fairy'
before he kept his appointment with Cathy. It was unlikely
there had been a relationship going on between Giles and his
boss, because Giles had obviously been a ladies man, but he
might have something to tell that would help.

Turning away, Ben's eye fell on something protruding from
beneath the sofa. He bent to pick it up, realizing that it was
a photograph, which was odd because he hadn't seen many
in the apartment. There was only a picture of Giles and his
father in a silver frame standing on top of the bureau – though
he had seen a rather nice box camera on the chest of drawers
in the bedroom. As he flipped the photo over, he saw that it
was of a naked woman. She was young, very attractive and
posing with one arm behind her head . . . and on this very
sofa! He could see the bureau and a small occasional table in
the background, leaving him in no doubt that the photograph
had been taken in this very room.

If it had been shot here, it probably meant that Giles had
been the photographer. Ben returned to the bedroom and
checked to see if there was a film inside the camera, but it
was showing empty. He left it on the chest of drawers and
returned to the bureau, slipping the picture inside an envelope
and sealing it. He would rather that Cathy didn't find it in his

pocket by accident, because she might get the wrong idea. He wrote 'Evidence' on the envelope, underlining it before putting it into his jacket pocket.

He had no idea who the young woman was, but he was pretty sure that the photo didn't just get on to the floor by accident. Someone had dropped it there – and it might have been the woman he had disturbed when he first entered the apartment that morning. If he could find her, Ben thought he might be halfway to solving the mystery of what had happened here.

Four

'Telephone call for you, Sarah,' Esther said, popping her head around the door of the dressing room. 'You'd better hurry, there's only twenty minutes to go before you're on.'

'Thanks,' Sarah said and went out into the passageway that led from the dressing rooms to the back of the stage. Esther had left the receiver dangling and Sarah picked it up, putting the black trumpet to her ear. 'Hello, Sarah Beaufort speaking?'

'Sarah?' Ben said. 'It's Ben Marshall. I hope this isn't inconvenient, but I'm bringing my wife to the show this evening and I wondered if we could meet afterwards – perhaps have a drink somewhere? Cathy would love to meet you and I need to talk to you about something.'

'Ben, it's so nice to hear from you! Yes, that would be lovely. If you go to the theatre bar and wait, I'll join you as soon as I am ready – it takes about ten or fifteen minutes for me to change, but I'll be as quick as I can.'

'No need to rush,' Ben said. 'We're making a night of it, staying at a hotel. Good luck for tonight, Sarah. It's the night before your last show, isn't it?'

'Yes,' Sarah said. 'We'll talk later, Ben. Tell Cathy I am looking forward to seeing her.'

'Right you are.'

Sarah was smiling as she went back to the dressing room she shared with Janey and two other girls. As she entered, she saw a huge basket of flowers. Esther was reading the card that accompanied them and looking like the cat that got the cream.

'They've just arrived – aren't they gorgeous?' she said, seeming very excited. 'He's asked me to supper at a night-club this evening too.'

'Lucky you,' Janey said with a wry look. 'I never get anything like that – who is he?'

'No one you would know,' Esther said and slipped the card into her purse. 'Besides, Sarah has a date too – don't you?'

'I've been asked to have a drink with a friend and his wife,' Sarah said. 'I'm sure you could come too, Janey, if you wanted. Ben and Cathy have come to watch the show. I think they would be pleased to meet my friends. I would have asked you as well, Esther, but you have something better in mind.'

'Yes, I have, much better.' Esther looked smug.

'I don't think I'll come if you don't mind,' Janey said. 'I have some things to do this evening, Sarah.'

'It's up to you,' Sarah said. 'I might be a bit late back so don't wait up for me.'

'Don't worry, I shan't,' Janey said and laughed. 'Have a good time though.'

'Yes, I am sure I shall. I met Ben last year, but this is the first time I shall have met his wife. I am looking forward to it.' She smiled at Esther. 'I hope you have a wonderful time.'

'I shall, don't worry,' Esther said. 'I've been living on cheese and toast all week. I could eat a horse – and I shall!' She picked up the basket, preparing to go back to her own dressing room next door, because she had just popped in to show off her wonderful flowers.

There wasn't much time to waste, because there was the usual buzz of excitement that pervaded the theatre as it began to fill up in the auditorium. It was time to get ready for the performance.

'It is lovely to meet you at last,' Cathy said as she and Sarah shook hands later that evening. 'Ben has talked about you a lot – he thought you were rather marvellous last autumn.'

'Oh no,' Sarah said and blushed as she leaned forward to kiss Cathy's cheek. 'I really didn't do very much at all, but it is kind of Ben to be so generous.'

'As a matter of fact, you practically solved the case for me,' Ben said. 'I was getting there steadily, but you were way ahead of me.' He smiled at her. 'I am working on something else now as it happens – and I believe you may know of Giles Henderson?'

'Yes, I do. The police interviewed one or two of the girls,

but I don't think they could tell them very much. Giles was a bit of a playboy I think. He liked women, which a lot of men don't really, do they?'

'That is a bit too deep for me at this hour,' Ben said, amused because she always went straight to the heart of things. 'Someone told me he might have been a bit of a gigolo?'

'Oh no, I wouldn't have thought that. He might have been nice to older women, taking them about, doing things for them. In fact I know—' she broke off and blushed. 'Perhaps I ought not to say . . .' She glanced over her shoulder. 'It is rather public in here and I wouldn't want to be overheard.'

'No, right,' Ben said. 'Perhaps we could talk more privately another day?'

'Yes, perhaps, though I'm not sure that anything I might have to tell you is relevant to the case. I wouldn't want to set you off on a false trail.'

'But you do know something about Giles Henderson, even though you refused to go out with him?'

'Yes, I do,' Sarah replied. 'But I would rather not say anything here.'

'I understand. Perhaps we could meet soon?'

'I am very busy tomorrow, with it being the last day for the show, and then I go down to visit with Amelia, before we both go to France in a couple of weeks.'

'Well, I think I might manage to get down at the weekend,' Ben said. 'Actually, there is a cat show in Norwich that I want to attend – if I could come on Sunday afternoon, towards the evening?'

'Why don't you come to tea?' Sarah said. 'I am sure Amelia would enjoy having you – and Cathy if you like?' She glanced at his wife.

'Yes, that would be nice,' Cathy replied. 'I usually go to the shows with Ben. It gets me out of the house a lot more and we enjoy staying at various hotels or guesthouses – don't we, Ben?'

'Yes, it makes a bit of an interest,' Ben said, which was, in his wife's opinion, a gross understatement.

'Well, I shall look forward to seeing you both again. Did you enjoy the show?'

'Yes, very much,' Cathy said. 'You have a really lovely voice, Sarah. I thought you were better than the star.'

Sarah laughed and shook her head. 'Oh no, I'm afraid that just isn't true, but I'm doing very well. I'm going to have a little holiday before I audition again, but I should like another London-based show if I can get it.'

'Ben is taking me to the South of France next month,' Cathy said. 'We went to Paris for our honeymoon but we've never been to the fashionable part of the coast. I'm beginning to get excited about it.' She gave her husband an affectionate smile. 'If I can drag Ben away from the cats long enough.'

'You know that's all arranged, Cathy,' Ben said, but they all laughed.

After that the talk became general until Sarah excused herself. Ben insisted on getting a taxi for her because it was late, and he paid the driver despite her protests.

Sarah was thoughtful as the taxi sped through streets that were gradually becoming emptier as people dispersed and went home. She was later than usual and she felt tired as she let herself in and went straight to bed. She wasn't sure whether she ought to tell Ben what she knew about Giles Henderson and Miranda. It felt like a bit of a betrayal, and it might not be wise, because Miranda was married now – and yet perhaps she ought.

There was something else, too. It might mean nothing but it was the kind of thing that could give Ben a lead. She would think about it carefully before she decided.

Miranda telephoned the next morning, asking to meet. Sarah was apologetic, but as she had told Ben, she was very busy that day.

'I did try to ring you a few days ago, but your housekeeper said that you were out. Did she tell you that I had rung?'

'No, she didn't actually, though she may have written it down somewhere. I have been caught up in something and I may have missed her message. I thought it would be nice to meet before we see each other in France?'

'Yes, it would. But I'm busy all day, because it is our last, and tomorrow I'm going down to stay with Amelia. I suppose I might get up to town sometime in the following couple of weeks to have lunch – if you wanted?'

'Why don't I come down? I haven't seen Amelia for ages. I could stay for one night – perhaps towards the end of next week? Peter is going away for a couple of nights on business . . .'

'I am sure she would love to have you. Why don't you give her a ring? I'm sorry but I have to leave now. We have a meeting at the theatre before the matinee show and I need to be there.'

'I mustn't delay you. I think you are marvellous, Sarah. It took a lot of courage to do what you have.'

Sarah made a wry face as Miranda hung up. If her grandmother's godchild was going to go out of her way to be friendly, it made her decision all the harder. How could she tell Ben that she knew Miranda had had a long-standing affair with Giles Henderson before her marriage? She didn't want to cause trouble for Miranda, and she was afraid that it might if Ben started asking questions. Of course it hadn't been much of a secret and if he started nosing around he would discover it for himself before too long . . .

Putting the problem from her mind, Sarah picked up her bag and went downstairs, hailing a taxi. She more often took the bus but she was a little late for the meeting and felt like being extravagant for once. After all, she only had to say the word and her father would restore her allowance. Not that she wanted him to just yet, because she needed to prove she could live on what she earned.

When she arrived on stage at the theatre, Sarah discovered that she was almost the last. The show director had already started talking. He was telling them that the show had been even more of a success than he had hoped at the beginning.

'Our angel is very pleased, because he didn't really expect us to break even let alone make a profit,' Marcus Hedges said. 'In fact, he is talking about taking the theatre for a longer run next time. We shall start auditioning at the end of August. I wanted to make sure that you all knew the situation, because some of you will probably be trying for pantomime and Christmas shows – but we are planning another variety show similar to this one, and the theatre will be booked for ten months next time instead of six.'

There was a buzz of excitement, because a lot of the girls knew that they would be in with a chance of getting a place in the next show. Marcus was talking about various things that had happened. One of the girls had landed a brilliant job in Vaudeville on Broadway and two others had been picked for a musical extravaganza in a West End theatre and were leaving that night to go straight to their next show.

'Isn't that exciting?' Janey asked, coming up to Sarah. 'I shall put my name down for next time – you will too, won't you?'

'Yes, of course,' Sarah said. She glanced round at the excited faces. 'Where is Esther? I thought I was late, but it looks as if she has missed the meeting altogether.'

'Big night out,' Janey said and laughed. 'I hope she turns up in time for the show.'

'Surely she wouldn't miss it deliberately?' Sarah frowned. She didn't know why, but she had an odd feeling about this. 'I mean, I know she was looking forward to going out with her new admirer – but it goes down as a black mark if you miss a performance without letting Marcus know.'

'Perhaps he does know,' Janey replied with a shrug. 'How did you get on with your friends last night?'

'Oh, very well,' Sarah said. 'Ben and Cathy are coming down on Sunday so you will probably meet them. Shall we have our coffee now? I skipped breakfast and I'm hungry.'

'That makes a change for you,' Janey said. 'I could do with a bacon roll – what about you?'

'Yes, good idea,' Sarah said. She took one more look around as they left the stage, making their way to the back of the theatre and the little coffee shop just outside. She couldn't help wondering why Esther hadn't bothered to turn up for the meeting. 'I wonder why Esther didn't come. Do you think we should telephone her?'

'She probably overslept,' Janey said. 'Don't worry about it, Sarah, she will be here later.'

Esther didn't arrive at the theatre for the afternoon perform-ance. The other girls covered for her as best they could, but Marcus was annoyed and asked questions afterwards.

'Has anyone seen her?' he approached each of them in turn. 'Has she let anyone know she is sick?' They shook their heads, feeling mean about letting Esther down, and yet not wanting to lie. 'Does anyone know where she lives?'

'Yes, I do,' Sarah said. 'I knew of a room going in a boarding house just round the corner from where we live and I told her about it. I could go round there in my break if you like?'

'Would you mind, Sarah?' Marcus said. 'I have tried ringing the phone number she gave me, but no one answers. I can't leave the theatre myself, because I have a meeting with someone.'

'No, I don't mind,' Sarah replied, because that horrid nagging feeling wouldn't let her rest. 'I'll ring you as soon as I discover what has happened – if I can. She probably just overslept or something . . .'

'For five hours?' Marcus was sceptical. 'If it wasn't Esther I'd say she had just run out on us – but she is normally reliable.'

'Yes, I know,' Sarah said feeling more worried than ever. 'I think I'll go straight away. I'll telephone the theatre if I discover anything.'

'Thanks, Sarah. I shan't forget this,' Marcus said and smiled at her.

Sarah went outside and hailed the first taxi she saw. Two taxis in one day was extravagant, but it would take too long to go there and back by bus. She was feeling worried about her friend, because it wasn't like Esther to let anyone down, and there was no reason for her not to turn up for the last day. Everyone looked forward to the last night of a show, because it was special.

Sarah paid her taxi and crossed the road to the house where Esther was staying. The owner lived in two rooms downstairs, and let out her bedrooms to girls who worked for a living. She was a friendly woman and Sarah had stayed here for a week or two until she met Janey and they moved into their small apartment. She answered the door a minute or two after Sarah rang, smiling as she recognized her.

'Well, if it isn't Sarah,' she said. 'It is nice to see you, my dear. Come in and have a cup of tea with me.'

'Thank you, Muriel,' Sarah said. 'But I really came to look for Esther. She missed the meeting this morning and the afternoon performance.'

'What a silly girl,' Muriel Browne said and shook her head. 'And it's the last day. She told me she was looking forward to the party.'

'Have you seen her today?'

'Now you mention it, I haven't seen or heard her,' Muriel said. 'That is rather odd. She owes me two weeks' rent and she said she would pay tomorrow – I hope she hasn't run off without paying.'

'I don't think Esther is the kind of girl who does things like that,' Sarah said. 'May I go up to her room and see if she is ill?'

'You think she might be unwell?' Muriel frowned. 'Surely she would have made a noise to attract my attention? I know I've had my wireless on, but I would have heard her. We'll both go up and see if she is there. I don't often go into the girls' rooms other than to clean them – but if she might be ill . . .'

Sarah ran ahead of her up the stairs. She knocked at the door, calling Esther's name, but there was no reply. Muriel looked at her and pulled a face, then inserted her key. She went into the room first and Sarah followed. Esther's suit-cases stood open and waiting, as if she had been almost ready to pack, but her clothes were still hanging in the wardrobe.

'Did you hear her come in last night?'

Muriel shook her head. 'I went to bed early with a headache. I took one of my pills and I slept through until about six this morning.'

'So we don't know if she came home last night,' Sarah said. She gave the landlady an anxious look. 'Do you think we should telephone the police?'

'Report her missing?' Muriel asked. 'I'm not sure, Sarah. It does seem odd that she didn't turn up for work today – and her bed hasn't been slept in by the looks of it.'

'I am very worried about her,' Sarah said, 'but I don't want to cause a fuss for nothing. Could you possibly ring me if she hasn't turned up by seven o'clock this evening? I am going back to the theatre now and I'll talk to some of the other girls, but if she is still missing by the time we go on stage tonight, I shall ask Marcus to telephone the police.'

'Yes, of course, my dear. You will want to be getting back to work – but I'll let you know at the theatre if she comes in before then.'

'Thank you,' Sarah said. 'If Esther had intended to run away and not pay you, I don't think she would have left all her things. So either she has had an accident or . . .' her words trailed away because she didn't want to think the unthinkable. 'I'll get Marcus to ring some of the hospitals . . .'

'You can leave that to me,' Muriel Browne said. 'Either way, I'll put a call through to the theatre before seven.'

'You are very kind,' Sarah said. 'I don't have time to do it myself . . .'

'You get off and stop worrying,' Muriel said. 'She is my tenant and it is probably my place to make the enquiries and to inform the police if it seems that she is missing.'

Sarah thanked her once more and went outside. She was going to ask around some more, see if any of the girls knew anything that they hadn't wanted to tell Marcus. If Esther had gone off without letting anyone know it was too bad of her, but Sarah had an uncomfortable feeling that something was wrong.

Sarah explained to Marcus that Esther's landlady was going to ring the theatre before seven o'clock and then went to grab a cup of tea and a sticky bun before the second show. She kept hoping that Esther would poke her head around the door as she usually did, but it didn't happen. Ten minutes before curtain-up, Marcus came to tell her that Muriel Browne had telephoned to say that there was no sign of Esther.

'She had no luck with the hospitals, Sarah,' he said, looking puzzled. 'So she said she thought she ought to ring the police and I agreed. It may be just a storm in a teacup, but I must admit I was surprised when she didn't turn up for the meeting this morning.'

'It isn't the sort of thing she usually does,' Sarah said and frowned. 'I am very worried about her, Marcus. Do you think something has happened to her?'

'What kind of thing?' he asked. 'If she'd been knocked down by a bus or something, she would be in hospital, surely?'

'Yes . . .' Sarah hesitated. She didn't want to say what was in her mind, because it was too horrible. 'Do you know who she went out with last night?'

'I was just going to ask you the same question. If she didn't tell you and Janey, she wouldn't have told anyone. You were the closest to her of all of us.'

'Yes, I know. She wanted to share with us, but we only have two bedrooms at the flat. If anything has happened to her . . .'

Marcus frowned. 'Why do you keep saying that? Good grief! You don't think she . . .' he shook his head. 'Why would anyone want to hurt Esther? She was pretty and full of life . . .'

'I don't know,' Sarah said, 'but I've had this awful feeling ever since she failed to show up this morning. It's the reason I volunteered to go over there . . . but I hope I'm wrong.'

'I'm sure you are,' he said. 'She has probably gone off somewhere without giving the rest of us a thought . . . but please don't say anything to the others. We don't want an atmosphere on our last night. Our angel is going to be out front tonight and we want everything to be perfect.'

'The backer for the show is going to be out front this evening?' Sarah was surprised, because it was a big secret. Marcus was the only one who knew who had put up the money for the show, and they had nicknamed him the angel. 'Is he finally going to tell us who he is?'

'I don't know,' Marcus said. 'He has sworn me to secrecy, but if he wants to reveal his identity to certain people no doubt he will.'

'It's a pity that Esther is going to miss it all,' Sarah said and sighed. 'I shan't say anything to anyone, but it is bound to cast a bit of a shadow with her having disappeared just like that, isn't it?'

'If anyone asks before the show, I shall say she went to visit a sick relative,' Marcus said. 'But they probably won't bother – they aren't all like you, Sarah. Besides, as I said, you and Janey were her best friends.'

Sarah nodded, because she knew it was true. She wished that Esther had told her the name of the man she was going out with after the previous night's show, but she had been secretive, as if she didn't want to share her good fortune.

What if the man wasn't a very nice person? What if he had hurt Esther in some way . . . or killed her?

Sarah tried hard to dismiss the thought as she went through the shadowy passageway to the stage. During the day and the performances, there were always people around, but she couldn't help feeling that it would be creepy here alone at night. For some reason she felt cold and shivery as she waited in the wings. She couldn't help thinking about Esther, wondering where she was and if she was all right.

It was perhaps one of the hardest things Sarah had ever done, to go on stage and sing her two solo songs as if she hadn't a care in the world. She wasn't quite sure how she managed to get through it, but she did, and she kept a smile on her face throughout the rest of the show, taking her bow at the end with the others. The audience stood to applaud them and they took three encores, which left everyone feeling excited as they laughed, kissed and hugged each other. It had been a successful show and everyone was delighted with the prospect of coming back again the next year.

Sarah had been lifted by the swell of appreciation from the audience and she made an effort to put her anxiety for Esther out of her mind as she changed into a pretty dress for the end of show celebration.

At the party afterwards, which was held on stage, but over-flowed into the auditorium, Amelia introduced Sarah to her friend, Rosalind Darby. Sarah liked her immediately, because she was a friendly, outgoing lady, and it was obvious that she and Amelia got on very well.

'I am so pleased you've come to live near my grandmother,' Sarah said. 'She was always so isolated there. I know she has Andrews and Millie to look after her – but you know what I mean?'

'Yes, of course,' Rosalind agreed. She was a head taller than Amelia, thin with a well-lived-in face and fine grey hair that she did up in a neat twist at the back of her head. She was that evening dressed in a long blue skirt and a beaded tunic, which she wore with a rather magnificent string of pearls. 'I must say that I had met Amelia before I took the lease, and she was one of the main reasons I decided to settle in the cottage. We share a passion for cards, you see – and she is kind enough to offer me a lift to the bridge evenings we both attend.'

'I see,' Sarah said and nodded. 'Yes, well, it is nice for both of you. You don't find it a little lonely living so close to the woods?'

'Not at all, my dear. I walk in them quite often . . . with the dogs, you know. Besides, I have company more often than you might think.' Rosalind laughed, her greenish eyes twinkling merrily. 'I have an unpaid gardener. At least, all he seems to want is tea and cake. He turned up one day this week and started tidying up my front garden. I had been meaning to do it since I moved in, but was still finding other jobs to do.'

'Tea and cake . . .' Sarah frowned and then nodded. 'I think that might be Ronnie Miller. Gran told me they were allowing him to come home, at least for a while.'

'Amelia told me about him,' Rosalind confirmed. 'I think she was a little anxious about him looking after the garden for me, but I've had no trouble at all. I know he is a tiny bit slow, and you have to tell him things at least three times before he understands what you want, but he works well and all he asked for was a cup of tea and a piece of cake. Naturally I shall give him a few shillings as well, because I rather like him.'

'He got into a bit of trouble last year, but apparently he was meeting someone who gave him whisky to drink. His mother was quite worried about him and at the time, the police thought he might have murdered Miss Bates – but it wasn't him and I'm glad they've let him come home again.' Sarah frowned, because she had suddenly felt icy cold.

'Is something the matter?' Rosalind looked at her. 'You are very worried about someone, aren't you? Is it a friend? One of the girls from the show, perhaps?'

'How did you know that? Yes, I am worried about her. She hasn't come in for work today, and it isn't like Esther to just go off without telling anyone.'

'I knew because . . .' Rosalind frowned. 'Please don't think I want to press my services on you, Sarah – but I am psychic. I sense things rather than see them most of the time, but occasionally I do have visions . . .'

'Really? How interesting – no, I mean it, I do think it interesting. I have always thought there might be something to all that stuff, though I know a lot of people think it is ridiculous, and that mediums make it all up.'

'Then we must have a little chat one day, quite soon I think.'

Something in Rosalind's eyes made Sarah feel cold again, but just at that moment Janey came up to them and she introduced her to Rosalind. Leaving them together, she went in search of Amelia and found her talking to Marcus.

'Ah, there you are, my dear,' Amelia said and kissed her. 'You were getting on so well with Rosalind that I thought I would have a word with this gentleman – and you'll never guess who I've seen tonight . . .'

Even as Amelia spoke, Sarah had spotted someone across the room. Her heart took a great leap of excitement as he began to thread his way through the crush of people towards her.

'Larch!' Sarah cried as he reached her. 'I didn't know you were back!'

'I got home yesterday,' Larch told her with a grin. He kissed her cheek and then hugged her. 'Amelia told me she was coming up and I managed to get a ticket at the last moment. I thought you wouldn't mind if I came backstage as well?'

'No, of course I don't,' Sarah said, feeling as if the black cloud that had hung over her all day had suddenly lifted. 'It's the most wonderful surprise, Larch. I want you to meet Marcus. He is our director and we owe the success of the show to him . . .'

'I think some of it is down to you and the other girls,' Larch said. 'I thought you sang very well, Sarah. It was an excellent show altogether.'

'You must meet all the girls,' Sarah said. 'Especially Janey – she always enjoys your postcards. She has been wanting to meet you for ages.'

Janey was coming towards them. She looked expectantly at Larch, a grin on her face as she shook hands. 'It is lovely to meet you,' she said. 'Sarah is very generous with your cards. She lets me read them, because as she says there's nothing that every postman between here and Venice hasn't already read.'

'Yes, well, I suppose not.' Larch looked a bit doubtful. The cards had never been more than a way of keeping in touch. 'I'm not good at writing letters.'

'Very few men are,' Amelia said. 'My husband was terrible. He would never write even a Christmas card unless I pushed him to it – though he was an excellent businessman.'

'I'm afraid I'm not that,' Larch said. 'Father despairs of my ever getting a proper job.'

'But your painting is a proper job,' Sarah said. 'You should see some of his pictures, Janey. Larch is a wonderful artist.'

'Well, it won't be difficult to see most of my work in the next few months,' Larch said. 'I've been offered a series of shows at various galleries all over the country. The first one is in four weeks in a Norwich gallery.'

'That is wonderful news,' Sarah said, her smile lighting up her face. 'I am so pleased for you.'

'I wasn't sure at first, but some of the work I've done lately isn't bad so I thought I might as well give it a go.'

'It is certain to be a success,' Sarah said. She caught sight of one of the other girls, realizing that Karen North was trying to attract her attention. 'Talk to Janey for a few minutes, Larch. Karen wants me.' She left him and made her way across the room to meet her colleague.

'Oh, Sarah,' Karen said as she went up to her. 'Marcus just told me that Esther's landlady has contacted the police because she is missing. I was wondering if I ought to tell them something . . .'

'Do you know where she went last evening?'

'Well, sort of,' Karen said. 'You know she had those wonderful flowers? She said she was going out with the man who sent them, but I saw her later. She was standing outside the theatre crying . . .'

'What happened to the man who was taking her out?'

'It seems the flowers weren't meant for her. She went down to meet him after the show, and he told her it was you he had wanted to take out.'

'Me? But I don't understand . . .'

'Apparently, the flowers were delivered to the wrong dressing room. Esther said she was upset and humiliated, because he was rude to her – said he didn't go out with girls of her class. He called her a slut and told her he wouldn't be seen dead with her at a nightclub.'

'Oh, that's wicked,' Sarah said, but at the same time she felt a flicker of relief. 'Do you think that's why she didn't turn up? She felt humiliated and didn't want to face any of us?'

'Well, it might be,' Karen said. 'If the police have been called in – should I say anything or not?'

'Give me your forwarding address when you leave here,' Sarah said. 'I shall go round to Esther's lodgings in the morning to ask if she has turned up – and see if I can soothe her feelings, because he must have been a spiteful snob to say that to Esther. If she hasn't been back to fetch her things, I'll speak to someone I know about this and I'll give him your number. He isn't in the police now, but he used to be – and he's really nice.'

'Oh yes, do that,' Karen said relieved. 'I suppose I should have said earlier, but she made me promise not to . . .'

'You've done just the right thing,' Sarah said. She took the scrap of paper Karen gave her, slipping it into her purse. 'I'll let you know if I discover anything.'

'Right.' Karen smiled at her and glanced across the room at Larch. 'I know why you weren't interested in Giles Henderson now.'

Sarah laughed. 'Larch is rather wonderful, isn't he? He has been travelling, painting, but I think he will be based here now for a while, because he is going to have a series of shows for his pictures.'

'That sounds hopeful,' Karen said. 'You will get to see him more often.'

'Perhaps,' Sarah agreed, 'though I'm going to France soon to stay with friends.'

'Well, that won't be for ever,' Karen said. 'We've haven't been close friends, Sarah, but I'm going to miss you.'

'I shall miss you – all of the girls,' Sarah said and then looked anxious again. 'I suppose Esther didn't tell you the name of the man who was so unpleasant to her?'

'No, though I know he was something out of the ordinary, because she was so bitter, said she had been an idiot to think a man like that would be interested in taking her out. Why?'

'I should like to tell him what I think of him, that's all,' Sarah said and looked angry. 'It was really mean of him to upset her like that just because of a mistake. If it had been Giles, he would simply have taken her out and given her a good time.'

'I thought you didn't know him?'

'Oh yes, I knew Giles,' Sarah said. 'I had met him several times, but he was never my friend – and I didn't want to be one of his conquests.'

Karen nodded. 'I see. I wondered why he kept asking when you repeatedly told him you weren't interested.'

'I think – at least someone told me once – that Giles is like that until he gets what he wants.'

'Yes, I can believe that,' Karen agreed. 'I went out with

him a couple of times . . .' Her cheeks were pink. 'It was
before he got interested in you, but there was nothing between
us. He bought me dinner, flowers and took me to a nightclub.
I enjoyed being with him, but neither of us was interested in
having sex as it happens. He told me that he had been dumped
by someone he cared about and was only interested in compan-
ionship, but it was nice while it lasted.'

'Yes, I think Giles was usually good company,' Sarah agreed.
'Although I wouldn't have trusted him – but he wouldn't have
hurt Esther the way this other man did. I wonder who it was.'

'None of the girls seem to know,' Karen said. 'The flowers
were delivered by a shop so they might know who sent them.'

'Yes, you're right,' Sarah said. 'I think it must have come
from one of the best flower shops in London, because Esther
was very impressed. If she doesn't turn up, that could be worth
investigating.'

'Your friend is looking this way,' Karen said. 'Perhaps you
had better go. You have my number. We can talk again if you
like?'

'Yes, I shall ring you,' Sarah said. 'I had better get back to
my friends.'

'Ah, there you are again, my dear,' Amelia said as Sarah
went back to them. 'Larch was just saying that we might all
go on somewhere to have a late supper. I am not sure that
either Rosalind or I would wish to eat this late, but perhaps
you three might?'

'I'm going home to have a bath and write some letters,'
Janey said, obviously being tactful. 'Why don't you go with
Larch, Sarah?'

'I don't fancy a nightclub, but we could go somewhere and
have a coffee,' Sarah said and smiled at Larch. 'If you wish?'

'Anything you want,' Larch said and glanced at Amelia.
'You don't mind my stealing her away now?'

'No, of course not,' Amelia said. 'Rosalind and I will go
back to the hotel and order a cup of cocoa or something in
our rooms.'

'As long as they brace mine with brandy,' Rosalind said, a
twinkle in her eyes. 'Have a good time you two.'

Larch took Sarah's arm, steering her towards the door. They
were stopped a few times by people wanting to say goodbye
to Sarah, because she had been popular with the other

performers as well as the crew, but at last they were standing outside in the fresh air.

'So,' Larch said, looking at her intently. 'Now we are alone, perhaps you will tell me what is on your mind?'

Five

'Is it so obvious?' Sarah grimaced. 'I am sorry. I thought I was putting on a brave face – but I should have known you would see through me. Yes, I am worried about a friend of mine. Esther didn't come to work today and it just isn't like her . . .'

'There is more to it than that. Where shall we go for our coffee?'

'Why don't you come back to the apartment?' Sarah said. 'Janey shares it with me, but she won't be back for a while.'

'Yes, all right,' Larch said and hailed a passing taxi. Sarah gave the driver her address and Larch followed her into the back seat. He looked at Sarah's face in the half-light, sensing that she was actually very anxious. 'What is her name?'

'Mary Tanner is her real name, but she uses Esther as her stage name,' Sarah said. 'We all call her Esther, and she is one of the dancers. The thing is that she was supposed to be going out to dinner last night. She had a big basket of flowers and there was a card asking her out . . .'

'Then perhaps she woke up with a bad head and just didn't feel like coming in?'

'I went round to her lodgings, but she wasn't there. Her landlady hadn't seen her all day – and her bed was made, as if it hadn't been slept in.'

'She might have made it before she went out,' Larch suggested.

'Perhaps . . .' Sarah lapsed into silence, gazing out at the streets, the theatres and the cafes, which were still busy even though it was late.

The taxi had come to a halt. Larch got out and paid while Sarah fished in her purse for her keys. The apartment was the middle floor in a converted house, and they went in through the communal hall, up the stairs to her front door. Sarah opened it and Larch followed her inside. He looked around. The furniture was old and a little the worse for wear, but the girls had made it their own, throwing bright shawls over the ancient sofa and filling it with personal clutter.

'I'm afraid we're a bit untidy,' Sarah apologized. 'We're always too busy to put things away.' She cleared a space on the sofa, which was littered with a collection of teddy bears. 'These are Janey's. She collects them and I rather like them too.'

Larch caught her arm as she headed towards the kitchen. 'Come and sit down. Tell me what is upsetting you, and we'll have the coffee afterwards.'

'Yes, all right.' Sarah sat on the sofa and he sat beside her, turning to look at her face. 'The thing is that Karen, another of the chorus girls, was later leaving the theatre than most of us last night and she saw Esther outside. She says that Esther was crying, because the man she was supposed to go out with had been unkind to her. Apparently, the flowers had been delivered to the wrong dressing room and he told her that he didn't go out with sluts . . .' Sarah sat up straight, suddenly angry. 'Why did he say that to her? It wasn't her fault that the flowers were delivered to the wrong person.'

'It certainly sounds as if he wasn't a very nice person,' Larch said. 'It's just as well she didn't go out with him . . .' He looked thoughtful. 'She might have been so upset that she just went off to be alone for a while.'

'Yes, I suppose that is possible,' Sarah said. 'She was very excited about getting the flowers and she might have felt embarrassed about it being a mix-up.'

'But you think something has happened to her – don't you?'

'Yes, I do. I know it sounds stupid but . . . I think she is dead.' Sarah gave a little sob. 'I've been fighting it all day, Larch. I didn't want to believe it, and I still don't. Perhaps I've got it all wrong because of . . .'

'Because of what happened last year?' Larch nodded as he saw her face. She looked upset, a little pale. 'Things like that are hard to shake off, Sarah. That's why I didn't want you to get too involved in the first place. It all seemed like a bit of a lark when we started, but it became rather nasty in the end. I daresay it has been playing on your mind a bit?'

'Yes.' Sarah shuddered. 'What happened to Morna Scaffrey and then Simon Beecham . . . it was horrible. I'm still not sure that all got sorted out, you know. Agnes certainly killed Miss Bates and her own sister, but I've never been sure who killed Morna and Simon.'

'I don't believe Agnes Browning killed Simon,' Larch said. 'The police seemed to think it was Jethro Scaffrey in revenge for Morna's murder – and Sir James Beecham clearly blamed him, because he shot him before he turned the gun on himself.'

'But you're not sure, are you?' Sarah nodded, because she knew without hearing his answer. 'It just didn't seem to fit to me, I don't know why. I had an odd feeling that we were all being led astray – and I've got a similar feeling now. It doesn't fit and yet I think they are connected . . .'

'Simon Beecham's murder and the disappearance of this girl?' Larch looked bewildered.

'No, of course not,' Sarah said. 'I'm talking about the recent murder of Giles Henderson . . . but you probably don't know anything about that?' Larch shook his head. 'He was one of Pamela Avery's crowd. He was a gossip writer. Pamela's brother writes articles too, but he is an expert on gardens and design. You might have met him at weddings or society affairs.'

'No, I don't think so, not that I can recall. None of those names rings a bell, I'm afraid. But then, I don't go to society affairs – not my style.'

'Well, Giles came to our show almost every day for weeks and he sat in the audience looking at me most of the time, at least while I was on stage. He kept sending me flowers, expensive flowers – and he asked me out several times.'

'You didn't go?' Larch said, because he knew it instinctively.

'No, I quite liked him but he wasn't my type – and I knew he wasn't to be trusted in that way. He was murdered just over two weeks ago. The police seem to think it was a burglary gone wrong, but Major Henderson asked Ben to investigate and . . .' She shook her head. 'I don't know who sent them, but the flowers that Esther thought were hers were meant to be for me . . .'

'What has that got to do with Giles Henderson's murder?'

'Probably nothing,' Sarah said. 'But I'm fairly certain the flowers came from the same florist that was sending mine. I told you, nothing fits, but I can't help feeling that somehow Esther's disappearance and Giles's murder . . . No, I'm being silly. I'm all muddled up because I'm upset.'

'They are completely unrelated,' Larch said. 'I don't know what has happened to your friend or why Giles Henderson was murdered, but I am sure that neither event has anything to do with you.'

Sarah smiled, feeling relieved. 'Yes, of course, you are right,' she said. 'I suppose the murder has been on my mind, because Giles was trying to date me – and it upset me this evening when Karen told me that Esther was made to feel humiliated because the flowers were for me.'

'I should just forget about it if I were you,' Larch said. 'You were not involved with Henderson so his murder has nothing to do with you. As for your friend, I should think she went off to lick her wounds. She will probably turn up in a day or two and wonder what all the fuss was about.'

'Yes, I expect so,' Sarah gave him a grateful look. 'I'm so glad you're home, Larch. Talking to you has made me feel so much better.' She got to her feet. 'I'll make that coffee now and then you can tell me about the exhibitions of your paintings . . .'

Sarah went into the kitchen. Larch was right. Esther's disappearance could have nothing whatsoever to do with Giles Henderson's murder. The two incidents were completely separate.

It was surprising how easy murder became after you had killed the first time. He smiled as he remembered the pleasure it had given him when he saw the surprise in that slut's face turn to fear. She had really thought that he was going to ask her out after all when he'd followed her back into the theatre.

It was so much bigger backstage than one would think from the outside – and so quiet after the noise and laughter of the show. She had gone back to her dressing room for something she had forgotten and he had followed her in. She was such a slut that she had smiled at him even after he had insulted her and he'd seen the hope in her eyes. It was pathetic the way women would do anything to please a man for money! He despised them all . . . except for one. Sarah was different. She had refused that fool Henderson. She'd seen how shallow he was, how worthless. It was her refusal to accept any of Henderson's invitations that had made him realize her purity.

He had taught that slut a lesson. She wasn't fit to breathe the same air as the woman he admired. Most of them were sluts . . . especially that other one. She hadn't given him what he wanted yet, but he would get it. There wasn't much he wanted that he didn't get in the end. He knew how to deal with sluts. He taught them a lesson and then he killed them.

Miranda Bellingham deserved all she got. As for Sarah Beaufort, well, he would have to go slowly. At the moment he was content to admire her from afar. It had been a mistake to send those flowers. He should have waited for the right moment . . .

'Muriel,' Sarah said a little breathlessly when the landlady opened her door the next morning. 'This is my friend Larch – we came to enquire if you had heard from Esther?'

'No, my dear, I am so sorry. I'm very worried about her. Esther was a nice girl. I don't think she would have gone off like this without saying goodbye or paying her rent.' She opened her door wider, inviting them into her sitting room. 'Would you like a cup of tea?'

'Thank you, no,' Sarah said. 'Larch is driving me down to my grandmother's home this afternoon, but I wanted to speak to you first. What did the police say when you rang them?'

'They seemed to think I was making a fuss over nothing.' Muriel sniffed. 'They said that Esther couldn't be considered officially missing until she had been gone for some days – a few hours doesn't count. I believe they thought I was chasing her for the rent, which I'm not, Sarah. I don't care if she never pays me, as long as she turns up all right.' She blew her nose hard. 'But I think something is wrong, because it just isn't like her.'

'No, it isn't,' Sarah agreed. 'I did wonder if the police might think we were making a fuss about nothing – and of course we might be. I think Esther may be upset over something. She may just have gone off for a few days.'

'Well, I hope you're right, but I don't know what else to do. I've tried the hospitals again this morning.'

'Yes, I thought you might,' Sarah said. 'I don't want to take up too much of your time, Muriel – but will you telephone me at Amelia's if Esther does come back?'

'Yes, of course, my dear. Give me the telephone number. I can't see it happening, because I think . . .' she shook her head. 'This isn't the first time a girl like her has disappeared, you know.'

'What do you mean?' Sarah felt the ice at the back of her neck as she handed Muriel a small piece of paper with the phone number.

'It was two years ago,' Muriel said. 'Neither of them were my lodgers, but I knew their landlady. Joan is a friend of mine and she couldn't understand why either of the girls would just go off that way . . . and in the end they found them. Alice was dead, strangled – and poor little Brenda was in a worse state. She had been raped and beaten, left for dead. They saved her life, but they couldn't bring her back from wherever she'd gone in her mind. I think she's in some sort of hospital for the insane now. Joan went to visit her a few times, but she didn't know her and in the end Joan gave up visiting, because it upset her too much.'

'Oh, the poor girls, both of them,' Sarah said. 'Who could have done such an evil thing?'

'The police never caught him. There was a lot of stuff in the papers for a while, but then it just got forgotten. They were both dancers, pretty girls but not like you, Sarah . . . a different class.'

'Yes, I see,' Sarah said and shuddered. 'It is all very unpleasant, especially since Esther is missing . . .'

'Yes.' Muriel sniffed again. 'You would think the police would remember, wouldn't you?'

'They probably do,' Larch said, 'but they may not have put the various cases together – because we don't know that anything has happened to Esther, do we?'

'No . . . but I feel it,' Muriel said. 'And Sarah does too, don't you?'

'Yes,' Sarah admitted. 'I don't want to but I keep getting this awful feeling that it is already too late.'

'Well, you just take care of yourself,' Muriel said. 'It would really upset me if anything happened to you.'

'Don't worry, it won't,' Sarah said and gave her a hug because she was so obviously distressed. 'None of this has anything to do with me.'

'No, of course it doesn't,' Larch said. 'Try not to be too anxious, I expect Esther will turn up soon.'

He nodded to Muriel, taking Sarah's arm as they left. She looked at him as he steered her towards his car, opening the door and holding it until she slid inside. He still didn't speak as he got into the driving seat.

'Do you really think she is going to turn up just like that?'

'I'm not sure. I think it might be a good idea to give Ben a ring, Sarah. He might know something about the other girls.'

'Yes, I was thinking the same thing. He's agreed to come down and visit Amelia on Sunday, but I'd rather talk to him sooner . . .'

'I rang him this morning before we came here,' Larch said. 'He suggested that we all go there for tea.'

'Janey won't mind,' Sarah said. 'She wanted to meet Ben, because her aunt breeds cats and she is very fond of them – and I'd told her all about what happened last year.'

'That's what we'll do then,' Larch said. 'Since we have a couple of hours before we leave, is there anything you want to do?'

'We could have lunch at the pub,' Sarah said. 'Janey as well . . .?'

'Why not?' he agreed. 'I like her. I'm glad you have a friend like that, Sarah.'

'Yes,' Sarah said. 'She wanted me to apply for the summer shows with her, but I decided not to. I wanted to see what else came up . . .'

'Getting fed up with it?' Larch asked, brows raised.

'Oh no, I loved the show we've just finished,' Sarah said. 'I've put my name down again. Our backer has agreed to a longer run next time – isn't that exciting? I feel I'm getting somewhere at last, and I do want to prove to my father that I can make a success of my career. I know he doubted it when all I could find last year was a job in the chorus of a seaside show.'

'What are you going to do until the autumn?'

'Well, I'm going to France for a holiday with Amelia in a couple of weeks' time. We are staying with Lady Avery – you know her, don't you?'

'We've met once I think,' Larch said. 'What about when you come back? Will you stay with Amelia?'

'Daddy wants me to go to him for a while. I'm not sure yet. I shall need some sort of a job to tide me over the summer, but it is too late for a show now, because the auditions are over. I might find something else . . . or I could be a waitress in a teashop for a couple of months.'

'Surely you wouldn't do that?'

'I might . . .' Sarah teased, but then shook her head as she saw alarm in his eyes. 'No, don't worry, Larch. I was only joking. I expect I shall find something.'

'If you're looking for a job you can come to me,' he said. 'I need someone to help me with the shows. I have to make up the various collections, design the posters – and someone has to be there at the exhibitions, and tell people about the paintings.'

'That sounds like something I would enjoy,' she said. 'But I don't want you to invent a job for me, Larch. I promise you that I can find something for myself. There are lots of opportunities for singers, not always in shows but at nightclubs and special occasions.'

'Your father would not approve of your singing in a nightclub and nor would I.'

'You sound just like Daddy,' Sarah said and laughed. 'I didn't say I would do it, just that there are a lot of opportunities. I might be interested in special occasions – weddings and local dances, things like that . . .'

'I suppose that might be all right,' Larch said and then laughed as he saw her expression. 'Well, all right, I know you don't need me to hold your hand all the time – but I could do with some help.'

'We'll see,' Sarah said, though she was quite pleased that he had asked her. It would be one way of seeing more of him. She had missed him while he was away, far more than she was willing to admit even to herself.

'Larch, it is good to see you!' Ben shook hands with them and then kissed Sarah's cheek. 'And you . . .' He looked at her friend, smiling and offering his hand as Sarah introduced them. 'It is nice to meet you, Janey.'

'And you, sir,' Janey said. 'Sarah told me you breed Siamese? My aunt Sally breeds Persian blues. She does very well at the shows – or she used to until a couple of years ago. She complains that a new crowd has taken over the judging and her cats have lost out to inferior breeders recently.'

'It is funny you should say that,' Ben said, a glint in his eyes. 'You must tell me more about that another time, Janey – but come in all of you. Cathy has the kettle on . . .'

After tea, Cathy took Janey out to see the cats, and Ben invited Larch and Sarah into his study. They all sat down in comfortable leather armchairs that had seen better days, relaxed and at home, old friends together once more.

'You wanted to talk to me about a friend who has gone missing?' Ben said, arching his brows. 'Is she one of the girls from the show?'

'Yes. Her stage name is Esther,' Sarah said. 'The night I met you, she had some lovely flowers delivered to her and the card asked her to meet the man who sent them at the stage door after the show. She didn't come to work the next day and she still hasn't been back to her lodgings.'

'You think that something has happened to her?'

'Yes, I have a horrible feeling about it. I hope I'm wrong but I think she has been murdered.'

'Why?'

'I'm not sure. I felt this way when Morna was found and to a certain degree over Miss Bates . . .'

'So it is just your instinct at the moment?'

'Yes. I expect I'm being silly – I hope I am!'

'You don't make too many mistakes,' Ben said with a frown. 'Is there anything else you want to tell me about this affair?'

Sarah told him what Karen had related to her. She gave him a list of phone numbers she had written down. 'That's Karen's new address. She wasn't sure if she ought to tell the police, so I said I would ask you – and that's Esther's landlady's number. And here's the number of a boarding house where two chorus girls disappeared a few years ago. One was found murdered and the other had been raped and is now in a mental hospital. I know we can't be sure anything has happened to Esther, and there's probably no link, of course, but I thought it might come in useful. The final number is for a florist. It may not be of any help, but I think the flowers that Esther received came from there. They were like some that Giles Henderson sent me . . . at least at the time I thought they came from him. However, at one period I was receiving flowers almost every day and I couldn't be sure they all came from Giles.'

'I should imagine these may all come in useful if your friend doesn't turn up,' Ben said, putting the paper into his jacket pocket. 'I shall make a few enquiries, though I am enquiring into Mr Henderson's murder at the moment, as you know.'

'That was awful too,' Sarah said. 'I know Giles was probably a bit of a rogue – but he was a likeable one.'

'Yes, I've discovered that most people liked him,' Ben said. 'I wanted to know your opinion of him, Sarah – and if there was anything you could tell me that might give me a clue about his lifestyle?'

'Well, I know that women liked Giles and he liked them,' Sarah said, wrinkling her brow in thought. 'I had only met him a few times before he started sending me flowers and waiting for me outside the theatre so I can't tell you much, but . . .' She stopped speaking and shook her head as if uncertain.

'You wouldn't go out with him – was there a particular reason?'

'Yes and no,' Sarah said. 'I refused him for personal reasons – but I would have hesitated to go out with him even if I had been inclined towards him.'

'Why?'

'Two reasons,' Sarah said hesitantly. 'I know that he had a long-standing affair with someone . . . someone I know quite well. And there was another thing but I'm not sure I ought to talk about it.'

'It concerns a friend?'

'Yes, in a way,' Sarah said and frowned. 'I will tell you some of it, but not the name of the person – if you don't mind. It was about some kind of jewellery. I can't say exactly what, but it had been stolen and this person was very worried, because she was afraid of what might happen if it was recovered by the police.'

'She was afraid it might be recovered?' Larch said, looking puzzled. 'I don't understand that bit, Sarah. How do you know this?'

'I overheard a conversation, at least part of it,' Sarah said. 'I've never been sure if I heard it exactly right you see. I think there was a reason why she didn't want it to be recovered ... something to do with insurance.'

'She was after the insurance money?' Larch suggested.

'No, I don't think so,' Sarah said and frowned. 'It was more about the scandal if the truth came out ...'

'Yes, I see what you're getting at,' Ben said and nodded his head. 'And this conversation was with Giles Henderson?'

'I'm damned if I follow,' Larch said, baffled.

'If she didn't want to claim the insurance I'm thinking that perhaps the necklace wasn't all it should be,' Ben said. 'It might have been a copy of the original perhaps, but still held on the insurance cover ...'

'Oh ... yes,' Sarah cried, looking at him in wonder. 'I've been puzzling over it, but that could be what she meant. This person – she said that her husband would be angry if he discovered what she'd done and ... Giles said not to worry, he could get her another one just like it, because he'd had two made at the time just in case.'

'Giles said that?' Ben's gaze narrowed. 'Are you certain he said that he had had them copied for her?'

'Yes, I'm fairly certain that is what he said – and she started crying and telling him how marvellous he was ...' Sarah blushed. 'I felt awful because I was stuck, you see. I was behind a huge palm in a conservatory. I heard them come in and I knew ... well, they kissed at first. I was embarrassed to go past them, because she was a married woman and ... then it got so much worse. Thank goodness someone came to call her and they both left.'

'Awkward for you,' Ben agreed. 'Did she say anything else?'

'No, not much – just that she would go to his apartment the next week as usual ...'

'Yes, I see.' Ben nodded. 'Well, that tells us quite a bit about Mr Henderson, doesn't it?'

'Does it?' Larch frowned. 'It sounds as if he was a bit of a rogue.'

'Yes, perhaps,' Ben agreed. 'But if he had the necklace copied for her to help her out of a scrape . . . he was clearly a useful person to know. Resourceful.'

'Yes, but the thing was, she was so grateful to him,' Sarah said. 'And someone else told me that Giles was useful to have around . . .'

'He liked women and he was willing to help them – and they gave him presents for the things he was able to arrange for them.' Ben looked thoughtful. 'Not so much the gigolo as a friend to those in need?'

'Yes, I think that was Giles,' Sarah said. 'I did tell you that I quite liked him. I just didn't want to go out with him.'

'I should think not!' Larch looked annoyed. 'That woman was deceiving her husband, Sarah – and the insurance company too if she could get away with it, I daresay.'

'Perhaps not,' Ben said. 'She may have put the story about that the theft was a mistake . . . that she had recovered her diamond necklace . . .'

'Yes, I think she did,' Sarah said and looked at him in surprise. 'How did you know it was a necklace?'

'Oh, just something I read somewhere,' Ben said and tapped the side of his nose. 'One of my hunches, Sarah.'

'That still leaves the deceived husband,' Larch muttered darkly.

'I am not saying that she ought to have done it,' Sarah said, 'but she might have had a good reason for disposing of the necklace in the first place. Perhaps she desperately needed money, couldn't ask her husband – and Giles said that she could sell it and replace it with a copy. Or maybe she decided that for herself, and he was the go-between. I don't know what happened to the necklace, but I am certain that she was terrified her husband would discover it was a fake.'

'Yes, well, we may never know,' Ben said, because he could see that Larch was still annoyed for some reason, though he wasn't sure it was the story of the necklace that was upsetting him. 'But it tells me a few things I needed to know about Giles. I'm afraid I don't have any ideas about your friend's disappearance at the moment, Sarah.'

'Perhaps she will turn up in a few days.'

'We must hope for the best,' Ben agreed. 'That sounds as if Janey and Cathy have come back. Shall we join them?'

'I think we should be on our way,' Larch said. 'It will be quite late before we get to Amelia's as it is. Shall we see you at the weekend?'

'Oh yes,' Ben agreed. 'We shall certainly come. Cathy is looking forward to having tea with Mrs Beaufort. She comes to the cat shows with me, although she isn't as interested as I am, but I know she is looking forward to meeting Mrs Darby.'

'Cathy doesn't believe in that mumbo-jumbo, does she?' Larch said.

'You shouldn't condemn it just like that,' Sarah said, mischief in her eyes. 'Besides, it is a woman's thing, having your fortune told. I think it is fun. I shall ask her to read mine as well, discover if I'm going to be a big star on Broadway.'

'You're already a star,' Ben said. 'I'll just say goodbye to Janey, and then you can be on your way . . .'

Sarah yawned and looked out of the window. It was very late, because she had sat up talking to Larch long after Amelia and Janey had gone to bed. She had sensed that he was upset after they left Ben's house, though he hadn't said anything all the way down here. He hadn't confided what was on his mind until they were alone in Amelia's parlour.

'Why wouldn't you tell Ben who the woman was?' he asked. 'And why didn't you tell me what you'd overheard?'

'Because I wasn't sure if I should tell anyone. It was embarrassing to overhear something like that, Larch. I wasn't sure it had any bearing on Giles's murder and it wasn't really my business. I ought not to have known anything about their conversation.'

'Who came to call them?'

'I don't know, I didn't see him. I was too busy keeping out of the way so that they didn't realize I was there.'

'You haven't told anyone else what you heard?'

'No, of course not. I only told Ben because . . . well, you know.'

'You can trust him,' Larch said. 'Be careful that you don't

mention this to anyone, Sarah – especially the woman whose necklace it was . . .'

'Why?'

'Because . . .' Larch frowned. He'd had an uncomfortable feeling ever since she had related the story. 'I think it might be dangerous. I don't know what is at the root of all this, Sarah – but someone killed Giles Henderson. It might have been for some other reason, but it could be because of the necklace. If he knew how to get copies of expensive jewels made . . .' He broke off, shaking his head. 'None of it makes sense to me, but I had an odd feeling that we were getting into dangerous waters . . . a premonition, if you like.'

'You don't believe in things like that, remember?' Sarah teased him.

'No, I don't,' Larch said. 'When you had feelings about various things that happened down here last year, I thought it was just your imagination playing tricks on you most of the time. But when you were talking to Ben about that necklace I had a sudden fear that you might be in terrible danger, because of something you know. You might not even realize that you know it yet, but if the killer thought you did . . . I don't want you to be his next victim, that's all.'

'Oh, Larch, I'm so sorry,' Sarah said. 'It's because I went haring off with Keith Bates, which made Agnes Browning try to kill me. I promise I won't do anything like that again. If I am bothered about something I shall tell you or Ben.'

'As long as you do,' Larch said and looked relieved. 'I think an awful lot of you, Sarah.'

'Yes, I know, and I'm sorry I made you so angry before.'

'I was frightened out of my wits,' Larch admitted ruefully. 'But we're friends again now, aren't we?'

'Yes, of course,' Sarah replied. 'Now tell me more about your shows . . .'

They had spent the rest of the evening talking easily about various things that they were both interested in, parting on good terms. Now, alone in her room, Sarah felt a little restless, though she wasn't sure why. Larch said they were friends, and of course they were – but did she want to be more?

Going over to the window, Sarah looked out at the garden at the back of the house. It was quite bright, because the moon was almost full, and she frowned as she caught sight of something moving in the garden. What was that? It looked like the shadow of a man . . .

She had seen it fleetingly, but even though she stood watching for some minutes, she saw nothing more. Had it been a man staring at the house, or was it just a trick of the moonlight?

Six

It was a luxury for both girls to get up when they felt like it and spend time over breakfast. They enjoyed simply sitting around, talking to each other, going for walks and being taken out in the evening by Larch, who had offered to drive them wherever they wanted to go. He had shown them some of his paintings, and Janey was in raptures, because she thought they were wonderful. Larch made her a present of a scene in Venice, and she hadn't stopped talking about it ever since.

'He is such a wonderful artist,' she told Sarah. 'And a lovely person. If I were you, I should give up the stage and marry him before someone else gets there first.'

'I might one day, if he asks me,' Sarah replied. 'But neither of us is in a hurry.'

On the morning of the third day, they walked to the village shop and had coffee with the owner, Mrs Roberts, and her sister, Jilly, who had come to live with her after she was attacked the previous year.

'Your grandmother told me you were coming down,' Mrs Roberts said, smiling warmly at Sarah. 'And this is your friend?'

'Janey,' Sarah supplied. 'How are you now, Mrs Roberts? Has Jilly settled in?'

'Yes, she has,' Mrs Roberts replied and looked at Janey. 'Sarah saved my life, you know. I was attacked out there in my back room, but Sarah came through to look for me and the murderer ran off.'

'You didn't tell me that bit,' Janey said, looking at her friend in surprise. 'She knows how to keep a secret, Mrs Roberts. I didn't realize she was a heroine.'

'I thought I heard voices,' Jilly said as she came into the shop from the back. 'I've made the coffee and I baked earlier.

Why don't you take your friends through and have a really good chat, Betty?'

'Yes please,' Janey said. 'I should like to hear all about what happened. Sarah only told me a little bit.'

'Janey, I'm sure Mrs Roberts doesn't want to talk about it,' Sarah said, because she was embarrassed.

'Oh, I don't mind,' Mrs Roberts said. 'It was all very frightening,' she told Janey as she took them through. 'People running around in devil masks and all those murders . . .' She glanced at Sarah as she invited them to sit down in ancient but comfortable armchairs. 'Did you know that Ronnie Miller was back? His mother was in here yesterday, telling me that she hadn't been sleeping well, needed some pills from the doctor to help her. I daresay that lad of hers is difficult to manage.'

'Yes, perhaps. I did hear he was back,' Sarah said. 'He turned up in Mrs Darby's garden and started digging one morning. She said all he asked for was tea and cake, and she seems quite pleased with him.'

'Yes, so she told me when she popped in earlier this morning,' Mrs Roberts said. 'I shouldn't fancy living in that cottage after what happened – but she isn't the nervous sort. And of course she has those dogs.'

'Amelia said they are lovely. I haven't seen them yet, but we might call when we go back.'

'They tell me Mr Larch is back home?' Mrs Roberts said as she poured tea and cut freshly baked sponge cake. 'You will be pleased about that, Sarah. How long are you going to stay here this time?'

'Oh, a couple of weeks. We're going to stay with friends in France after that, just for a few weeks.'

Mrs Roberts nodded. 'Did you know there are new people at the manor? Lady Beecham sold up you know. Well, you can't blame her after what happened . . . it was the shock of my life when I heard that Sir James had shot that gypsy and then himself. I suppose it was in revenge for what he did to Simon Beecham, but . . . well, it wasn't what you would expect of a man like that.'

'No, it wasn't,' Sarah said, wishing that Mrs Roberts wouldn't keep going on about the unpleasant incidents that had taken place the previous year. 'Have you met the new people yet?'

'No, not yet. I've seen their car. I think they have plenty of money, though there's no title. They might be American. Someone said they've spent a lot of money tarting the manor up. I should think Sir James would turn in his grave if he could see it now.'

'Yes, I daresay,' Sarah said. 'At least it is better than leaving it empty, and I suppose Lady Beecham couldn't manage it on her own. She was stuck in that wheelchair and it must have been lonely for her up there.'

'She went to live with a cousin, I think – her cousin, not her husband's – and these new people bought it straight away.'

'Well, that is interesting,' Sarah said and put her cup down. 'I must tell Amelia, because I am sure she didn't know. I think we have to be going now, Mrs Roberts. It was lovely to see you.'

She got up and went through to the shop, buying some pear drops from one of the jars on the back shelf, while Janey stopped to chat with Mrs Roberts for a few seconds longer. When her friend came through, they left the shop and went outside to the High Street.

'Mrs Roberts certainly likes to gossip,' Janey said with a grin, 'but I liked her.'

'She sometimes comes out with a lot of useful information. She supplied the reason for Morna Scaffrey's murder. At least, we thought it was the motive at the time . . .' Sarah shook her head, dismissing her thoughts. 'And Amelia hasn't mentioned her new neighbours, so I'm sure she didn't realize they had moved in.'

'Shall we call on Mrs Darby?' Janey asked. She glanced at her watch. It was rather a nice watch in the art deco style with small diamonds set in platinum around the dial. A present from her aunt Sally for her twenty-first birthday, she had told Sarah. 'Do we have time or shall we be late for lunch?'

'I think we might be if we stop now. Besides, we could walk down this afternoon and have tea with her. She said come any day we felt like it.'

'Yes, that might be better,' Janey agreed. She put a hand to Sarah's arm as an expensive-looking silver and grey car came towards them down the hill. As it went by, they could see that a woman was driving. She was wearing a red jacket and her

hair was a pale, silvery blonde. 'Do you think she is one of
your new neighbours?'

'Yes, possibly,' Sarah said, though she had only noticed the
car, which was, she thought, an American marque. 'Oh, look,
I think that must be Ronnie.'

'Where?' Janey followed the direction of Sarah's gaze and
saw a man sitting on an upturned crate in the front garden of
what everyone still called Miss Bates's cottage. 'Oh, yes. What
is he doing?'

'I think he is sharpening his spade by the looks of it. Don't
stare, Janey. He has noticed us . . .'

Ronnie had got to his feet and stood watching them as they
walked past up the hill. Janey put up her hand and waved to
him, and to her surprise he waved back.

'I know he looks normal,' Sarah said as they continued
on up the hill, 'but his mind is still very childish. I gave
him a bun once and he said he liked me. He couldn't understand that Miss Bates was dead, and I think he still believes
he is working for her. Perhaps he thinks Mrs Darby is Miss
Bates.'

'It is a shame,' Janey said. 'He looked nice . . . attractive.'

'Yes, he does, but if you speak to him you will understand.
I think he is quite harmless, but apparently he causes trouble
if he has too much to drink.'

'A lot of people do that,' Janey remarked.

They were nearing the bend at the top of the hill now. One
way led on to the manor and the other to the Dower House,
which had once belonged to the Beecham family. Amelia's
husband had bought it years before, intending to move on one
day, but she had refused to leave the house she had loved as
a bride – and still loved even now her beloved husband was
dead.

Sarah hesitated as she saw a man walking down the hill
towards them. For a moment she was reminded of Sir James
Beecham, but he had worn the clothes of a country squire
easily. This man looked as if he were all dressed up with
nowhere to go, his riding breeches, boots and hacking jacket
all obviously expensive and brand new. As he came closer,
she could see that he was younger than Sir James had been,
a tall man with dark hair and blue eyes.

'Good morning, ladies,' he said, a slight twang in his voice making Sarah think that once again Mrs Roberts had got her intelligence right. 'I'm Harvey Ashton. We've just moved into the manor and I think you must be the young ladies who have come to stay with Mrs Beaufort?'

'Yes, we are,' Sarah said and smiled at him. She held out her hand, which he took and shook warmly. 'I'm Sarah, Amelia's granddaughter – and this is my friend, Janey.'

'Nice to meet you,' he said and grinned. 'I've just been to introduce myself to Mrs Beaufort and now I'm on my way to Mrs Darby. I thought I would walk because it is a nice day, and it's the best way to meet your neighbours, don't you think?'

'Yes, I do,' Sarah said, a naughty twinkle in her eye. 'You must go and buy something from the local shop, sir. Mrs Roberts knows everyone and she will be pleased to meet you.'

'Thank you, I shall,' he said. 'But please call me Harvey. I should like to make friends. You must come to tea one day soon – isn't that the right thing to do, come have tea with us? We're new to your English customs, but we want to fit right in with everyone.'

'Oh yes, we should love to,' Janey said, 'wouldn't we, Sarah? But not today, because we are having tea with someone else.'

'Come tomorrow then,' he said. 'Nancy has gone off to Norwich for the day. Something to do with the curtains not being quite what she ordered. She wasn't too pleased about that, I can tell you – but she'll be pleased to have you come for tea tomorrow.'

He nodded and set off down the hill once more. Janey turned her head to watch him, suppressing her giggles until they were inside the gardens of the Dower House.

'I wonder what Mrs Roberts will have to tell us about him next time? She's sure to know his life history before she lets him leave her shop.'

'Janey, you are wicked,' Sarah said, but her eyes were bright with laughter. 'He is very nice and friendly.'

'I'm not sure Nancy will be as friendly,' Janey said and gave a little moan as her stomach grumbled. 'I'm so hungry and it isn't long since we had breakfast. It's because of Millie's cooking. If I stayed here long I should get fat!'

Sarah shook her head, because Janey ate far more than Sarah ever did, but she was always the same weight. Perhaps because she did so much exercise and rehearsing for her dancing.

'Millie told me she thought you were too thin and needed proper food,' Sarah said, teasing her. 'Be careful or you will have to live on gruel for a month to get your figure back.'

As they approached the house, the front door opened and a woman came out. Sarah smiled as she saw her. Vera Hayes was the vicar's wife and one of her grandmother's regular visitors.

'Ah, there you are, Sarah,' Mrs Hayes said. 'Amelia told me that you had gone for a walk with your friend. You just missed your grandmother's new neighbour.'

'Actually, we met him as we came up the hill,' Sarah said. 'He seems nice, doesn't he?'

'Well, yes, he is nice enough,' Mrs Hayes said with a little frown. 'I called on her first thing this morning but Mrs Ashton told me she didn't have time for visitors just yet. You never quite know when to call on newcomers.'

'I think she may have been upset over some curtains,' Sarah said. 'No doubt she will be pleased to see you another day.'

'It isn't just the curtains,' Vera Hayes said. 'I think something happened just before they moved here from somewhere near London. Someone broke into their house and some valuable jewellery was stolen, when they were out at a charity affair apparently.'

'Oh, how unpleasant for her,' Sarah said, instantly sympathetic. 'That would be enough to upset anyone. Who told you – was it her husband?'

'No, I heard it from someone else,' Vera said. 'I'm not quite sure who . . . Oh yes, it was Mrs Harlow from Thorny Bridge. Her cousin had a break-in recently while she was at a similar affair, but she lives in Hampshire, and of course the two incidents are quite separate.'

'I don't think I know Mrs Harlow,' Sarah said. 'Is she new here too?'

'Yes, she bought the house early this year. I suppose you wouldn't have met her, but it seems that Mrs Ashton knows her through various charity events that they both attend.' Vera shook her head. 'Well, I mustn't stand here gossiping all day, I have things to do.' She straightened her bicycle, which had been leaning against the house, and mounted it, peddling off with a wave of her hand.

'Another of your grandmother's neighbours?' Janey asked. 'They do seem to talk a lot, don't they?'

'Perhaps there isn't much else to do here. Vera Hayes is a bit like Mrs Roberts. She knows everyone, but where Mrs Roberts has to wait for people to come to her, Mrs Hayes is busy riding from house to house spreading the news. But being burgled might explain why Mrs Ashton is so upset over her curtains.'

'It must be awful to know someone has been in your house, going through your personal things,' Janey said and shivered. 'I think that is worse than losing your jewellery, because I expect it was insured.'

'Yes, I expect so,' Sarah frowned. That was the third time she had been told about stolen jewellery in the past few days, and it seemed that at least two of the thefts had happened when the owners were at a charity affair.

For some reason that stuck in her mind, though of course, as Vera Hayes had said, the two thefts were unrelated incidents.

Rosalind Darby rang just after they had finished eating lunch. She asked to speak to Sarah, and sounded a little strange when Sarah answered.

'Sarah! Were you thinking of coming to see me soon?'

'Janey and I were hoping to have tea with you this afternoon?'

'Oh, good. I would rather have seen you alone, but your friend will be welcome. We can always have a few moments together while she is looking at some of my treasures.'

'I'm intrigued,' Sarah said. 'What kind of treasures?'

'You will see,' Rosalind said and laughed. 'I shall expect you at three this afternoon then.'

Sarah went back into the sitting room. Janey had her head in a recent copy of *Vogue*, and Amelia was setting the cards on a small table as she prepared to play solitaire.

'Rosalind wanted to ask if we were going to visit her,' Sarah said. 'Apparently, she has some treasures to show you, Janey.'

'I think she means a collection of jade,' Janey said, looking interested. 'She was wearing a pretty bracelet the other night. I noticed it and she told me it was part of a large collection.'

'Oh, I see.' Sarah nodded. 'I'm afraid I didn't notice.'

'I've always liked jade,' Janey went on, 'so she said that she would show me her collection.'

'Rosalind has some very nice jewellery,' Amelia observed, looking up from her cards. 'I don't mean diamonds or anything like that, but nice wearable things, nothing too valuable – which is perhaps a good thing at the moment. Vera was telling me about what happened to Mrs Ashton's jewellery. It must be most upsetting for her – but she isn't unique. I believe there have been quite a few robberies lately, all over the country, though particularly in London.'

'Who told you that, Gran?'

'I've read about them in the paper,' Amelia said. 'And Miranda mentioned something about one of her friends losing a valuable diamond necklace.'

'Yes, I see. I suppose she didn't say whether her friend was at a charity do?'

'No, I don't recall that she did.' Amelia looked at her curiously. 'Is there any reason why you wanted to know?'

'No, just curious. Things going on in my head.'

Amelia gave her an old-fashioned look. 'I hope you're not starting to get involved in something, Sarah? Remember what happened last time you turned detective.'

'No, of course not,' Sarah said. 'But I think I shall telephone Muriel before we leave – if you don't mind, Gran?'

'I never mind what you do, as long as it doesn't land you in trouble, my dear.'

Sarah smiled at her grandmother. She could hear Janey and Amelia talking as she went out into the hall. They got on very well, which was nice, and Amelia had already asked Janey to come and stay whenever she had the chance.

Sarah asked for Muriel's number and the exchange put her through after a couple of minutes. It was obvious straight away that Esther's landlady hadn't heard anything, and Sarah spent several minutes reassuring her that Esther must have gone off somewhere, though she wasn't at all sure that her friend would turn up.

Janey looked at her anxiously as she returned to the sitting room. 'Still no news?'

'No, none,' Sarah said. 'Muriel says that she is going back to the police if Esther doesn't turn up by tomorrow. I think she is really worried about her now.'

'As you are,' Amelia said and looked anxious. 'I am beginning to think you must be right, Sarah. It is very odd that she should disappear like this.'

They talked about Esther for a few minutes longer, but there wasn't much any of them could say or do, except repeat the same things over and over again. Sarah glanced at the time, and then suggested that they ought to leave, because Rosalind Darby would be waiting for them.

Andrews was working in the garden as they left the house. Sarah smiled and waved to him. He hesitated and then came towards her.

'I think someone has been interfering with the lock on our shed,' he told Sarah. 'It looks as if they tried to break it but couldn't.'

'That's odd. I did think I saw someone in the garden late one night – it was the night I came home, but then I looked again and no one was there so I thought I must have imagined it.'

'I can't think what they hoped to find in there,' Andrews said. 'It's just the gardening tools and some seeds and bits and pieces. Nothing of any value.'

'It might have been a tramp,' Janey suggested. 'My aunt had trouble with a tramp sleeping in her garden shed a year or two ago. She had to get the police to come and scare him off.'

Andrews nodded, as if he believed she might have hit the nail on the head. 'Well, no harm was done. I haven't told Mrs Beaufort. I don't think I should – do you?'

'It isn't really necessary for her to know,' Sarah said. 'If he didn't get in, no harm was done, was it?'

'No, not really,' Andrews agreed and looked at Janey. 'It might have been just a tramp.'

The two girls continued on their way, walking down the hill past the woods. A cloud of birds rose suddenly into the air, making Janey jump because the noise of their wings was startling.

'Oh, it was only some rooks,' she said, looking relieved as she saw the birds. 'I wondered what had happened for a moment.'

'Something must have disturbed them,' Sarah said, a little shiver running down her spine, because the incident had brought back memories. 'It's nothing to worry about, Janey. Come on, I'll race you to Mrs Darby's house.'

Janey laughed and started to run, Sarah following. She had seen someone in the trees, but it could have been anyone and she didn't want to make her friend nervous. They were out of breath and giggling as they turned into the front garden. Sarah thought it was looking remarkably neat, which meant that Ronnie Miller had been busy.

'Ah, there you are,' Rosalind said, coming to her front door. 'I thought I heard something. It is so nice to see you both again. Is Amelia well?'

'Yes, she is fine,' Sarah said. 'Vera Hayes came to see her this morning and so did Mr Ashton. Did he call on you as well?'

'Yes, he did,' Rosalind said. 'Come in, both of you. I've set my collection out on the table in the parlour, Janey. Why don't you amuse yourself for a few minutes while I have a word with Sarah?'

'Oh . . . yes, of course,' Janey said and went into the room her hostess indicated.

Rosalind led the way into the kitchen before turning to look at Sarah. 'I hope your friend doesn't feel shut out, but I have to talk to you.'

'Is something wrong?' Sarah felt icy cold all of a sudden, because the expression in the older woman's eyes was disturbing.

'The friend you were worried about – did she have dark hair?'

'Yes, but . . .' Sarah stopped. 'What have you seen? That's why you want to talk to me alone, isn't it?'

'Yes. Some people are frightened by things like this, and I thought Janey might be one of them – but I don't believe you are?'

'It depends,' Sarah said, 'but I don't scare easily.'

'I think your friend died the night she was supposed to have met someone,' Rosalind said. 'I saw something last night. I suppose you might call it a dream . . . but I saw a girl being followed into a dark place. She turned and spoke to the man, because she knew him – and then he attacked and killed her.

It was quite shocking and I felt ill for an hour or so after-wards. I always do when I have one of these visions . . .'

'No!' The colour drained from Sarah's face. 'I've been trying to deny it for days, but I've thought she was dead from the beginning. I don't know why. The feeling just wouldn't go away however hard I tried to tell myself she was safe . . .'

'That's how it is when you sense things,' Rosalind said. 'As soon as we met, your fear communicated itself to me and I couldn't help thinking about Esther. That was the name you called her, wasn't it?'

'Yes, though her real name was Mary.'

'He called her Esther, the man who killed her.' Rosalind's hand crept to her throat and Sarah knew that she was upset. 'It isn't pleasant when you see things like that, because it isn't quite like a dream. I was there. I saw it all so clearly and then it faded . . .'

'But where was she? You said it was dark?'

'Yes, very dark, but there were ropes and screens . . .' Rosalind frowned. 'It may be because we came behind the curtain at the theatre the other night. It might all be in my mind, just my imagination, but I think she is there somewhere. I think he killed her and hid her body somewhere in the theatre.'

'It can be very creepy backstage sometimes,' Sarah agreed and then looked at Rosalind in wonder. 'I felt something that last day when I was walking from the dressing room to the stage. Do you think . . .?'

'Yes, it is possible,' Rosalind said. 'I believe that the spirits of the departed stay around for a while, a few hours perhaps, and Esther might well have been trying to communicate with you.'

Sarah shivered. She wasn't sure whether she believed all this, and she was certain that Larch would call it mumbo-jumbo, but Rosalind was very believable – and Sarah had felt something at the theatre the day that Esther didn't turn up for work.

'What should I do?' she asked. 'Is it worth going to the police?'

'They probably wouldn't believe you,' Rosalind said. 'And if they did they might think you had something to do with the murder, because most of them refuse to listen to us. A friend of mine, who has much stronger powers than my own, has offered her services more than once to track down a killer, but they laughed at her.'

'I know someone who wouldn't laugh. He will be here for tea tomorrow. Would you tell him what you told me?'

'Yes, of course,' Rosalind said. 'If you think he would listen.'

'Oh, I am sure he would,' Sarah replied. 'Come and have tea with us. I know Amelia would be pleased, and Cathy, Ben's wife, would love to meet you, I'm sure.' She glanced round as she heard a whistling sound. 'The kettle is boiling. Should we make the tea? Do you have it here or in the parlour?'

'The table is spread with my collection at the moment,' Rosalind said. 'We'll join Janey for a few minutes, shall we? And then we'll have our tea in here.'

Sarah followed her into the parlour. It had shocked her to hear Rosalind declare that Esther had been murdered that first night, even though she had been thinking it herself for the past few days. But hearing someone else say it was different, and she found herself hoping that it was all just nonsense.

Sarah looked around the parlour with interest. Rosalind had changed all the furniture. Janet Bates had had some nice pieces of antique furniture, but Rosalind's things were all more modern. She had gone for the art deco style and the room looked very stylish, with a lot of ebony and satinwood furniture; the sofas had bright shawls thrown over them, and there were lots of cushions everywhere. On a square dining table, the top inlaid with a chequered pattern, she had set out a huge collection of jade objects.

There were all kinds of things, from little Japanese netsuke to miniature animals, all sorts of jewellery, buttons and belt buckles. Sarah admired some pretty vases and a little mirror on a stand of jade.

'Oh, that is lovely,' she said. 'How delicate it is!'

'Yes, it is one of my favourite pieces,' Rosalind replied with a smile. 'I would like you to have it, Sarah – and perhaps Janey would like to choose something for herself?'

'Oh no, you can't!' Sarah cried, horrified. 'You just said it was a favourite thing. I didn't admire it so that you would give it to me.'

'Of course you didn't, Sarah. But I have so much of it,'

Rosalind replied. 'I assure you that this isn't the whole of my collection. I sent some of the more valuable things into storage when I came here. We had a large house, you see, and I couldn't bring everything to this little cottage. I have decided to sell or give away some of my things – and I really would like you to have the mirror.' She smiled at Janey, who had been admiring a beautiful string of dark green beads. 'They might come in useful for you for your stage work, my dear. Please accept them as a gift from me.'

'Are you sure?' Janey blushed. 'I've never had any beads as good as this necklace, though my aunt has promised me a bracelet one day.'

'Of course I am sure,' Rosalind said. 'I have plenty more. My husband wanted to buy me diamonds when we were married, but I preferred jade. I have been collecting all my life, but one can't go on adding all the time. I've decided to give some things to Mrs Hayes for her next bring-and-buy bazaar.'

'Oh, these are much too good,' Sarah said. 'You would do better to sell them to a shop in Norwich and give the money to the church, if that is what you want.'

'Some of the pieces are worth very little,' Rosalind said. 'I promised her she should have a few things, and I shall keep my word. But now I think the kettle will have boiled nearly dry and we ought to have our tea . . .'

Sarah decided not to say anything to her friend about what Rosalind had told her in the kitchen. If Janey believed it to be a true vision it might frighten her. Besides, Sarah wanted to hear what Ben had to say when he came to tea before she spoke to anyone else.

She knew a lot of people would say that Rosalind had invented it all, but Sarah was certain she had actually seen something. It might be that Rosalind had been influenced by what she'd noticed backstage at the party, but Sarah had felt something . . . unpleasant . . . that same day.

Larch might dismiss it all as nonsense, but Ben would listen and give Rosalind's dream – if it was a dream – proper consideration.

Sarah wondered if she ought to tell him what else was in her mind, but the jewel thefts could have nothing to do with what had happened to Giles, despite the conversation she had overheard concerning a stolen necklace.

She wished that she had looked to see who had called Pamela Avery that day in the conservatory. She knew that it had been a man, but she didn't think it was Lord Avery, because she was sure he had been away somewhere that day. Besides, would Lady Avery have dared to kiss her lover if her husband had been at home?

Had someone else heard them talking that day? Had Giles been murdered because of the necklace? Sarah's thoughts were confused, twisting and turning as if she were trapped in a maze. She knew that she was searching for a link, and that was ridiculous, because there was nothing to find. After all, why should there be? She was just upset over Esther and all the rest was imagination.

She decided that she would keep her ideas to herself for the moment, though she would ask Ben what he thought she ought to do about Rosalind's vision.

'There you are,' Cathy said as they left the show in Norwich, Ben carrying his prize cats while she carried the ribbons. 'I told you it wasn't all fixed, didn't I? You won first and second prizes today.'

'Bella deserved the first prize, but Sukie was lucky to get second,' Ben said. 'But did you notice that Lady Avery wasn't there today? I think that made all the difference.'

'What does it matter?' Cathy asked. 'At least the judging was fair.'

'Yes, it was,' Ben agreed. 'Though I think Harry Carter's Jenny should have got the second prize – and he thought so too.'

'There's no satisfying you, Ben Marshall,' Cathy said. 'If you lose you grumble and when you win . . .'

'I still grumble,' Ben said and grinned at her. 'I like to see fair play, love – and I still think there's something going on . . .'

Cathy shook her head, because when it came to the cats, there was no arguing with him. 'I'm looking forward to seeing Mrs Beaufort and Sarah again,' she said to change the subject.

'Yes, so am I,' Ben agreed. 'I wonder if she's heard any news about that friend of hers. If she's still missing I think

I'll give Gareth a ring and ask him if they can start an investigation.' He deposited the cages in the back of the car, making sure that they were secure. 'I'll give them some food and water when we get to Mrs Beaufort's house. She might let me take them into the kitchen, give them a little run around for a few minutes if I ask her.'

'You can't do that, Ben,' Cathy said. 'She might not like to say no.'

'She's got a cat of her own,' he said. 'He is usually around somewhere so I think she will understand. Anyway, I'll ask and see what she says . . .'

Cathy looked at him disapprovingly, but she knew that Ben was always concerned to see that his cats had the best attention he could give them on long journeys. Glancing over her shoulder, she saw that Bella had settled down to sleep as she usually did, but Sukie was making plaintive noises.

'Well, maybe she won't mind . . .'

'I'm sure she won't,' Ben said. 'I've got their trays so they won't make a mess.'

'Just make sure they don't,' Cathy said, but she knew he would look after the cats, because he always did. 'Have you made up your mind whether you will take the villa that Major Henderson offered you?'

'I haven't made much headway with the case,' Ben said. 'I think I would rather stick to a hotel, Cathy. It was good of him to offer, but I prefer to pay my own way.'

'I thought you might say that,' Cathy replied and smiled. 'I'm glad. I think I would rather stay in a hotel anyway.'

'That's settled then,' he said. 'I shall arrange it on Monday, because I told Henderson that I couldn't guarantee a result and I'm not going to cancel our holiday. If I come up with something in the meantime, I'll set things in motion, but so far I'm working in the dark.'

Ben frowned, because he was aware that he was searching for something, a link that would make sense of the bits and pieces he had learned so far. It might help if he could break the code in Giles's notebook but as yet his expert hadn't got back to him. Perhaps the police were right after all and it was just down to the burglary. Yet his instincts were telling him the link was there – if he could find it.

* * *

Amelia said straight away that it was all right for the cats to be in the kitchen. She followed Ben into the large, comfortable room, as he took the cages through and let the two cats out, having first made sure that Mr Tibbs was shut in the sitting room.

'We don't want any accidents,' she told Ben with a smile. 'Mr Tibbs is very precious to me, but he might not take kindly to having strangers on his territory.'

'This is very good of you,' Ben said and smiled at her. 'I like to let them out for a bit when I can, but if they got into the garden they would be off like a shot. They aren't used to it, you see. I have a special run for them at home where they can play safely.'

'I suppose you have to be careful with pedigree cats like this,' Amelia said. 'But they will be all right here, won't they, Millie?'

'Oh yes,' Millie said. 'They are beautiful, especially that one – what is her name?'

'She's Bella and she's my best cat,' Ben said with pride. 'She took first prize today and Sukie took the second, though I'm not sure she deserved it.'

'You'll hurt her feelings,' Millie said and bent down to stroke the smaller cat. 'She is beautiful too, aren't you, my precious?'

'Come into the sitting room,' Amelia said. 'Millie will make sure they are all right. She will give them some milk and water – and some of that chicken we had for lunch, if that is all right?'

'That's very kind of you. I'm sure they would enjoy that,' Ben said. 'I'll come back in a few minutes and put them back in their cages.' He followed Amelia out into the hall, carefully shutting the door behind him.

'Millie will wait to bring in the tea trolley until you've put them back safely,' Amelia said. 'Come and talk to Sarah, Mr Marshall. I know she is very worried about something, but she won't tell me what.'

'I expect it is that friend of hers,' Ben said and frowned. 'I suppose she hasn't turned up?'

'No, I'm afraid not. It is rather worrying, isn't it? Sarah has something on her mind, but she won't talk to anyone until she has seen you.'

Ben nodded his understanding. When he saw Sarah's expression, he knew it was serious, and when she asked him if he would like to have a walk about the garden, he agreed at once.

'Something has happened,' he said. 'Tell me what has upset you, Sarah. I'll do what I can to help.'

'I know it may sound strange or even foolish,' Sarah said, 'but I have thought Esther was dead from the beginning . . .' She explained about Rosalind's vision and he listened in silence. 'I don't know if it is a dream or a true vision – but I have a horrible feeling she is right. I felt something backstage at the theatre that day . . . a creepy feeling . . .'

'Are you sure you felt it then and not afterwards?'

'Yes, quite sure. I know that I may have communicated my fear to Rosalind, and she may have imagined it all . . . but I can't help thinking that she is right and that Esther is in the theatre somewhere.'

'Then I think I should ask a colleague of mine to start an investigation, don't you? I believe we'll keep Mrs Darby out of it for the time being, because policemen in general are a bit sceptical about these things. However, I could suggest that the last time she was seen alive was outside the theatre. It would be the logical place to begin the search . . .'

'Oh yes,' Sarah said, smiling in relief. 'Rosalind is coming now. Oh dear, she is heading round to the back of the house and she has her dogs . . .'

'Bella!' Ben cried and made a sprint round to the back door. He was just in time to see Rosalind open it, and then the dogs started barking madly and a cat came streaking out towards him. He snatched Bella up in his arms, holding her away from the dogs Rosalind was trying desperately to control.

'I'm so sorry,' Rosalind said. 'I didn't know they were in the kitchen. Mr Tibbs takes no notice of them . . .'

Ben had no time to answer. He saw Sukie squeeze out of the door that Millie had tried to shut and go streaking across the garden. He gave a shout of alarm and Sarah set off after the terrified cat, she shot out of the gate towards the road.

'You look after Bella,' Sarah called out. 'I'll try and catch Sukie . . .'

'I am so very sorry,' Rosalind apologized, having finally got her dogs to sit and stop barking. 'I'll take them home . . .'

'No, don't do that,' Ben said. 'I'll pop Bella in her cage

and put her in the car. And then I'll go after Sarah and see if she's had any luck. You take the dogs in, Mrs Darby. It wasn't your fault.'

'Oh but . . .' Rosalind sighed as he disappeared into the kitchen. Now she would be in Mr Marshall's black books and she had particularly wanted to make a good impression.

Seven

S arah saw the cat heading for the road and hurried after her. She was not certain what to do for the best, because the poor thing was clearly frightened and unused to being outside. If she got into the woods, it might take weeks to find her and she could be lost for good.

As she reached the grass verge, Sarah breathed a sigh of relief as she saw that Sukie had crouched down in the middle of the road. Perhaps if she coaxed her, she might get near enough to grab her. Making soothing noises, she inched towards the cat, trying not to startle her, and then suddenly she saw the car coming down the hill. The cat flattened itself, caught in the headlights, seeming too terrified to move. Sarah no longer had a choice. She made a dive across the path of the oncoming vehicle and scooped Sukie up in her arms as the car screeched to a halt and slid across to the grass verge.

'It's all right, I've got you now,' Sarah said, holding the cat protectively and rubbing her face against its soft fur. Sukie made a hissing sound and her claws snaked out, scratching Sarah's cheek, but Sarah held on, even though her captive made a desperate attempt to struggle free. 'Hush now, you're safe.'

'What the hell did you think you were doing?'

Sarah became aware that the driver of the car had jumped out and was coming towards her. She glanced at the woman's furious face, belatedly realizing that her act of instinctive courage might have caused an accident.

'I'm terribly sorry,' Sarah said. 'But the cat got out and she was terrified. She couldn't move and you would have hit her—'

'Stupid cat,' the woman said. 'Why can't you keep it under control? You might have caused an accident, to say nothing of the damage to my car!'

'Sarah!'

Sarah turned in relief as she heard Ben's voice just behind her. 'Oh, Ben, it's all right. I managed to get her. She is quite safe.'

'But you very nearly weren't,' Ben said. He took Sukie from her, soothing her quivering body for a few moments before putting her into her cage. 'If that car hadn't swerved you might have been killed.'

'Exactly,' the woman said. 'I don't know who you are, young woman, but if my car is damaged I shall expect you to pay for it.'

'My name is Sarah Beaufort. I think you must be Mrs Ashton. You are my grandmother's new neighbour. I met your husband this morning – and of course if there is any damage I should expect to pay.'

'Oh . . .' Nancy Ashton looked slightly taken aback. 'I see . . . well, I suppose there was no harm done, but you should be more careful in future.'

'Yes, of course. I am so sorry if I upset you.'

'It doesn't matter.' Nancy Ashton turned and walked back to the car, driving off without another glance in their direction.

'Not exactly friendly, was she?' Ben said as the car shot off down the hill. He looked at Sarah and frowned. 'I have to thank you for saving Sukie – but it was a bit reckless. I would rather have lost the cat than seen you knocked down and badly injured.'

'Well, it didn't happen,' Sarah said. 'Please don't tell Amelia – or Larch. They would both scold me and they don't need to know.'

'Providing you promise to think first next time,' Ben said. 'It scared me, Sarah, but I shan't scold you. I know why you did it and I am grateful.'

'I'm afraid I've upset Amelia's neighbour,' Sarah said, looking rueful. 'Her husband told us this morning that his wife was upset over some curtains and now I've ruined her day – and the poor woman had some jewellery stolen recently.'

'How do you know that?' They walked back to Ben's car. He popped the cat's cage inside and locked the door, pocketing the key. 'We don't want any more accidents.'

'No, I was worried about poor Sukie, but she seems all

right now,' Sarah said. 'Vera Hayes told me about the theft. She is the vicar's wife – do you remember that she was the one who came to tell us about Morna Scaffrey?'

'Ah yes, her husband was having a problem with the pagan rites in the churchyard . . .' Ben looked at her. 'I suppose all that stopped after what happened to Madeline Lewis-Brown and Simon Beecham? They were clearly the mainstay of the coven, or whatever they called it.'

'Yes, I am sure that has all finished,' Sarah agreed. 'And I think the cats have stopped disappearing.'

'I'd forgotten about that,' Ben said, looking thoughtful. 'You have a good eye for detail, Sarah. I valued your opinion very much over that business last year.'

'I wish I could help you more with Giles Henderson's murder. I keep thinking it has something to do with that necklace, but I don't know why.'

'That's interesting,' Ben said. 'The same thing occurred to me.' He smiled at her. 'I must admit that I haven't made much headway with this case – so if you think of anything, you will let me know?'

'Yes, of course,' Sarah said. 'But now I think we've kept everyone waiting long enough. Perhaps we ought to go in and have our tea . . .'

After tea, Amelia took Janey and Cathy into the dining room to look at some photographs, leaving Sarah, Rosalind and Ben together. Sarah asked Rosalind to repeat what she had told her at the cottage, and Ben listened to her in thoughtful silence.

'Well, Mrs Darby,' he said when she had finished. 'I have heard of things like this before, and I'm not going to dismiss what you've seen out of hand – especially as Sarah has a feeling about this too. I shall ring a friend of mine in the morning and ask him to start a search for Esther. I think we have reason enough to suspect that there might be something wrong about her disappearance.'

'Thank you for listening,' Rosalind said with a smile. 'I know it sounds as if I'm a silly woman with an overworked imagination, but I assure you I wouldn't upset Sarah for the world.'

'Yes, I believe that,' Ben replied. 'Well, I shall set things in motion in the morning and we'll see what happens.' He looked at Sarah. 'I'm not sure where – or if – this fits in with the rest of my investigations, but I've got a feeling it might. I am taking Cathy away soon, but I shan't just forget what I've discovered, and I'll come back to it when we return from France.'

'Oh, Amelia and I are going to France for a few weeks,' Sarah told him. 'I'll give you the address, shall I? Just in case either of us thinks of something . . .'

Ben stared at her. He was certain she hadn't told him all her thoughts on the case, because he had seen that look in her eye once before.

'I don't know why, but I am going to ask you not to do anything that Larch wouldn't approve of,' he said. 'And that means going off and trying to solve a mystery all on your own, Sarah.'

'Oh no,' she said, and laughed huskily. 'I promise I shan't, Ben. I've already told Larch that I won't follow any leads alone. I'll keep in touch with you or him if he is around – that is why I've given you that address. I am not sure of the telephone number out there, but Lady Avery is sure to have one connected.'

'Lady Avery?' Ben said and frowned. 'Her name keeps cropping up. I don't know why . . . You're not holding out on me, are you, Sarah?'

'Oh no, of course not. It is just that . . .' She shook her head. 'None of it fits and yet I think it has to . . .'

'Yes,' Ben agreed. 'I have been trying to find a link myself, but there probably isn't one, you know.'

'Yes, I expect you are right,' Sarah said and gave a little sigh. 'I wish Esther would turn up and everything else would just go away. I know I wanted to discover things when Miss Bates was killed – but I don't this time. I haven't tried to get involved, but . . .'

'You feel as if you are?'

'Yes, I do,' Sarah told him seriously. 'The flowers Esther thought were for her were meant for me. If I had agreed to meet whoever sent them . . .' She shook her head. 'I just keep thinking that he might have been angry because it wasn't me that night. Might he have killed Esther because she wasn't me?'

'You mustn't think that, Sarah,' Rosalind said. 'I believe

that you are involved in this, whether you like it or not – but it isn't your fault.'

'Mrs Darby is right,' Ben agreed. 'Personally, I am glad you didn't get the flowers. I shouldn't want you to be the one who disappeared.'

'I wouldn't have met him, whoever he is, but supposing he was expecting me that night . . .' A cold chill went down her spine. 'Do you think . . .'

'That he might try again?' Ben asked. 'You must be careful, Sarah. I am sure you are safe enough for the time being, but if you go back to the theatre . . .' Ben broke off as the door opened and his wife, Janey and Mrs Beaufort entered the room. 'Keep in touch, Sarah. I think we ought to be on our way now. Mustn't keep the cats shut up for too long.'

'I'll see you off,' Sarah said, and got up to go to the door with him. She hesitated in the hall for a moment, then: 'I can't help thinking that Giles may have been killed because of that necklace . . . and that his death may be connected to the jewellery thefts. Several of them have happened while the owners were out at a charity affair. You might ask your friend at the Yard if there is a pattern to those thefts . . .'

'Yes, I could do that,' Ben agreed and looked serious. 'It is odd how often we think alike, Sarah. We make a good team.'

'Thank you,' she said, feeling relieved that she had told him at least a part of what was in her mind. 'It was lovely to see you again, Mrs Marshall. I hope you will enjoy your holiday in France.'

'Please call me Cathy, my dear. It was very nice to see you. Ben thinks so highly of you, and I can see why.'

Sarah shook her head. She watched as they walked to the car together and then drove away. She shivered as a cold breeze came into the house. It would be so much better if Esther turned up alive.

Miranda looked at her husband as she came downstairs that evening. She was wearing a new evening dress, which she had purchased from Worth; it had a low waist with a fringed sash and a cutaway back. She had twisted her pearls twice about her throat. She saw Peter's eyes narrow as he noticed that she was not wearing her emeralds.

'The clasp has been a little awkward on my emeralds,' she told him. 'I didn't want to wear them this evening in case I lost them.'

'You should have told me before,' he said, his frown easing. 'I'll take them in to the jeweller's for you when I come home from my business trip and have them repaired. What is the trouble?'

'Oh, it keeps coming undone,' Miranda lied. 'It might just be me – but I think the clasp is a little weak.'

'I'll have another safety clasp fitted.' He smiled at her. 'Are you ready to leave, my dear?'

'Yes . . .' Miranda hesitated. She had invented the weak clasp because she was beginning to think that she would have to lose the emeralds. She was going to have to do something, because her tormentor had phoned her again that morning, warning her that she had a little over two weeks left. 'I'm going down to visit Amelia Beaufort tomorrow. I shan't take the emeralds.'

'No, no, don't wear them again until I have them fixed,' her husband said, his gaze narrowing. 'You look very nice, as you always do, Miranda – but I have thought you seemed a bit distant of late. Is something worrying you?'

'No, of course not. Why should I be worried?' She felt coldness at the nape of her neck. Had he heard something? Did he suspect her of lying about the emeralds? Yet why should he? She smiled up at him, her mouth soft and slightly open, seductive. 'I'm fine, darling. I had thought that I might be . . . well it is several months now and I know you would like an heir . . .'

'If that is all, you can stop worrying,' he said and laughed. 'A child of any sex would be welcome, Miranda – but it isn't the reason I married you. Surely you know that I adore you? I just want you to be happy.'

'I am very happy,' she assured him. 'I love you, Peter. I wanted to give you something in return for all you have given me.'

'You don't have to give me anything,' her husband told her, a serious expression in his eyes. 'I want you just as you are.'

Miranda was tempted to tell him that she was being black-mailed. She knew that he would sort it out and that she wouldn't have to find the money or worry about it any more

– but he wouldn't look at her that way again. He would be hurt and angry, and he might stop loving her. Miranda didn't want to lose what she had – and she wasn't going to! As she saw it, she had two choices. One was to give in to her black-mailer; the other was to discover his identity and kill him, before he ruined her life.

She couldn't be sure that the blackmailer was Tommy Rowe, but she was beginning to think it might be. Miranda had been looking at the code in Giles's address book again. She was pretty sure that 'F' stood for friend and the 'XX' just meant a very good friend. Pamela had mentioned that Tommy didn't much like Giles – so that 'S' might stand for snob or snake. Tommy was sure to visit his sister at her villa in France and that would give Miranda a chance to study him, listen to his voice – and perhaps catch him out. If it came to a choice between losing Peter's respect and killing a blackmailer, Miranda thought she knew what to do.

'What time is Miranda coming?' Sarah asked that morning. 'I was thinking of walking down to the village. I have a letter to post and I thought I might call and have a word with Mrs Darby.'

'Miranda said she should be here for tea,' Amelia told her. 'She said she would come down on the train. Andrews can fetch her from the station.'

'Oh good. I don't want to be out when she arrives,' Sarah said, 'but Larch suggested lunch. I wasn't sure whether to go or not . . .'

'Yes, of course you should go. What about Janey?'

'She wants to go shopping in Norwich for the day,' Sarah said. 'Andrews said he would take her to the station. If she comes back on the afternoon train he may be able to pick her up at the same time as Miranda.'

'He can always go twice if not. He is always so obliging,' Amelia said. 'Ring Larch and tell him to pick you up from Rosalind's. He will think you are avoiding him if you don't go. You haven't been alone with him since that night at the theatre.'

'I was wondering if Ben might telephone . . .'

'If he does, I'll tell you anything that he might have to say, Sarah. You can't sit around all the time waiting for news.'

'No, I can't. I'll just have a word with Janey, and then I'll ring Larch before I walk down to Mrs Darby's.'

'Yes, do that,' her grandmother said. 'I am sure Rosalind will be pleased to see you.'

Sarah went into the hall and rang Larch at home. Lady Meadows answered and they talked for a few minutes before Larch came to the telephone.

'I'm going to Mrs Darby's house,' Sarah said. 'Could you pick me up in half an hour or so?'

'Yes, of course.' Larch sounded pleased. 'I've discovered a new place for lunch, Sarah. Mother told me about it. We'll go there.'

'Lovely. I shall look forward to it,' Sarah said. 'I'll see you soon.'

She replaced the receiver, picked up her softly-fitting jacket and called goodbye to her grandmother as she left the house. The wind was cool as she walked down the hill so she went at a brisk pace. As she passed a certain spot in the woods, her eyes strayed towards the trees, seeking something, but there was no shadow lurking there that morning. She had probably imagined it the day the birds went up suddenly, Sarah thought. It was a pity that she should feel this way about the woods, because she had always loved them – but she still wondered about Morna Scaffrey's murder. Everyone seemed to think that Simon Beecham had killed her and that Morna's brother had taken his revenge by brutally decapitating Simon, but a doubt still lingered in Sarah's mind, though she didn't know why.

As she approached Mrs Darby's cottage, she saw a man in the garden. He was bending over to fuss one of the dogs, but as he straightened she saw that it was Ronnie Miller.

'Hello,' she said and smiled at him. 'How are you, Ronnie?'

He turned his vacant eyes on her, and then a slow grin spread over his face. 'I like you,' he said. 'I remember you . . . you gave me a bun.' He looked at her expectantly, as if he hoped for another. Remembering a small bar of Fry's chocolate in her pocket, she took it out and offered it. Ronnie grinned, taking it and tearing off the paper at once, cramming half of it into his mouth, a blissful smile on his face as he spluttered, 'You're nice . . . like she was . . .'

For a moment there was a strange expression in Ronnie's

eyes, but Rosalind Darby had appeared at the door of her cottage and she waved at Sarah.

'Have you come to visit me, my dear?'

'Yes, I have. Goodbye, Ronnie,' Sarah said, walking past him towards Rosalind. The dog bounded after her, panting, its tongue hanging out. 'Just for a few minutes, Rosalind. Larch is picking me up soon. He is taking me to lunch.'

'How nice,' Rosalind said. 'I like that young man – rather intense, of course, particularly where you are concerned, but trustworthy.'

'Oh yes, that describes Larch very well,' Sarah said and laughed. 'I was pleased to see Ronnie getting on so well with your dogs. He hates cats, you know.'

'Does he? Well, I can't blame him. I'm not a cat person myself,' Rosalind said. 'I felt awful about Mr Marshall's cats, though. It would have been a disaster if that poor thing had been lost or knocked over.'

'Poor Sukie was terrified. She just froze in the middle of the road.'

They were inside the cottage now, which was spick and span and smelled of lavender polish. 'Sit down, my dear. Have you time for coffee?'

'Not unless you were making some for yourself,' Sarah told her. 'I would rather talk. I've been wondering if you . . .' She shook her head. 'No, of course you haven't. It doesn't work like that, does it?'

'If you mean can I conjure up my visions at will, the answer is no,' Rosalind said. 'They come out of the blue, sometimes at the most awkward moments. No, I haven't had any more for the moment . . .' She hesitated and then frowned. 'Mr Marshall is very pleasant, isn't he? I should imagine he was good at his job?'

'Yes, I expect he was. Sir William – he is Larch's father – well, he thinks that Ben should become a private investigator.'

'I should imagine most of that is humdrum stuff,' Rosalind said. 'Why did he give up his work at the Yard, do you know?'

'I think he was ill,' Sarah said. 'He is fine now though. I know what you mean. He is too clever to be retired so young, isn't he?'

'Exactly. It seems a waste – and yet perhaps it was meant to be. We never know these things . . .'

'No . . .' Sarah shook her head, drawing a little picture on the kitchen table with the tip of her finger. 'I can't rest. I'm waiting for news. I don't want them to find Esther and yet I know she is there . . . in the theatre.'

'I have been thinking about it,' Rosalind said. 'I mean, why should he have killed her – if he did? She wasn't the girl he wanted to date, but he didn't have to kill her.'

'Esther's landlady told us that two other showgirls were attacked a couple of years ago. One of them was found strangled, and the other had been badly beaten and is still in a mental home because of what happened to her.' She frowned. 'I wonder if either Ben or I should visit her . . .'

'Do you think there is a connection? Be careful, Sarah. I am sure Ben will have thought of it.'

'Yes, I expect so,' Sarah said. 'I know there are killers who strike repeatedly, of course – like Jack the Ripper to quote a famous case – but why wait for two years before killing again? And if Esther has been murdered it must surely have been an impulse killing? He hadn't planned to kill her, because he meant to send the flowers to me.'

Rosalind looked at her. 'Are you afraid he will come after you next?'

'No! I am not sure . . . it doesn't make sense though, does it?'

'Perhaps it does if you think it through,' Rosalind said, surprising her. 'If the murders were committed by the same man . . . perhaps he thinks that showgirls are sluts and that is why he kills them.'

'Sluts . . .' Sarah's face turned pale. 'That is what he called Esther. Karen said it made her cry . . .' She explained about Karen meeting Esther outside the theatre that night and Rosalind nodded, her expression thoughtful.

'Esther was eager to go out with him because she thought he had sent her the flowers and that he would take her somewhere nice. You, on the other hand, had turned Giles down several times, even though he had sent you flowers and asked you to dinner . . . it might be that he admires you but despised her.'

'That is horrible . . .' A shudder went through Sarah. 'You are saying that he killed Esther because she dared to think she could take my place?'

'Well, yes and no,' Rosalind said. 'No sane person would kill for such a reason – but how can anyone understand the mind of a killer? If this man admires you, thinks that you are different from all the others . . . he might have been very angry when Esther turned up instead of you.'

'Yes, that is what has been bothering me,' Sarah said. 'I feel as if I am responsible for what happened to her, though I know that is silly – but I can't help it.'

'You mustn't think like that. We don't know if any of this is right – for the moment it is just speculation, and if it does turn out to be correct it still isn't your fault.'

'Not strictly speaking, but if I am somehow the reason for Esther's murder . . .' Sarah shook her head. 'We're talking as though we know she is dead, and we can't know for sure yet.'

'Of course not. I may just have had a bad dream and Esther will turn up and ask why you were worried.'

'Yes . . .' Sarah knew that Rosalind was merely trying to comfort her. However, at that moment they heard a car draw up outside and she got to her feet, glancing out of the window. 'Larch is here.'

'You go and have a nice lunch with him,' Rosalind told her. 'Remember that whatever the truth, it wasn't your fault, Sarah.'

'Yes, I shall,' Sarah said and impulsively kissed Rosalind's cheek. 'Thank you so much. It has made me feel better talking to you.'

'We must talk again another day,' Rosalind said.

Sarah went out into the garden. Larch had got out of the car and was speaking to Ronnie, who had an odd, sulky expression on his face, as if he didn't like what had been said to him.

'Are you ready?' Larch asked, unsmiling.

'Yes, of course,' Sarah said. She looked at him as he held the door for her, wondering why he was looking so stern. She waited until he was in the car with the engine running before asking, 'Is something wrong?'

'I am surprised they let Ronnie Miller come home, that's all,' Larch told her. 'I thought he would stay in that secure hospital for good.'

'Oh, but why?' Sarah was surprised because Larch had championed Ronnie from the start, one of the first to claim a miscarriage of justice when the police took him away the previous year. 'He didn't do anything wrong, except cause a little disturbance at the pub when he'd been drinking.'

'I'm not sure that is all he did,' Larch replied. 'I think he may have killed Miss Bates's cat . . .'

'I suppose he might have done that,' Sarah admitted, feeling a little sick at the idea. 'I know he doesn't like them, and it was horrible if he did – but not wicked enough to be shut up for the rest of his life, surely? I can't see him killing anyone. I don't think he would know what to do – though someone told me that once Ronnie learns something he never forgets it.'

'No, I doubt if he would know what to do, but if someone told him . . .' Larch debated whether to tell her that he suspected Ronnie of something much worse than killing cats, but decided against it. All he had to go on was a certain look in Ronnie's eyes when he had visited him at the home – and he might have imagined that, of course. At the time it had sent a chill down Larch's spine, but since then he had wondered if he'd been mistaken. 'No, of course not. I hope you will like this new restaurant, Sarah. Mother thinks it is very good.'

'Then I am sure I shall like it,' Sarah said. 'Anyway, being with you again is lovely.'

'Same here.' Larch grinned at her. 'I sort of missed it when I was travelling.'

He had missed her a great deal more than he was prepared to say, because he didn't want Sarah to feel that she was being pressured. He knew that she wanted to make a go of her career, and he felt a bit like that himself – not that it would stop him painting if they married. It might make Sarah think she ought to give up the stage, however, especially if they were to have a child. All in all, it was probably best to let her get the singing bit out of her system.

Sarah was feeling happy when Larch drove her home after lunch. The new restaurant he'd taken her to was situated by the river, and they had been given a table by the window, which looked out on a gorgeous view. It had been pleasant to sit and watch the ducks and swans on the water, and the occasional houseboat passing by. The food was rather special too, making it a treat she wouldn't forget.

After lunch they had gone for a stroll by the river, talking mostly about Larch's travels, because for some reason he seemed reluctant to mention the show.

'I've never been to Venice,' Sarah told him, 'though of course I've seen paintings. Daddy wanted to take me last year but I had other things on my mind.'

'You ought to see it for yourself,' Larch told her. 'I don't think anyone has ever really done it justice – not even Canaletto. The light over the Grand Canal has to be seen to be appreciated . . . something magical that I couldn't quite get, however much I tried.'

'Yes, I envied you that when you sent that card,' Sarah said. 'Perhaps I shall go another year. As you know, I have accepted an invitation to stay with Pamela Avery and I must find a job when I get back.'

'I've already offered you one,' Larch said as he held the car door for her to get in. A cloud had come over and there were a few spots of rain starting to fall. 'I didn't mean you to do it for free, Sarah. I'll pay whatever the going rate is for the job.'

'You are sure you weren't just inventing it for me?' she quizzed him with a teasing smile. 'I shouldn't like that, Larch. I'll do it if you really need someone – but I won't take charity.'

'I really do need help,' Larch said, avoiding her eyes. He felt a bit guilty, because of what she had just said, but he didn't want her to know anything about that . . . 'Besides, it would mean we should spend more time together this year.'

'Yes, it would,' she agreed. 'All right, that's definite then. I'll help you with the shows when I get back from France.' He had drawn up outside the house, stopping the car to look at her. 'Are you coming in?'

'No, I won't this time if you don't mind,' Larch said. 'I have something to do this evening and I had better get back.'

'Yes, of course. Give me a ring when you have time.'

'Yes . . .' He leaned towards her, kissing her cheek. 'I've enjoyed today, Sarah.'

'So have I, very much,' Sarah told him. She stood waving at the door as he drove away, and then turned and went into the house. The shadow that had been hovering at her shoulder for days had lifted while she was with Larch, but quite suddenly she felt cold all over.

Amelia had come out into the hall, having heard Sarah arrive. The expression in her grandmother's eyes told Sarah that her worst fears had been confirmed.

'You've heard something,' she said. 'Is it Esther?'

'Yes, my dear.' Amelia looked upset. 'Mr Marshall rang earlier. He said that her body had already been discovered when he went to the Yard to ask if an investigation could be started. Apparently . . . some of the cast from the new show had noticed an unpleasant smell and one of the stagehands found her under a pile of ropes.'

'Exactly where Rosalind said,' Sarah gasped, feeling light-headed for a moment. 'That is horrid, Gran.'

'Yes, my dearest, it is,' Amelia said. Her hand trembled a little and Sarah was immediately concerned.

'Gran,' she cried, 'all this has upset you, hasn't it? Come and sit down. Millie can bring the tea – or something stronger. Perhaps a little brandy?'

'A cup of tea will do very well,' Amelia said, straightening her back. She was very sprightly for her age, still young in her outlook, though her old-fashioned clothes made her look as though she belonged to a more elegant age, and not the roaring twenties.

'I am distressed, as anyone would be – but I cannot help thinking that it might have been you, Sarah. If those flowers were for you—'

'I shouldn't have accepted the invitation, Gran,' Sarah assured her as they went into the comfortable sitting room. The chairs were deep with cushions and a welcoming fire burned in the hearth, a faint scent of polish and potpourri lingering in the air. 'Truly I wouldn't . . . I had lots of flowers and several invitations to dinners, but I never went out with anyone alone. It was always Janey and me – and quite often Esther and some of the other girls came along. We were quite safe like that, dearest.'

'Yes, I am sure you were,' her grandmother said and sat down in a Georgian elbow chair near the fire. 'But one cannot help being a little anxious . . . with you living alone in London.' She fingered a copy of the *Tatler* on the table beside her.

'I wasn't alone, Gran. Janey was with me.'

'Yes, I know, and I am being silly,' Amelia said. 'Mr Marshall would like you to telephone him later. He was going to be out this afternoon, but he said he would be at home this evening.'

'Then I shall ring him after I have rung Rosalind,' Sarah

said. 'I must tell her, because she will be anxious to know. You haven't done so already?'

'No, I didn't feel I ought,' Amelia said. 'I think—' She broke off, listening, and then Sarah heard the crunch of tyres on gravel. 'I think that must be the car. Andrews has fetched Miranda from the station. I don't think we should say anything to her.'

'No, of course not,' Sarah said, though she thought that perhaps she might mention it if she got a chance to be alone with Amelia's god-daughter.

Eight

Miranda had turned lighting a cigarette into an art form, Sarah thought as she watched her take a gold and enamelled cigarette case, which looked as if it might be Russian and was probably Fabergé, out of her bag. A matching lighter followed and finally an elegant black holder, with a band of gold at the thicker end. She fitted a cigarette into the holder and then flicked her lighter, drawing smoke into her mouth and exhaling a little cloud with evident relief.

'I am so glad you don't mind me smoking, Amelia,' she said. 'I didn't on the train, of course – it isn't quite nice – and I've been dying for one since.'

'No, of course not, my dear,' Amelia told her with a smile. 'I don't myself, but Sarah does occasionally, and most of my gentlemen friends do – though not cigars in my presence. I cannot tolerate them.'

'Did you have a good journey down?' Sarah asked, shaking her head as Miranda offered her a cigarette. 'No, thank you, not just at the moment.' She glanced at the clock on the mantle. It was a little past five o'clock and Janey still wasn't back from her shopping trip to Norwich. 'Do you think Andrews went down to the station again?'

'You are thinking that Janey might have missed the last train?' Amelia said. 'It is possible I suppose, though you did tell her that the four fifteen was the last, because I heard you. Andrews is back now so you can ask him.'

'Yes, I did tell her,' Sarah agreed. She glanced up as she heard the car outside the house. Her grandmother was always aware of these things just seconds before Sarah. 'I'll go and speak to him now.'

Miranda looked at Amelia as Sarah left the room. 'Is Sarah upset about something? She seems a bit quiet. I hope she isn't put out because I came down?'

'No, of course not,' Amelia assured her. 'She has something on her mind, but I know she was looking forward to seeing you. She thinks it will be nice to catch up before you meet at Lady Avery's next week. After all, you hadn't seen each other for a couple of years, had you?'

'At least that,' Miranda said and took another puff of her cigarette. 'I hear voices. It sounds as if her friend has turned up safely.'

'Thank goodness for that,' Amelia replied. 'I'll ask Millie to bring some more tea. I daresay Janey could do with one.'

Amelia got to her feet and left the room. Miranda could hear her speaking to someone in the hall. She glanced at herself in the mirror, touching her pearls and smiling. She had made up her mind now. She would not sacrifice any of her jewellery unless she was forced. Why should she? She turned as the parlour door opened and Sarah returned with another girl. Miranda knew at once that she was a girl from the show, and not quite her sort, but she put on a smile, because she could hardly be rude to her godmother's guest.

'Janey, this is Lady Bellingham,' Sarah said. 'Miranda is staying with us for one night – and we shall both be guests of Pamela Avery next month in France. I told you that Miranda was Amelia's goddaughter, didn't I?'

'Lady Bellingham,' Janey said and held out her hand, clearly not certain whether she ought to curtsey. She did a sort of bob and laughed awkwardly.

'Oh no,' Miranda said, 'none of that, Janey. We are amongst friends. I am just Miranda here, you know.'

'Oh, thanks,' Janey said, relieved. She looked at Sarah. 'I only just caught the train back, and I had walked most of the way here when Andrews saw me. Apparently, we missed each other at the station. My fault, because I didn't think he would come to fetch me unless I rang . . . but it was very nice of him. I was relieved, because . . .' She looked as if she wanted to say more, but glanced at Miranda and didn't, sitting down instead on the sofa. 'Did you have a good day, Sarah?'

'Yes and no,' Sarah said, because she hadn't yet told Janey about Esther's body being found. 'Did you get the things you wanted in Norwich?'

'Oh yes,' Janey said. 'I've left everything in the hall, Sarah. I got you something, and Amelia – just small things.'

'That sounds as if you are leaving soon?'

'Well, yes, as a matter of fact, I've decided to go tomorrow,' Janey told her. 'I met a girl I know in Norwich and she suggested that we room together – and she is going tomorrow. I've arranged to meet her in Norwich and we'll go on from there.'

'Anyone I know?'

'No, I don't think so,' Janey said and smiled. 'I knew her from before. She wasn't in the London show but we've been friends a long time.'

'I am so pleased for you,' Sarah said. 'It is good to have a friend to share things with – and it cuts down on the expenses.'

'Yes, it does,' Janey said. 'I shall miss you though, Sarah. Will you come down and see me at Yarmouth? If you let me know, I'll get you a free ticket for the show.'

'If I can when I come back from France,' Sarah said. 'But I've agreed to help Larch with his shows at various galleries so I can't promise.'

'Come if you can,' Janey said. 'I'm going upstairs now to unpack my things. I'll be down again in a few minutes.'

'I'll come with you,' Sarah said as Amelia returned to the parlour. 'Excuse us for a moment – we shan't be long.'

She followed Janey out to the hall, helping her with her various parcels as they walked upstairs. Janey went into her bedroom, and Sarah followed her in, carefully closing the door.

'I didn't want to tell you down there, because Amelia doesn't want to say anything to Miranda – but they've found Esther.'

Janey went white with shock. 'Are you telling me that she is dead?'

'Yes, I'm afraid so,' Sarah said. 'Her body was discovered under some ropes backstage – and she had been strangled.' She saw Janey put a hand to her throat and nodded. 'Yes, I know. It is awful, though I've been expecting it for some days.'

'I kept thinking she would turn up,' Janey said and shuddered. Her eyes filled with tears, which trickled down her cheeks. She scrubbed them away with her hand and sucked in her breath. 'Poor Esther! Who could have done that to her?'

'I wish I knew,' Sarah said. 'I've been racking my brain for some clue, but I can't think of anything . . .' She saw something in Janey's face. 'What have you thought of? Do you have an idea who it might be?'

'I don't know his name,' Janey said, 'but I have seen him

hanging about outside the theatre on several occasions – and I've seen him in the audience at our show too.' She took a deep breath. 'I hadn't thought about it until today, but he might have been in the wood when I walked past, talking to someone . . . your grandmother's new neighbour.'

'You mean Mr Ashton?' Sarah was puzzled. 'What has he to do with all this? I don't understand . . .'

'Nor do I – and it probably has nothing to do with Esther being killed. It is just that I remembered seeing a man outside the theatre sometimes, and I think it was you he was interested in, because he asked me once if you had left the theatre.'

'You didn't tell me about him?'

'No. I didn't like him much, though he was a gentleman – at least he spoke posh,' Janey said. 'I just said you'd gone, though I don't think you had – but I knew you wouldn't want to go out with him.'

Sarah nodded. 'I wouldn't, whoever he was – but you said you had seen him again here? Do you mean today?'

'Yes. It was a bit creepy actually,' Janey said. 'That's why I was so glad that Andrews turned up when he did. I was at the bottom of the hill – the bit where the wood is so close to the road?' Sarah nodded. 'I saw them talking. They were in the woods and they seemed to be having a bit of an argument about something. I heard shouting . . .'

'What did they say?'

'Something like, "You won't get away with it. I want my share." It was odd really.'

'Yes, that is odd,' Sarah agreed. 'Who said it? The man from outside the show or Mr Ashton?'

'I'm not sure. I didn't linger or look at them much. I was frightened and I was just thinking of walking a bit faster when Andrews stopped the car and told me to get in.'

'Tell me, what did the man you saw outside the theatre look like?'

'Well, he is quite attractive really,' Janey said. 'Not my type, because I like dark men and he has blond hair, but I think a lot of girls would find him interesting. He has that English gentleman look about him: smart suit, classic shoes, good silk tie . . . class, I suppose, is the word I'm looking for.'

Sarah nodded. 'I know the type, and it isn't my type either – but he doesn't sound like a murderer.'

'Who does?' Janey asked. 'They don't go around with it stamped on their foreheads, do they?'

'No, I suppose not . . . I wonder what their argument was about.' Sarah looked thoughtful. 'I had better go down, because Miranda will think I am avoiding her. Do you think you can manage to sit through an evening without mentioning Esther? I know it won't be easy.'

'No, but I can do it for Amelia's sake,' Janey said. 'She has been so nice to me. I bought her some lace hankies – do you think that is all right?'

'She will say you shouldn't have bought anything,' Sarah told her. 'But they will be perfect. No one can have too many nice handkerchiefs.'

'I bought you some of the perfume you like.'

'You really shouldn't have,' Sarah said. 'I haven't anything for you at the moment, but I'll bring you something nice from France . . .'

Andrews drove Janey to the station early the next morning. She left one of her suitcases with Amelia, because it contained her winter clothing and she wouldn't need it for the next few months.

'It is no trouble to me to store it for you,' Amelia told her when she asked rather tentatively, 'and it will give you a reason to come and stay with me again.'

'I don't need a reason,' Janey told her and kissed her impulsively. 'I've really enjoyed these few days, and I should love to come again.'

Sarah went to the station with her friend. She didn't feel that she was deserting Miranda, because she never got up much before eleven and Sarah would be back long before then. She kissed Janey before she boarded the train, giving her a hug because she sensed that her friend was upset that they were parting.

'It is only for a while,' Sarah said. 'The summer will soon go and then with any luck we'll be together in the show in London.'

'Yes, I know,' Janey said. 'Enjoy your stay in France – and be careful, Sarah. Don't go out with any strange men.'

'No, I shan't do that,' Sarah said and laughed. 'Not if they are the least bit peculiar – and especially not if they have odd twitches or weird eyes.'

Janey shook her head, because she knew she was being teased. 'Oh, you! I meant strangers – but do be careful, won't you?'

'Yes, of course, love. You too, Janey.'

Sarah stood back as the guard blew his whistle and the engine let off a huge cloud of steam. She waved to her friend until the train had moved down the line and then went out to join Andrews in the car, sinking into the luxury of her grandmother's indulgence. There was nothing quite like a Rolls-Royce for comfort.

'Everything all right, Miss Sarah?'

'Yes, of course.' She smiled at him. 'Will you drop me in the village, please? I want to buy something from the shop and I'll walk home afterwards.'

He nodded, glancing at her in his mirror as he drew away from the station. If he were any judge, Sarah was up to something again . . .

'So your friend has gone then,' Mrs Roberts said when she finished serving Sarah with a quarter-pound of Tom Thumb drops and a packet of Bourbon biscuits. 'You will miss her, I daresay?'

'Yes, I shall,' Sarah agreed. 'I think I'll take one of those sticky pink buns as well.' She glanced through the headlines of a newspaper on the counter. It appeared that another leading churchman had denounced women for wearing their clothes too short. 'Did Mr Ashton come in to see you the other day?'

'Oh yes, he did, lovely man,' Mrs Roberts said enthusiastically. 'I was only saying to Jilly how nice it was to have someone new in the village – and a man like that is always an asset. He seems very keen to get to know people and he was asking me all sorts of questions.'

'What kind of questions?'

'He wanted to know about the bridge club, and the best places to meet nice people. He plays golf, you know, and he's a bit of an amateur dramatic . . . likes acting and singing, he says. Well, of course I told him about Lady Meadows and her charity affairs, because she puts on a show at the village hall in Thorny twice a year, doesn't she? He seemed very interested in getting to know people.'

'Yes, I expect he is,' Sarah said. 'You have to make a bit of an effort when you come to a new place, don't you?'

'I think he will blend in quite well,' Mrs Roberts said, 'but I am not sure about his wife. She came in earlier this morning. I daresay she is nice enough in her way, but . . . you know what I mean?'

'Yes, I think perhaps I do,' Sarah said and smiled. She paid for her purchases and left, walking thoughtfully along the street in the direction of Thorny Woods and Rosalind Darby's cottage. It was surprising how much you could learn in a few minutes.

Ronnie Miller was sitting in the front garden of Rosalind's cottage on an upturned orange box, busily sharpening his spade. He seemed very intent on his work, using the file steadily, going over and over the edge of the tool, as if he wanted it just so.

'Hello,' Sarah said, and he looked startled, but grinned as he saw it was her. 'I bought you a sticky bun, Ronnie. You look as if you're busy this morning?'

'I like you,' he told her. 'It has to be sharp, see. Cuts through the earth then, cuts deep and easy . . .' For a moment there was a strange expression in his eyes. 'They put her in the earth, you know. I didn't like that. She was nice to me . . . like you.' His gaze narrowed. 'If they put you there I'll dig you up again. I like you . . .'

'Thank you.' Sarah gave him the paper bag. For a moment she had felt chilled, because she knew he must be talking about Morna Scaffrey, the gypsy girl who had been strangled in Thorny Woods the previous year.

Rosalind had come to the kitchen door and was waiting for her. 'I thought you would come this morning,' she said. 'Have you time for coffee – or tea if you prefer?'

'Coffee please, though it ought to be tea, because you could tell my fortune.'

Rosalind laughed. 'I told Janey's for her, you know. She was so keen to have it done, and of course I discovered that she was going to meet someone who would make a big difference to her life.'

'Oh, good,' Sarah said. 'I am not sure I want to know mine. I would rather it came as a surprise . . .' She sat down at the large pine table as Rosalind put water on to boil. 'You know why I came, of course.'

'Yes. When you telephoned last night I realized that you couldn't talk – that is why I expected you this morning.'

'Miranda is staying,' Sarah said. 'Lady Bellingham now, of course. Amelia didn't want her to hear in case it upset her.'

'I'm more worried about you. How are you coping?'

'Actually, I feel better this morning,' Sarah said. 'I knew Esther was dead but I kept hoping. Now I'm angry. I want the man who did this to her caught and punished.'

'Yes, I thought you might feel that way,' Rosalind said. 'It is exactly how I would feel myself. What did Mr Marshall have to say about it?'

'No more than I've told you. He says that the police are starting an investigation, but for the moment they have no clues . . . or none that they are prepared to talk about.'

'They could start with the florist,' Rosalind said. 'If they could trace who sent her those flowers it might help.'

'Yes, it might,' Sarah said. 'Tell me, what do you think of our new neighbour? Do you like him?'

'Mr Ashton?' Rosalind was startled. 'Well, yes, I think so . . . As a matter of fact, he has invited me to tea tomorrow. I had a phone call from him this morning. He said he was going to invite you and your friend, Amelia too.'

'Janey left this morning, but I shall go and I expect Gran will too. I was going to ask her to break the ice, but if the invitation has come from him it will be all the better. I should like to see what they've done to the manor.'

'People say it has been tarted up,' Rosalind said. 'But each according to their own taste. Oh, that reminds me. I told you that I had given some pieces of jade to the vicar's wife, didn't I?' Sarah nodded. 'Well, apparently Mrs Ashton bought them all and paid a fair price. It seems she has a good eye for things like that . . . with a bit of age to them.'

'Does she?' Sarah was thoughtful. 'That is interesting . . . yes, very interesting.'

'Sarah, my dear, what are you up to?' Rosalind asked as she put a cup of fragrant coffee in front of her. 'Will you have cream and sugar?'

'Yes, please – two sugars.' Sarah smiled. 'I'm not up to anything, but I think I have the instinct of a squirrel at times. I store away pieces of information, and sometimes they come in useful . . .'

'Yes, I am sure they do,' Rosalind said. 'Would it help you

to know that although I like Mr Ashton I think he goes deeper than he lets people believe?'

'Yes, it would help,' Sarah said. 'I haven't spoken more than a few words to him, but that was what I was hoping you would say.'

Rosalind arched her brows. 'I don't suppose it is any use asking you to explain?'

'I would if I could,' Sarah said and laughed huskily. 'I know Ben thinks I am holding out on him, but I don't know anything for certain, Rosalind. At the moment it is just feelings . . . a sense of something not quite right.'

'Yes, I do know exactly what you mean,' Rosalind said and sighed. 'Last night I had a vision . . . or maybe it was a dream . . . but nothing was clear to me. I've tried to make sense of it this morning, but nothing fits . . .'

'That is it exactly,' Sarah said. 'I have lots of bits and pieces jumbled up together and at the moment I can't see where they fit – and perhaps they don't.'

Rosalind nodded. Her dream had concerned a death, and the awful thing was she didn't know whether it was her own – or if she was the cause of someone else's death. But it was so muddled, so unlike the vision she had had concerning Esther's murder that she could not be sure just what she had seen. She didn't want to tell Sarah anything more at this stage, because there was no point in upsetting her for no reason.

'Well, I had better get back,' Sarah said, putting her cup down. 'That was lovely coffee, Rosalind. I shall visit you again if I may?'

'You know you are always welcome. I shall see you at the manor tomorrow I expect – but if you ever feel anxious and you think I can help . . .'

'Yes, I know,' Sarah said and got up. 'I shan't hesitate, Rosalind. You have already helped quite a bit, though you might not think it. I shall see you tomorrow. I must go, because I want to have a talk with Miranda . . .'

'This is nice,' Miranda said when they were alone in the parlour. Amelia was in the kitchen talking menus with Millie, but also giving them the chance to converse on their own. 'So how are you getting on with your singing career, Sarah?

I think you must be very brave. I couldn't stand up in front of a crowd of people and sing – even if I could sing well, which I can't.'

'I have always enjoyed singing,' Sarah told her. 'I was nervous the first time I appeared on stage, but it was just something I wanted to do.'

'Peter took me to see Josephine Baker in Paris last year. She was wonderful, of course . . .' Miranda looked thoughtful. 'Someone told me that you knew Giles Henderson?'

'Yes, though not well,' Sarah replied. 'We had met a few times socially, but he had started coming to the shows and sending me flowers. He asked me to dinner twice but I turned him down.'

'You were probably very wise,' Miranda said. 'Giles was a dear and we were good friends, but he wasn't the marrying kind. I thought once that he might ask, but it didn't happen – and then I met Peter.'

'And you are very happy?' There were faint shadows beneath Miranda's eyes, as if she had not slept well recently.

'Yes, I am actually,' Miranda said. 'A lot of people imagine I married Peter for his money, and I admit that he spoils me – but I love him. I am in love with him, despite the age gap.'

'That's lovely,' Sarah replied. 'I am so glad, Miranda. I wasn't sure whether I dare ask – but perhaps if your romance with Giles was over, you wouldn't mind talking about his murder. A friend of mine is investigating it and I knew that you went out with him for a while . . .'

'Oh, it was only a light-hearted affair,' Miranda lied. 'Nothing serious at all. I can't imagine what I could tell your friend, Sarah. I know nothing about his murder.'

'No, of course not. I just meant you might know if he had any enemies – anyone who might have wanted him dead? Or perhaps you might tell me something about his friends? Ben looked for his address book but it was missing. I thought that was odd, because a man like Giles would certainly have kept one.'

'Giles knew everybody,' Miranda said and reached for her velvet bag, opening it to fish out her smoking paraphernalia. Sarah sensed that she was nervous. 'I have no idea what happened to the book, but he knew all the crowd you will meet at Pamela's – and a host of others. I can't think that any of them would have killed him. Surely it was a burglary gone wrong?'

'Yes, that is the story the police have put out,' Sarah said. 'But Ben doesn't think so and neither do I, Miranda. I am certain there is a lot more to this, but as yet I haven't a clue what has been going on.'

Miranda gave her an odd look. 'What difference can it make to you? You weren't in love with him?'

'No, I wasn't,' Sarah agreed. 'But I didn't dislike him either. His father is very distressed and Ben is trying to get to the truth.'

Miranda lit her cigarette. Her hand wasn't quite steady. She drew deeply and blew a tiny smoke ring, trying to appear nonchalant.

'Well, I think you are wasting your time, Sarah. Besides, if there was something more to discover it might be dangerous to delve too far, don't you think? Surely you should leave it to the police – or your friend.'

'Yes, of course I shall. But I feel involved because . . .' She didn't want to tell Miranda about Esther's murder for some reason. 'Because he had been sending me flowers, I suppose.'

'Oh, Giles sent flowers all the time,' Miranda said airily. 'Pamela told me that he often sent her the most beautiful bouquets. She was devastated by his death, of course, because they were such good friends.' She wrinkled her smooth brow. 'Can't we talk about something else? Have you bought yourself some decent clothes for France?'

'Not very much as yet,' Sarah said. 'I shall probably pop in to Norwich and pick up a few things before we go. I didn't have much time before I left London.'

'I'm not sure you will find much of any use in Norwich. Don't worry, Sarah. We are much the same size, after all. I always take far more than I need anyway, and you can borrow some of my things if you need to.'

'That is extremely generous of you,' Sarah said. 'I don't have a lot of spare money at the moment, and I might take you up on the offer – if you really mean it?'

'I'll pack a few things that might suit you,' Miranda said. 'Our colouring is different but I am sure I have something you would like.' She smiled, feeling pleased, because she had got through the awkward bit and was sure that Sarah believed everything she had said.

Their conversation came to an end then as Amelia entered the room, but Miranda was feeling satisfied that the trip down had been well worth her while. She had been afraid Sarah might know that she and Giles had been lovers, but now she felt that she could stop worrying, because Sarah had seemed to accept all she told her. It was obvious that she knew nothing about Giles's private life, and therefore she could not reveal any embarrassing details.

Miranda had wondered if Sarah had known about those photographs, but she was sure now that she didn't, which meant that the only person she needed to worry about was the man who was blackmailing her. It was just luck that she had got to Giles's address book first, because it had given her the clue she needed. She would be seeing Tommy Rowe very soon, and she thought it would be easy enough to discover if he really had the photographs. She had to get them back somehow and then . . . her mind shied away from what she was planning to do.

Miranda wasn't a natural killer, and sometimes her thoughts horrified her, but she had made up her mind that she was going to do whatever was necessary to protect her marriage.

He was alone in his special place – the drug-induced world that he allowed himself to enter only when he needed to open his mind. It was odd but he seemed to recall seeing the girl before. He had a good memory for faces, though he was sure that he didn't know her name. He half closed his eyes as he tried to place her, his head against the chair back, letting the drug take him. It came to him then, as he had known it would.

He had spoken to her once outside the theatre where Sarah Beaufort was singing on stage. He had asked her if Sarah was still there and that bitch had told him she had already left. He had been sitting in a taxi, being driven away when he saw Sarah leave by the stage door. That bitch deserved to be taught a lesson just for lying! If the car hadn't come along that morning and picked her up he might have followed her and . . .

For a moment he let himself enjoy the thought of teaching another little slut a lesson. The last one had been so pathetically eager that it hadn't given him the thrill he had known at least twice before. There had been more, of course, over the past couple of years, but some of them died so easily that it gave him little pleasure. He wanted them to put up a fight so that he could indulge himself longer.

He thought about the girl from the show again. He was almost sure that she was a dancer. He wouldn't have bothered about her normally, but he was angry – angry with the man who was demanding more than his fair share. After all, he was the one who supplied all the information. He knew who had jewels worth stealing and who didn't – though he'd made one mistake. How the hell was he to know that the Avery diamond necklace had been copied? It ought to have been worth taking, because he had a good eye for quality. And he knew when the owners were going to be out for the evening, which was the most important part.

That slut from the show had seen something she ought not to have seen. He might have to do something about her, but not yet. He had more important business for the moment.

His mind was very clear at that moment. Smoking opium always gave him such clarity of thought, though he was careful not to do it too often. He used the drug; it did not use him. So, he decided, it wasn't worth wasting time over the dancer, at least for the moment. He was looking forward to getting those emeralds from Miranda Bellingham, but perhaps he would get something more . . .

He smiled at his thoughts. It would give him so much pleasure to bring that bitch down to her true level. After what she had done with Giles Henderson, she was no better than any of the other sluts.

There was only one woman he admired, because she had turned Giles down. She had turned all her admirers down, including him – though she wouldn't have known it was him, because he never signed his cards. He thought that perhaps he would get to know Sarah a little better when they were in France.

Nine

'How odd,' Amelia said, looking at Sarah as she came into the parlour the next morning. 'That was Pamela Avery on the telephone just now. She said that her brother was chartering a small aeroplane to fly out to France next week, and he has invited us to go with him.'

'Goodness,' Sarah said, 'how unexpected! Or do you know him well?'

'Only as Pamela's brother,' Amelia said. 'We've met a few times socially, of course, as you have – but I wouldn't have expected anything like this. I was so surprised that I hardly knew what to say. I admire his work, because I have visited some of the gardens he designs or writes about.'

'Did you refuse to fly?'

'Well, no, actually I said I would think about it,' Amelia said. 'It was very kind of him to ask us, Sarah. I believe one or two others are going with him. It seems that Mr Ashton is one of them . . .'

'Your new neighbour?' Sarah looked thoughtful. 'Are the Ashtons part of Pamela's crowd? I wouldn't have thought they were her sort . . . although perhaps . . .' She frowned and shook her head at her own thoughts. She mustn't let her imagination take over!

'Oh, Pamela collects all sorts,' Amelia said. 'I wonder if Mr Ashton was aware that we were all to be her guests? He has tried to be friendly, calling on me and then asking us to tea.'

'Yes, I am looking forward to meeting them this afternoon,' Sarah said. 'Would you consider flying, Gran?'

'Do you know, I think I might,' Amelia said, surprising her granddaughter. 'It is all very new and exciting, and some people say it is dangerous, though there has been a regular service between London and Paris since 1919. However, I dislike sea voyages. I have often wished that one might simply get in a train and arrive in Paris, but unfortunately that is never going to happen – at least in my lifetime. Yes, I think I might ring Pamela back and tell her that I should like to join her brother's party – providing that you have no objections?'

'None at all,' Sarah said. 'Do you think he has invited Miranda too?'

'I don't know. I'll ask Pamela,' Amelia said and went back into the hall to make her call. She was looking pleased with herself when she returned. 'Well, that is all settled then, Sarah. And Miranda is coming with us so that will be very nice. It will be Mr and Mrs Ashton, Miranda, us and Tommy . . . and there will be a car waiting for us at the other end. He has also arranged a car to pick us up and drive us to the airport.'

'How thoughtful of him,' Sarah agreed. 'I've never quite liked him. I thought he was arrogant and selfish, but perhaps I've misjudged him – of course I hardly know him.'

'I would have said the same myself,' Amelia told her. 'But if he has gone to the trouble of chartering a private plane for us I think I must also have misjudged him.'

Unless he has a particular reason for doing so, Sarah thought, but didn't say. She was trying to remember something . . . something that she had heard quite recently and might be important, but for the moment the elusive thread had escaped her.

Sarah looked around her as they were welcomed into the manor by Mr Ashton. She wasn't sure what she had expected, but in actual fact she was pleasantly surprised. Everywhere had been recently painted, and there was some rather expensive silk wallpaper on the drawing room walls. It had a fresh, modern appeal, all the old furniture having been either removed by Lady Beecham or thrown out by the new owners. Some of the furniture was in the art deco style and looked as if it might be expensive, and there were some very good pictures on the walls. Sarah recognized them as Impressionist and decided she liked them.

'Of course, it isn't finished,' Mrs Ashton told them as she welcomed them into her home. 'Those curtains are definitely not what I ordered – and if that shop imagines I shall pay for them they can think again.'

'Now, now, Nancy,' her husband said playfully. 'You don't want our visitors to get the wrong idea, sweetie. We shall negotiate, see what can be done to sort this mess out.'

'If you think I'm going to give in over this, Harvey, you are quite wrong,' his wife told him. 'But I shan't go on about it today.' She smiled at Amelia. 'Please do come and sit down, Mrs Beaufort. We haven't met, but my husband told me all about you.' Her eyes were slightly above freezing as she looked at Sarah. 'I believe we have met, Miss Beaufort, but we shall not talk about that now. There was no damage done after all.'

Sarah nodded, but didn't say anything. Her grandmother gave her a look, which meant explanations would be needed later. Sarah sat down just as they heard voices in the hall and then the housekeeper showed Rosalind in. For a few minutes the greetings went on, though Sarah noticed that Rosalind seemed a little quiet, her expression guarded. She smiled at Sarah, but it didn't quite reach her eyes, and Sarah sensed that she was anxious about something.

However, there was no time to talk privately. Nancy Ashton was busy talking about herself, and the house. Her husband looked at her oddly a few times, but he didn't interrupt or contradict her. Sarah thought that perhaps she was a difficult woman to please. Judging by the way the house was furnished, and the clothes she was wearing, she was a woman who expected the best of everything.

Sarah noticed that she had some lovely diamond rings, and her pearls were good too. She had been robbed of some of her jewels, but obviously she had more or she had replaced them. Sarah waited until the chance arose, then made a remark about her rings as Nancy passed her a cup.

'What beautiful rings,' she said. 'That diamond cluster is very pretty.'

'It isn't a patch on the one I lost,' Nancy said, with a sulky look at her husband. 'But it is pretty, I suppose.'

'We were unfortunate enough to be burgled when we were out at a charity affair,' Harvey Ashton said. 'Nancy doesn't like to talk about it, of course. It was the reason we moved. She couldn't bear to think someone had been going through her things.'

'That would be awful,' Amelia said sympathetically. 'I am so sorry to hear about your loss, Mrs Ashton.'

'Please call me Nancy. It made me angry,' she said. 'We got the insurance money, but you can never replace the memories – and it isn't easy to find replacements.'

'That ring is just temporary,' her husband told her. 'You'll get something better soon, my dear.'

'So I should hope.'

'Did the police have any clues as to who was responsible for the burglary?' Sarah asked. 'I mean . . . how did whoever it was know you would be out that night, and where to find your jewellery? You didn't just leave it lying around for him to take, did you?'

'That is what I want to know,' Nancy said, her eyes bright with anger. 'The safe was hidden and no one but us knew the combination . . . but the police told us that some thieves can crack almost any safe going.'

'I see . . .' Sarah nodded. 'That explains it, though not how he knew you would be out that particular night.'

'I daresay he read it somewhere,' Nancy said and frowned. 'Charities publish lists of celebrities in advance sometimes. I really have no idea, and what does it matter? I suppose these sorts of people watch decent houses and take the opportunity when it arises.' Her mouth curled in disgust.

'Yes, I am sure you are right,' Amelia said and gave Sarah a warning look. 'Tell me, where did you get that lovely dress, Nancy? I love the colour.'

'Yes, so do I,' Nancy agreed. 'The designer called it desert sunrise or something fanciful like that, but I bought it for the style as well as the colour.'

The conversation steered into calmer waters, and Sarah was content to sit and listen. She was convinced that Nancy Ashton's indignation was real, not assumed, but she wasn't so sure about her husband. Something about his manner was too good to be true, though he had probably learned to pacify his wife. It couldn't be that easy being married to Nancy!

Walking home with Rosalind after leaving Amelia at the Dower House, Sarah asked her what was wrong, and she pulled a wry face.

'I was hoping it didn't show. I didn't want to say anything in front of Amelia . . .'

'Have you had another one of your visions?'

'Sort of,' Rosalind told her. 'It wasn't as vivid as the one about your friend – but I saw another murdered woman. She had been strangled. At first I wasn't sure if it was me ... but I had it again earlier today and I know it was someone else. I couldn't see her face, because she was lying face down. I don't know why I felt it had something to do with me ...'

'That must have been horrible for you,' Sarah said. 'Has she already been killed?'

'I think that is why I felt I was involved,' Rosalind said, 'because it was different this time. I believe I have been given a warning – but I don't know what to do, Sarah. How can I warn anyone when I don't know who she is or when she is going to be murdered?'

'You can't. And you mustn't be upset about it, Rosalind. If you could do anything you would.'

'Yes, and it may just be a dream after all,' Rosalind said. 'I wasn't intending to tell you. I didn't want to upset you before you went away on holiday.'

'You haven't,' Sarah said and smiled. 'I can't be upset if I don't know who it is – and as long as it isn't you, you must try to put it out of your mind.'

'Yes, of course. I shall,' Rosalind told her. 'But I wondered if you would give me Mr Marshall's telephone number just in case?'

'I am sure he wouldn't mind,' Sarah replied. 'I'll walk down and give it to you in the morning – if that is all right?'

'Yes, of course,' Rosalind said. 'Now tell me, what did you make of Nancy Ashton?'

'I imagine she is difficult to please,' Sarah said. 'Her husband must be wealthy to keep up with her demands.'

'Yes, exactly,' Rosalind said. 'Which begs the question – where does he get his money? He has no visible income, unless of course he inherited a fortune.'

'He probably did,' Sarah said and then frowned. 'It might be hers, of course. Yes, I think perhaps it is ...' She nodded as a little bit of the puzzle clicked into place. 'That is why he is so careful to please her ...'

'I think you are right,' Rosalind said and looked thoughtful. 'Yes, I believe you have hit the nail on the head. It is her money ...'

*   *   *

Sarah telephoned Ben that evening. He told her that the police were now convinced that Esther's murder had been one of several.

'They won't be giving that piece of information to the press, Sarah, so keep it to yourself. However, they do think he may have killed at least twice before and it might be more. The pattern seems to be that they are either showgirls or, in a couple of cases, prostitutes.'

'Yes, that fits with what Karen told us,' Sarah said. 'Some people think that a girl who goes on the stage must be a slut and no better than she ought to be, which means the killer – if it is the same man – may class them all as sluts. He probably thinks they deserve what they get, or that he is doing society a service by getting rid of undesirable women.'

'Yes . . .' Ben sounded grim. 'He must be a pretty nasty piece of work. I'm going to ask you to be very careful of men you don't know, Sarah. I've been trying to trace the florist who sent those flowers. One of them told me they had been asked to deliver a large basket of flowers to you that evening, but they didn't have the man's name. He paid in cash, as he always did – so that means he had bought flowers for you before.'

'Yes, I have wondered about that. It sounds terribly vain, but I had so many for a while that I hardly looked at the cards. I just took it for granted that Giles Henderson had sent most of them.'

'Well, it seems likely to me that our man has an interest in you, Sarah. Be on your guard for anything out of the ordinary, and don't walk in lonely places on your own.'

'No, of course I shan't,' Sarah said. 'Don't worry, Ben. I promise not to be careless or impulsive.'

'I should hate anything to happen to you.'

'Thank you, but there's no need to worry.' Sarah laughed huskily. 'We are flying to France the day after tomorrow. I shall be with friends for two weeks, and when I come home I am going to be helping Larch with his shows.'

'Good. I like the sound of that,' Ben said. 'Did you ring for anything special?'

'Well . . . I'm not sure,' Sarah hesitated, then, 'Rosalind had a vision or dream, whatever you call it – she saw another murdered woman, but not her face. It was different this time, because she felt she was responsible in some way, but doesn't understand why.'

'She probably feels bad because she saw what happened to Esther. Don't let it worry you, Sarah. It probably doesn't mean anything.' He paused for a second. 'Is there anything else you want to tell me now?'

'I wondered if you had any thought of visiting the girl who was attacked before?'

'I did ask if I might see her, but the doctor at the home thought it unwise for her sake. I doubt she could help. Now tell me what is really on your mind.'

'I can't put it into words. It is there in my head, and it concerns the jewel thefts – but I don't know anything. I just have a feeling that something is going on under our noses and that we ought to see it but can't.'

'Frustrating, isn't it?' Ben chuckled. 'Ninety per cent of the national police force feel like that every working day of their lives. Don't push it, Sarah. Just let it all ferment and tell me when I see you. I have that address you gave me, and I shall find out if there is a telephone. Otherwise I may come along and see you while we're in France. We go a few days after you – just for ten days, but Cathy is really looking forward to it.'

'Have you got anywhere with Giles Henderson's murder yet?'

'I've been contacting a lot of people. The editor of the magazine he wrote for gave me several names, but as yet I haven't come up with much – though he seems to have been a popular man. Apparently, Giles was the person to go to if you were in a fix. He helped various friends and acquaintances out with problems, for which they gave him presents. He liked expensive trifles. Must have been a good customer for Asprey's and Garrard's I imagine.'

'Yes, I know Giles always liked the best. It is odd that his address book disappeared. I am sure he had one. Everyone who mixes in society keeps a list of contacts.'

'I didn't tell you about that,' Ben said. 'When I first went to Giles's flat there was a woman there. I called out and she tricked me by opening the French doors into the garden. By the time I realized what was happening, she had fled. I saw her disappearing into the crowds.'

'What did she look like?'

'Young, well dressed – no, better than that, elegant. I think her hair was blonde but she was wearing a hat so I couldn't be sure. Oh, and she wears very strong perfume. It was her perfume that told me she was there.'

'It sounds as if she was one of Giles's crowd. If she was able to get out without you seeing her, she knew his home well. That should narrow it down quite a bit, and she is likely to be a lady he knew socially. I shall be seeing Miranda soon and I'll see if she knows who Giles had been dating recently.'

'Who is Miranda?'

'Oh . . . Lady Bellingham. She married Lord Peter Bellingham a few months ago. She and Giles were . . . good friends. I think it may have been more than that, but I wouldn't like to swear to it – she is Amelia's goddaughter.'

'I knew you were holding something back,' Ben said with a little crow of triumph. 'She wouldn't be very pretty and blonde, would she?'

'Well, yes . . . but whatever she had with Giles was over. She is in love with her husband. She wouldn't have been in Giles's home . . .'

'She might if he was blackmailing her.'

'What do you mean?' Sarah frowned. 'Now who has been holding out?'

'I found a picture – one that a newly-married lady wouldn't want her husband to see, especially if she cared for him . . .'

'Ben!' Sarah was shocked. 'You can't think that she . . . No, she wouldn't! I am sure she couldn't do anything like that . . .'

'Sometimes desperate people will do things that are completely out of character,' Ben told her. 'I should like to meet Lady Bellingham. Even if she is completely innocent, she might have something to tell me.'

'Oh dear,' Sarah said. 'I was afraid of this happening. It's why I didn't tell you. It was a slip of the tongue . . .'

'I daresay she is innocent. But if the pictures were of her she might have gone to his apartment after the murder to see if she could find them. And if Giles wasn't blackmailing her, someone else might be – and that someone could be our man.'

'Yes . . .' Sarah clutched at that idea, because she felt guilty for telling him about Miranda. 'You will be careful, Ben?

Don't say anything to your friends at the Yard just yet please. And don't do anything that would ruin her marriage.'

'If she is innocent she is in the clear,' Ben said. 'And I certainly wouldn't want to ruin anyone's life – but if she did . . . well, we'll face that one when we come to it.'

'Yes. I think I had better go now,' Sarah said and hung up abruptly. She was feeling upset, because she hadn't meant to tell Ben about Miranda . . . even though she suspected that Miranda had lied to her about Giles. It was very possible that she had taken his address book. The only question was why . . . but if as Ben had suggested she was being black-mailed, she might have been looking for a clue to the blackmailer's identity.

Sarah was thoughtful as she left the house to walk down to visit Rosalind again. Some of the pieces were beginning to fit at last . . .

'Come in, Sarah,' Rosalind said, smiling at her as she opened the door. 'I'm glad you found time to call. You must be busy getting ready for your trip to France?'

'It won't take me long to pack,' Sarah said. 'I haven't spent a fortune on new clothes, because I shan't use half of them after-wards – and Miranda said I could borrow something of hers if I need to. I might if I get into difficulty, but not otherwise.'

Rosalind looked at her sharply. 'Worried about something?'

'No, not really,' Sarah said, because she couldn't talk about what was on my mind at the moment. 'I came to see if you were feeling any better?'

'The answer to that is yes and no,' Rosalind said and pulled a wry face. 'I haven't had any more visions and the last one has faded so perhaps it was just a dream – but I am bothered about something.'

'Is there anything I can do?' Sarah asked, seeing that her friend was actually rather upset.

'No, it was my own silly fault, but I feel annoyed,' Rosalind told her. 'I didn't notice until last night . . .' She shook her head. 'I hate to accuse anyone, and especially that lad, because he has earned it in the garden – but I don't like thieves.'

'I'm not quite sure I understand,' Sarah said, frowning. 'Are you talking about Ronnie Miller?'

'Yes . . .' Rosalind sighed. 'It was yesterday morning. I

invited him in for a mug of tea and some cake, but the telephone rang and I left him alone. When I returned he had gone. I didn't notice then, but when I looked for it last night I discovered that a new bottle of whisky had gone. It was standing on the kitchen dresser. I think he must have taken it.'

'Oh dear,' Sarah said. 'It isn't what he took, of course, but the fact that he did. Yes, I understand why you are upset.'

'I would have given him money. I've been thinking that I should speak to his mother – but someone told me not to pay him, because he might spend it on alcohol. Didn't you tell me that he causes trouble when he drinks too much?'

'Yes, that is what people say. I know his mother doesn't like him to drink – especially not whisky.'

'Then that makes it worse,' Rosalind said. 'I shall take him his tea and cake outside next time he comes. I don't feel I want him in the house again . . . you never know what else he might take.'

'I've never heard anyone say he was a thief before,' Sarah said. 'I don't think he would take anything of value, Rosalind. I don't believe he would even know what a piece of jade or silver was . . . but the whisky was probably too great a temptation.'

'Yes. I know that it was my fault for leaving it where he could see it, because I had been warned, but I just didn't think – and I'm upset because I like Ronnie. He always seems such a nice lad. I know he is slow and he only does what he feels like doing, but I felt sorry for him.'

'And now you feel as if he has let you down,' Sarah said. 'But try to think of it his way, Rosalind. He probably doesn't know what he did is wrong . . . at least, he doesn't fully understand.'

'Yes, I expect you are right,' Rosalind said. 'Oh, well, it has taught me a lesson. I just hope he doesn't drink it all at once and get into trouble.'

Ronnie sat on the upturned orange box in the garden shed behind his home and looked at the bottle of whisky. He had known it was the good stuff as soon as he saw it, because it had the same picture on the front as on the bottle Jethro had shared with him. He had acted on impulse when he snatched it, because he sort of knew he shouldn't have taken it from the nice lady without permission. He was sorry now, because maybe she would have given him some if he'd asked.

He liked her, because she talked to him and smiled. She didn't turn away as some people did, looking down their noses at him as if he were a piece of dog mess. Ronnie didn't forget the people who were nice to him. He still remembered the one he had liked best; she had given him his first taste of the good stuff in her caravan. A scowl came over his face as he remembered what Jethro had told him. They had put Morna in the ground. He didn't like that! When Jethro told him that she was there and would never come back he had been upset – and angry when he was told who had put her there. Jethro had said that they ought to teach him a lesson. Ronnie hadn't been sure what that meant, but he remembered that Jethro said they should go there together . . .

Ronnie's mind veered away. He was getting the bad thoughts again. Sometimes, his mind was like one of those things that made pretty patterns and changed when you shook it. He had been given one as a small boy, but another boy had taken it and smashed it. Ronnie had cried then. He had cried a lot when he was a child – but he didn't cry now. His mother used to beat him with a stick she kept in the corner of the kitchen, but he'd taken it away from her and told her no more. She didn't try to hit him now. She didn't say much to him at all, just put his food on the table and left him alone.

Ronnie picked up the bottle and looked at the cap. It took him a few minutes of trying, but he managed to open it at last. He held it to his mouth and swallowed several mouthfuls. It felt good as it trickled down his throat, warming him. His mind was beginning to clear, and he knew the bad thoughts would come back, haunting his dreams. But if he drank the good stuff he would sleep and they would go away.

Sarah was just about to leave the house the next morning when she saw Vera Hayes come cycling up the front drive. Something made her stop and wait, instead of just saying hello and walking on, and as the vicar's wife dismounted, leaning her bicycle against the wall, she felt an icy tingling sensation at the nape of her neck.

'Oh, I am so glad I caught you,' Vera said. 'I thought you might have left already. It is today you go, isn't it?'

'Yes, later this afternoon. The car is coming to collect us at half past one.' Sarah studied her face for a moment, seeing the expression of anxiety in her eyes. 'Has something happened, Mrs Hayes?'

'Well, yes . . .' She shook her head. 'I didn't want to bother you, but it looks as if it is all starting again . . .'

'I'm not sure . . .' Sarah felt as if she had been punched in the stomach. 'There hasn't been another murder?'

'Not that I know of,' Vera said. 'But the vicar found a cat with its head chopped off in the churchyard. He was most upset, because he had believed that all that unpleasant nonsense was over.'

'Oh . . .' Sarah felt slightly sick, but also relieved that it wasn't a woman who had been found dead. 'Yes, that is nasty.'

'Yes, it is. I thought immediately of Amelia, because I know how worried she was about Mr Tibbs the last time the cats were mutilated.'

'Yes, she is very fond of her cat,' Sarah agreed. 'I'll go and have a word with Andrews and we'll tell Millie he isn't to be allowed to stray from the garden. Fortunately, he is a lazy cat and doesn't often run off.'

Mrs Hayes looked relieved. 'Yes, that would be sensible, my dear. Now, do you think I should tell Amelia or not?'

'Oh yes, she will want to know. She will need to talk to Andrews and Millie herself I am sure.'

'As long as she isn't worrying all the time she is away.'

'I think she would be cross if we kept it from her,' Sarah said. 'Please go in, Mrs Hayes. I just have to walk down to the village to post a letter.'

She nodded to Vera and walked on, her brow creased in a thoughtful frown. She knew that Larch suspected Ronnie had killed Miss Bates's cat – and he had taken Rosalind's whisky. It was possible that he had got drunk and . . . she shook her head, not wanting to think about it.

As she returned from the village she saw Rosalind leaving her house. She smiled and stopped to say hello, but decided not to say anything to her about the cat. It was best not to accuse someone of a crime if you weren't sure of your facts.

'How are you this morning?'

'Oh, much better,' Rosalind said. 'I think I was making a fuss about nothing. So you are off this afternoon?'

'Yes. I posted my letter and popped into the shop for some humbugs. The car will be here in a couple of hours.'

'Well, have a lovely time, Sarah – and try not to worry about things too much.'

'I know Amelia is looking forward to it,' Sarah said. 'I am sure it will be very nice.'

'That sounds a bit forced?'

'Oh, I'm not sure if I really fit in with Pamela Avery's crowd,' Sarah said and shrugged. 'But I expect I shall enjoy myself when I get there.'

'Yes, I'm sure you will. Come and see me if you can when you get back.'

'Yes, I shall. Take care of yourself, Rosalind – and don't leave bottles of whisky standing around.'

'Ronnie hasn't come this morning. Perhaps he won't dare to show his face again – but if he does I shall just ignore what happened. As you said, the poor lad probably didn't realize it was stealing.'

Sarah agreed and walked on up the hill. She hoped she was right not to tell Rosalind about the mutilated cat in the church-yard. Yes, she was, because it would only upset her, and it might not have been Ronnie at all. It could well be the devil worshippers who had desecrated the churchyard before. She decided to put it all from her mind and start thinking about the fun she was going to have in the South of France.

'It is very generous of you to arrange this for us,' Amelia said as she got into the car later that day. 'I certainly didn't expect you to come and fetch us in person, Mr Rowe.'

'It is no trouble at all, Mrs Beaufort,' Tommy Rowe said and smiled at her. 'Pamela is very fond of you, and when she told me that both you and Sarah were coming to stay, I imme-diately thought of the idea. Besides, Pamela told me you have a lovely garden. Perhaps you would let me write a piece about it one day?'

'How kind,' Amelia said.

He turned his brilliant blue eyes on Sarah, his smile warm but not encroaching. 'I haven't had a chance to tell you, Sarah, but I came to see your show twice. I was very impressed.'

'Yes, it was a good show,' she said. 'I am glad you enjoyed it, Mr Rowe.'

'Oh, do please call me Tommy,' he told her with an engaging grin. 'I hope we are going to be friends now? We've only met once or twice I know, but we shall see a great deal of each other at the villa. Do you swim, Sarah? Pamela has a pool and there is a lovely private beach as well.'

'That sounds idyllic,' Sarah said. 'Yes, I am quite a strong swimmer – though it is ages since I've had time. It must be three summers ago when I went to Torquay with my father.'

'I think you will find it far nicer in France,' Tommy said. 'So much warmer – and the beach is secluded, no day trippers.'

Sarah was tempted to tell him that she had no objection to day trippers and that she considered his remark to be snobbish and uncalled for, but she held her tongue. It wouldn't do to get off on the wrong foot, and it was very generous of him to go to all this trouble for their sakes. She just smiled, getting into the back seat of the comfortable car. Amelia was in the front and had begun to tell Tommy how excited she was to be flying for the first time in her life.

Sarah looked at the back of his head as he got into the car. His grooming was immaculate, dark blond hair slicked back with pomade that smelled faintly of something pleasant, and must have been expensive, just as his clothes were. Tommy was certainly attractive; perhaps a little too polished for Sarah's personal taste, but he was clearly generous towards his friends. She knew that he was exerting himself to please Amelia, and that pleased her. Yes, all in all, she thought that perhaps she had been a little hard in her previous opinion of him; he could be arrogant on occasion, and he was a snob – but he could also be charming.

It would be interesting to get to know him better.

Ten

Sarah could just make out the villa through the trees as they drove along a road that twisted and turned its way to the top of the hill. Sometimes, she caught sight of other white-washed buildings or a sudden splash of blue sea shimmering in the sunshine. The scenery was certainly beautiful on this part of the coast, and she had enjoyed the short drive from the small private airport where their plane had landed. They had passed some charming villages and wonderful chateaux that she thought she might like to explore while she was here.

The flight had been very exciting, though she had seen the colour leave her grandmother's cheeks as the plane took off. However, Amelia had enjoyed herself, and she had got into the back of the first car with Miranda quite happy to be driven to the villa. Sarah was in the second car with Mr and Mrs Ashton. She had sat next to Mrs Ashton on the flight, but all her efforts to make conversation had met with mono-syllabic answers and she had given up trying. Nancy Ashton really was a disagreeable lady. Sarah had decided to stay clear of her as much as possible at the villa. Her husband, however, had gone out of his way to be pleasant, so much so that Sarah found it a little embarrassing. She was sure his attentions to her were a part of the reason that Nancy was ignoring her.

It was a relief to arrive at the villa and rejoin the rest of the party. The first car had already deposited its passengers, and Lady Avery was at the front of the villa, greeting her guests. She kissed Amelia and then Miranda. In her late thirties, she was elegant and attractive, her blonde hair twisted in a smooth pleat at the back of her head. Her eyes were a greenish colour and intensely curious as she turned to look at Sarah.

'How lovely that you could come,' she said and kissed her.

'I have heard how wonderful you are in that show of yours, Sarah. Tommy kept telling me that I should go and watch you, but somehow I never had the time. Perhaps you will sing for us one evening?'

Sarah smiled but made no promises. She hated being asked to sing for friends, because it was embarrassing. On stage you were hardly aware of the audience until the end, but in a drawing room it was somehow too intimate.

Following the others into the villa, she was already wishing herself back in England. She had joined the party because her grandmother had asked her and she would stick it out, but it wasn't going to be easy. She found herself wishing that Larch were here, because they could have gone off exploring together, but she knew he was busy. She'd tried telephoning him before they left but Lady Meadows had told her he was away for a day or so. Oh well, she thought, if things got too awful she would disappear on her own for a while, go for walks and visit places of interest.

The villa itself was beautiful, the walls white but draped with curtains of pale turquoise, which gave it a restful atmosphere; the floors were of marble with a hint of rose in the grain; and the furniture was pretty. Soft chairs in shades of turquoise or pale pink, blended with lacquered cabinets with an inlay of mother of pearl, jade and other semi-precious materials; occasional tables, bronze figures and huge porcelain vases filled with flowers were scattered about the place. Lady Avery had eclectic taste, and it showed in her collection of valuable items, which ranged from silver objets d'art to carved wooden plaques.

Lady Avery led the way up the curved marble staircase to the bedrooms. Sarah's was the first of the guestrooms, with Amelia further along, and Miranda next to Sarah. Mr and Mrs Ashton had been given a room in the guest annexe, which was on the ground floor, as had Tommy. Lady Avery had the last of the bedrooms on the first floor.

'My husband won't be joining us,' she said, 'so I thought all the ladies together – except for Mrs Ashton, of course, because she is with her husband.'

Sarah looked round the room she had been given. It was smaller than her own room at Amelia's, but adequate and furnished in a comfortable style without being overly fussy, which Sarah liked. She had carried her suitcases herself, because she thought there was too much to expect Lady Avery's servants to cope with everyone's bags at once. Much easier for her to unpack for herself. She had just begun when someone knocked. The door opened to admit Miranda as Sarah gave permission for her to enter.

'Oh, are you unpacking for yourself?' Miranda asked. 'Pamela told me to leave it. Her woman will do it later, after she has seen to Amelia.'

'I don't mind doing it,' Sarah said. 'I'm used to looking after myself.'

Miranda pulled a face. 'I just came to ask what you thought of Ashton and *her* . . .'

'Nancy Ashton?' Sarah said. 'You didn't meet them when you came down, did you? They have moved into Beecham Manor you see – Amelia's neighbours. I don't know if that is why they were invited . . .'

'Pamela said Tommy asked her to invite them,' Miranda replied, her eyes thoughtful. 'I really don't know why. I mean, Ashton is all right I suppose – but she is going to be a pain to have around.'

'She may get easier as she begins to know people,' Sarah said. 'I think she is used to having her own way. He seems to give in to her most of the time.'

'I daresay she is the one with the money,' Miranda said. She picked up a pretty dress Sarah had laid on the bed. 'This is nice. Did you buy it in London?'

'My father bought it for me for my last birthday,' Sarah replied. 'I think it came from Paris.'

'Yes, I would imagine so,' Miranda said. 'I haven't unpacked yet, but when I do you can have a look through the things I brought specially for you.'

'Thank you, but I shan't borrow unless I run out or need something special,' Sarah said. 'I've been thinking about Giles again, Miranda. You don't know if anyone was blackmailing him by any chance?'

'Blackmail . . .' Miranda went pale. 'What are you talking about? I have no idea. Why should I know about something like that?'

'Oh, I just wondered,' Sarah said. 'People do get black-mailed sometimes for silly little things. It is always best to ignore it or tell the police. If you give in to a blackmailer he will come back again.'

'Yes . . .' Miranda's eyes glinted angrily. 'Unless he can't . . .'

'What do you mean?' Sarah stared at her. 'Oh, I see . . . Could Giles have been blackmailing someone, do you think? Is that why he was murdered?'

'Oh for goodness' sake!' Miranda snapped. 'Can't you talk about something else? Giles wasn't being blackmailed. No one is being blackmailed. I don't want to talk about this! I came here to have some fun.'

'Sorry,' Sarah said. 'It's just that it has been on my mind. I'll try not to talk about it again, Miranda.'

'Thank you, I'll see you later.' She went out of the room hurriedly, letting the door slam after her.

Sarah knew that she had touched a raw nerve. Ben was right. Miranda was involved in this business somewhere. From the expression in her eyes a few seconds earlier, Sarah would guess that she was being blackmailed – but she wasn't sure if Giles had been doing the blackmailing or someone else. Miranda certainly didn't want to talk about it, but she hadn't looked guilty – just angry.

She walked over to the window to look out, gasping with pleasure as she saw the wonderful view over the hillside and the bay. The sea was a deep turquoise colour, moving gently as it glistened in the sun. It was so much warmer here than it had been at home, Sarah thought. In the distance she could see a yacht; it was probably heading towards its moorings in the harbour a little way down the picturesque coast.

She was about to move away from the window when she heard loud voices from below, and recognized them as belonging to Nancy and Harvey Ashton. It sounded as if Nancy were complaining about something.

'I've told you before, these things take time,' he was saying. 'As soon as the money comes through I'll get you a replacement for everything you lost.'

'That just isn't good enough,' Nancy's voice rose shrilly. 'They are your friends, not mine. You wanted to come here – and you can see what snobs they are. She doesn't really want us here and I feel at a disadvantage without any decent jewellery.'

'You have some nice things . . .'

'They don't compare with what I lost or with the rings she was wearing! It is your fault, Harvey, and you'd better do something about it.'

'You can't blame me for the burglary!'

'Whose fault was it then? You suggested we go to that damned charity event that night – and you were the last one to open the safe. You must have left the picture off the wall so that they could see it.'

'Don't be so ridiculous! You talk as if I invited them in!'

'That wouldn't surprise me in the least,' Nancy snapped. 'If you hadn't got involved with the wrong crowd you wouldn't have lost so much money gambling . . . and don't think I don't know about the rest of it . . .'

'Don't start that again, Nancy. I've made up for it since haven't I . . .'

Sarah moved away from the window. There was really no excuse for her listening to their private quarrel, except that they should have remained in their room if they had wanted to keep it private. Anyone in the house might have heard them, because their voices were raised.

Sarah felt a little guilty about eavesdropping on their argument, and yet she had known something was wrong between them even before the journey. Nancy had obviously been sulking about her jewellery. It must have annoyed her to hear her husband being pleasant to the other ladies on the aeroplane – but clearly it was Miranda's jewellery that had upset her. Sarah had noticed that Miranda was wearing some very expensive diamond rings as well as her pearls, but of course her husband was a wealthy man. Everyone had assumed that Mr Ashton was wealthy, because they had bought the manor, but Sarah wondered if that were quite true. Lady Beecham had possibly sold cheaply because she wanted to get away after the gruesome events of last summer. Sir James had shot the gypsy he blamed for his nephew Simon's murder and then turned his gun on himself. It must have been hard for his wife to bear, especially as she was stuck in a wheelchair.

So many thoughts chasing around in her head! Sarah wasn't sure where all this was leading her, but her instincts told her that she had overheard something important, though at this moment she didn't know why.

She turned as someone tapped the door and then Amelia came in. She smiled at her granddaughter.

'Are you settling in, Sarah dear?' She walked over to the window. 'Ah yes, you have a beautiful view. My room is larger, but I look out at the gardens and can only just glimpse the sea.'

'Yes, it is a nice view,' Sarah agreed, giving Amelia an affectionate look. 'Are you ready to go down, Gran?'

'Yes, my dear, if you are. Pamela said tea would be waiting.' She laughed. 'We English just cannot do without our tea, even when we are abroad. I think we shall enjoy our stay, my love, don't you? It will be so peaceful here.'

'Yes,' Sarah said. 'It will be lovely, Gran. We can go for nice walks and explore the little villages and the chateaux. It will be very relaxing.'

'Yes, Sarah. I've worried about you since those dreadful murders last year – and then your friend. Well, at least out here you are well away from all that . . .' Amelia looked at her anxiously.

'Yes.' Sarah smiled at her, wanting to reassure her. 'We don't have to think about any of those horrible things here, do we?'

Miranda went for a walk after she left Sarah's room. She was feeling restless, on edge, because she couldn't help thinking that Sarah knew something. Why did she keep on about Giles's murder – and why had she mentioned blackmail? What was she keeping back? And if she knew something, what did she intend to do about it?

And yet what was there for her to know? If Giles had shown her the pictures surely she would have said . . . unless she was in collusion with the blackmailer? For a moment Miranda's green eyes were as hard as emeralds, but then she realized it was unlikely. Amelia's granddaughter wasn't the type, and Miranda quite liked her. In fact, she was tempted to confide in her, to tell her that she was being blackmailed, and ask her advice.

If only Giles hadn't been murdered! Miranda knew in her heart that he had been her friend. He would have helped her to find a way out of this mess. She still hadn't worked out why Giles had been murdered, because she couldn't see the connection . . . unless . . .

'Miranda, how nice,' Tommy's voice startled her and she turned to see him coming towards her. For a moment her heart raced with fright. She wasn't ready for this! When the confrontation came, she wanted it to happen on her terms. Her suspicions had grown during the journey, because although the voice on the phone had been disguised she was fairly sure that he was her blackmailer.

'I came out for some air,' she said, a note of accusation in her voice. 'Are you following me?'

'Why should I do that?' he asked with an air of injured innocence. 'You are rather out of bounds these days, aren't you, darling . . . or has the gilt begun to wear off the ginger-bread?'

'No, it has not,' Miranda said angrily. 'I am in love with Peter – and I was never interested in you, Tommy. You simply aren't my type.'

'I think you made that clear once before,' he said. 'You preferred Henderson, as I recall . . . until something better came along.'

Miranda flushed. 'It wasn't like that. Peter is such a generous, good man – but you wouldn't understand that . . .' She gasped as she saw something in his eyes, realizing belatedly that she was on dangerous ground. 'No, I didn't mean that,' she retracted hastily. 'It makes me angry because everyone thinks I married for money and I didn't . . . I love Peter.'

'Yes, of course you do,' he said, a purring note in his voice. 'And all the beautiful things he gives you.'

Her eyes narrowed, slanting and green like a cat's. 'Peter may give me things but they aren't mine to sell or dispose of. He just likes to see me wearing them.'

'A woman like you should know how to get what you want. Make sure of your future before it is too late, Miranda.'

He turned and walked away, leaving her to stare after him. She was sure now in her own mind that he was the black-mailer . . . and a little voice in the back of her mind was telling her that he might have murdered Giles.

When she thought about it, it fitted. Giles had discovered the photographs were missing when she telephoned him. He had promised to look for them, but supposing he had realized that they had been stolen . . . and guessed that it was Tommy?

She was certain now that he hadn't liked Tommy. He would have rung Tommy and demanded their return. Had Tommy gone round to have a row about them and shot Giles in a temper? She knew that Giles had had a pistol somewhere. He might have threatened Tommy with it and . . . She could visualize the scene and it all fitted. Tommy must have taken the gun with him afterwards and got rid of it, because the police hadn't found it – at least she didn't think so.

Miranda felt quite certain that Tommy was blackmailing her. She had begun to suspect that Giles had discovered the truth and been killed because he had demanded the return of the photographs. She felt queasiness in her stomach, and yet it had hardened her resolve. If Tommy Rowe had murdered Giles, he deserved all that was coming to him.

Somehow she had to get her photographs back and then . . . she would kill him.

'It isn't much to go on,' Gareth Hughes said as he looked across the pub table. 'But I got the old files out last night and went through them – in each one a witness mentioned a well-dressed man, a gentleman. The description isn't much use, because one said dark-haired and the other said dark blond – but he had blue eyes; they all agreed on that much.'

'I don't suppose you have a name?'

'Nothing concrete,' Gareth said, 'but the florist sort of remembered sending that basket of flowers, and she said the man was well spoken, smart, and a gentleman, with dark blond hair and blue eyes. She said that he had sent several baskets of flowers to the theatre – all of them to Miss Sarah Beaufort.'

'To Sarah?' Ben asked, frowning. 'She was sure about that?'

'Yes, because she said she hadn't connected the murder with the flowers, because they weren't meant for Esther – they were meant for Sarah. You already knew that, of course, but you may not have known that he had sent others – quite a few actually. And he never signed his cards with his name. It was just from an admirer. He paid in cash, of course.'

'So we still have no idea who he was,' Ben said and pulled a face. 'He has covered his tracks too well.'

'Perhaps not,' Gareth said. 'It was the reason the florist rang me again – because she had seen his photograph in a society magazine. She never takes them as a rule, but one of her customers left it in the shop and she put it to one side for her.'

'She looked through it of course,' Ben said. 'A natural thing to do, and she saw a picture of the man who had sent all those flowers – so did she give you a name?'

'The Honourable Tommy Rowe,' Gareth said. 'It isn't enough to convict him, of course. Sending flowers to a singer you admire isn't a crime, but we shall be watching him. If he is our killer he is going to make a mistake sooner or later.'

'Oh, my God . . .' Ben looked sick. 'I know him – at least, I know of him. He is Lady Avery's brother . . . and Sarah has just gone to stay with her in France . . .'

'And she has no idea that he could be a murderer,' Gareth said. 'Do you know where to reach her?'

'She gave me the address,' Ben said. 'We leave for France in the morning. I'll go and see her straight away. All this could be speculation, of course, but at least if she knows what we know . . .'

'She can be on her guard,' Gareth agreed. 'You can trust her not to say or do anything stupid? I mean, we could be barking up the wrong tree and I don't particularly want to get sued for defamation of character.'

'Sarah knows that,' Ben said. 'If I had my way she would come home immediately, but knowing her she will stay, not just because she can't let her friends down, but because she will want to discover the truth.' He was silent for a moment. 'I can't invite myself along to Lady Avery's party, but I know someone who could . . .'

'Good.' Gareth nodded his approval and finished his warm beer. 'I don't want to read about your friend being murdered over there. As soon as her name came up, I decided to bring you in on this, Ben.'

'Thank you. I appreciate this,' Ben said. 'I'm still thinking about Henderson's murder, but so far I haven't made much headway, although . . . I have a funny feeling that the answer may be closer than I imagine . . .'

Sarah glanced out of her window the next morning. She saw Tommy and Lady Avery standing together in the garden. They appeared to be arguing, but her window was closed, and in any case they were too far away for her to have heard what they were saying.

As she stood watching, Tommy glanced up at her window. He stared at her for a moment and then said something to his sister. Sarah waved, because she didn't know what else to do. Pamela waved back and Sarah moved away from the window, feeling a bit embarrassed.

She ought not to have stood watching them, of course – but she couldn't help wondering why they were arguing. She picked up her bathing things, deciding to go down to the beach.

It was as Sarah was walking back from the beach that she saw Tommy coming to meet her. He was wearing a towelling bathrobe, clearly intending to go for a swim himself. He smiled as he saw her.

'I wish I had known that you were intending to swim this morning, Sarah,' he said. 'We could have come down together.'

Sarah smiled but said nothing. She had purposely stolen away, because she had hoped to be alone for a while. Dinner the previous evening had been difficult, because half the guests seemed not to be speaking to the others. Nancy and Harvey Ashton were glaring at each other the whole time. Miranda seemed lost in thought, and Pamela's attempts to get everyone talking had fallen flat. Afterwards, in the salon, she had begged Sarah to sing for them, and seeing how distressed her hostess was at the way her guests were behaving, Sarah had given in. Her performance had broken the ice and everyone had been very complimentary. In fact their praise had been so over-whelming that Sarah had escaped as soon as she could.

'Oh, I was up very early,' she said easily. 'Pamela was talking about getting a beach party up after lunch. I daresay we shall all come down then.'

'Yes, of course,' he said, nodded and walked on.

Sarah continued up the hill, walking through the trees that covered the hillside. She had enjoyed her swim more than she expected to enjoy the beach party that afternoon, but she couldn't just disappear on her first day at the villa.

She approached the side of the house, passing the guest annexe on her way. She was startled to see Miranda emerge just ahead of her, looking guilty, and hurried to catch up with her.

'Is something wrong?' she asked.

Miranda turned to her, and she caught the odd expression in her eyes. 'Oh, no, nothing. I just wanted to speak to ... Nancy, that's all ...'

'Oh, I see.' Sarah had the strangest feeling that she was lying, but why should she? 'I've been swimming. It was lovely.'

'Yes, I'm sure it must be,' Miranda said. 'I've picked out a couple of things you might like, Sarah. I really have no use for them. Shall I bring them to your room later?'

'Well, yes, if you really don't need them,' Sarah agreed and smiled at her. 'You know, Miranda, I might be able to help you – if you told me what was wrong.'

'Nothing is wrong,' Miranda said, and there was a gleam in her eyes that might have been triumph. 'It is kind of you to offer, but I don't need help.'

'Sorry, I didn't mean to pry,' Sarah said and went into the house, running up the stairs to her room.

She had taken a bath and changed into a cool green linen dress with wide shoulder straps when Miranda knocked at the door. She was carrying two pretty silk afternoon dresses, which she laid on the bed.

'I am sorry if I was a bit sharp earlier,' she said. 'I did have a problem, and I was going to ask you something – but it is all right now.'

'I'm glad,' Sarah told her. 'I didn't mean to pry – but you had seemed a bit anxious.'

'Yes, I was,' Miranda said. 'But it is fine now.'

Sarah nodded. Miranda did seem to have shed her cares, and perhaps Sarah had been wrong to think that she was being blackmailed.

Miranda was feeling on top of the world as she left Sarah's room. It had been so simple after all. She had taken the chance to search Tommy's room as soon as he left to go to the beach, and she'd found her photographs in the top drawer of his dressing chest. She hadn't been able to believe that he had left them lying there where anyone could see them, and she'd snatched them up and run. She hadn't noticed Sarah until she caught up with her. It was a nuisance that Sarah had seen her, of course, but she had accepted her excuse. Besides, what did it matter? The pictures were destroyed and she knew for certain that there was only one set. Giles had burned the negatives in front of her.

She was in the clear. The relief was overwhelming. Peter would never have to know about that foolish incident, and she would make very sure that nothing like that happened again. She loved her husband and she knew how lucky she was to be loved in return.

She couldn't help laughing as she thought of Tommy's anger when he got back and found the photographs had gone. He had nothing to blackmail her with now, and she hadn't had to kill him after all.

She frowned as she remembered that she had thought he might have murdered Giles, but of course she had no proof. Besides, she couldn't bring Giles back, and she wasn't going to risk shooting Tommy now that the photographs had been destroyed. She could forget it all and enjoy her visit with Pamela – she could enjoy the rest of her life.

Sarah met Nancy Ashton as she came downstairs after changing. She had obviously had her breakfast and was just leaving as Sarah entered the room.

'Oh, have you finished?' Sarah said. 'I went for a swim on the beach, I suppose that is why I am late.'

'The coffee will be cold,' Nancy told her sourly. 'The water in our bathroom was tepid this morning. I hate cold baths – and I hardly slept at all last night.'

'Oh dear, I'm sorry to hear that,' Sarah said. 'I slept very well. Perhaps you could change rooms with someone?'

'I doubt any of the beds are much better. Besides, Harvey wouldn't like it if I made a fuss. He wanted to come here. I have no idea why.'

'I expect he is friendly with Tommy, isn't he?'

'God knows why. It is all his fault for leading Harvey astray. I've told him he's being used, but he won't listen.'

'Pamela is arranging a beach party this afternoon,' Sarah said, hoping to distract her. 'Shall you come?'

'I prefer the pool,' Nancy said. 'I hate getting sand under my clothes. Besides, I don't like sitting in the sun. I shall probably stay in the house until the evening.'

Sarah gave up and went into the breakfast room. Harvey

Ashton was sitting there alone, staring in front of him. She couldn't help feeling sorry for him, even though she suspected that he might not be quite the genial, pleasant man he appeared. She had a feeling he might know more about his wife's stolen jewellery than he was saying, but perhaps she had got it all wrong.

'I thought I was the last,' Sarah said as she inspected the silver chafing dishes and helped herself to a little scrambled egg and some bacon. 'I went for a swim on the beach.'

'That must have been lovely,' Harvey said and smiled at her. 'I think I might do that myself another morning. Nancy prefers a pool if she swims, which isn't often, but I don't think you can beat the sea.'

'It was refreshing,' Sarah said. 'I saw Tommy going down to the beach as I came back.'

'Oh, I didn't realize,' Harvey said and frowned. 'So, what are we all going to do today?'

'I think Lady Avery is arranging a beach party for after lunch. I suppose we can please ourselves pretty much until then. There is a tennis court at the back of the house – if you play?'

'Are you offering to give me a game?'

'Why not? I don't know if anyone else wants to make up a foursome or if it is just us . . .'

'Nancy doesn't play,' he said. 'I don't know about Tommy or Miranda.'

'I think Miranda used to play. If not I don't mind playing singles. I'm not sure if I'm good enough to challenge you, but we could have fun.'

'You're on,' Harvey said. 'Shall we say in an hour? Give us time to get breakfast down?'

'Yes, that would be lovely.'

'Good, well, I'll go and make sure Nancy is all right and then get changed.'

'In an hour then,' Sarah said. 'If you are sure?'

'I couldn't be surer,' Harvey said. 'You are a nice person to be around, Sarah. I shall enjoy playing a game of tennis with you.'

Amelia had been having breakfast in her room. She was just coming from it when Sarah emerged wearing her tennis things, a knee-length white skirt and cotton shirt, also new plimsolls and short white socks.

'You look fresh and energetic,' her grandmother said, smiling. 'Who are you playing?'

'Harvey Ashton at the moment, though Miranda and Tommy are welcome to join in if they wish. Mrs Ashton doesn't play, apparently.'

'One wonders what that woman does do, apart from complain,' Amelia said. 'I daresay that is being uncharitable, but she created such an atmosphere last night. Poor Pamela was at her wits' end until you agreed to sing for us, dearest. She was so grateful. She told me she hadn't realized how well you could sing until last night.'

'Well, I hope she doesn't ask every night,' Sarah said. 'I came here for a holiday, not to sing for my supper.'

'Oh, I am sure she won't,' Amelia said. 'Besides, we shall be going out this evening. We've all been invited to a party at a villa somewhere further down the hill. I think it will be an open-air feast and there will be entertainment, music, dancing for those who wish – and fireworks at the end, apparently.'

'Oh, that sounds more interesting. I don't think I could bear another night of Nancy's sulks.'

'Go along then, dearest,' Amelia said. 'Don't keep Mr Ashton waiting.'

'No, I shan't,' Sarah said and went out of the side door and round to the back of the villa where the tennis court and swimming pool were situated. She saw Tommy Rowe coming from the annexe, noticing that he was scowling. He passed her but hardly looked her way. 'It must be catching . . .' Sarah murmured as she continued on to the tennis court.

Harvey Ashton had just arrived. He waved at her cheerfully and Sarah warmed to him. She wasn't sure that she entirely trusted him, but at least he was cheerful company.

'I hope I haven't kept you waiting? I stopped to have a word with my grandmother.'

'She was well, I hope, slept all right?' Harvey frowned. 'Nancy is lying down in her room. She says she has a headache.'

'Oh, I am sorry to hear that,' Sarah said. 'Do you want to serve first or shall I?'

'Ladies first,' he said. 'Unless you would rather not?'

'Oh, I don't mind,' she said. 'We'll have a knock up first and then I'll start. I hope you won't be disappointed. I'll do my best.'

Sarah won her first service game easily. She suspected that Harvey wasn't trying too hard, but when she took his first service game he looked surprised and after that he got into the match, contesting it fiercely. Sarah won the first set, but Harvey took the second. They were about to start the third when Miranda turned up and asked if she could join in.

'Why don't you take my place?' Sarah asked. 'Call it a draw, Harvey. I'll watch you two for a while, and then I'll go and change.'

Sarah watched until Miranda had lost the first three games. She wasn't really up to Harvey's standard, and was beginning to get cross. Sarah waved and set off back to the house. If Harvey knew what was good for him, he would start losing a few points.

She would have gone straight upstairs, but Tommy saw her come in and waylaid her in the hall.

'You are energetic, Sarah,' he said, humour in his eyes. 'No wonder you are in such demand. Pamela tells me that there have been two telephone calls for you this morning. She left a message for you in the front hall apparently.'

'Oh, thank you,' Sarah said, feeling surprised. 'I'll pick it up before I change. Harvey is a good player. I seem to remember that you won an amateur challenge cup once, Tommy. You should challenge him to a game one day.'

'Yes, perhaps – but only if you and Pamela make up a four-some. Pam is pretty good too, you know.'

'That would leave Miranda out,' Sarah said. 'But we could share games. Yes, that would be nice. Excuse me, I must pick up my messages.'

She went out into the hall and discovered an envelope addressed to her. It was sealed, and two messages were inside. She discovered that one was from Ben Marshall and the other was from Larch. Ben would be calling to see her either that evening or the next morning, and Larch was arriving the following day. Pamela had scribbled a message of her own underneath.

*   *   *

I've asked Larch to join us at the villa, Sarah – and your friend Ben knows about the party this evening, so he said it would probably be tomorrow morning instead.

Sarah wondered what had made Larch decide to come over, because she knew he had a lot of work on to prepare for his shows later that summer – and Ben was breaking into his holiday with Cathy to visit her. He must have discovered something important. She was glad he was coming, because she wanted to talk to him about some thoughts of her own.

Eleven

The beach party was fun, mainly because Harvey Ashton and Tommy organized a game of cricket. Everyone present joined in, because Amelia was happy to take a turn with the bat, and Sarah did her running for her. Miranda was out first ball from Tommy, and retired to sit on a deckchair and watch, refusing to field, but Pamela was very good and she hit the ball for what they had decided would count as a six three times. Harvey wasn't sure of the rules, but went along with everyone else, accepting his dismissal in his usual cheery manner.

Afterwards, they drank lemonade and rested before Sarah, Tommy and Harvey went for a swim. Miranda took her shoes off and paddled at the edge, but refused to come in. Nancy had declined to come at all, and was, according to Harvey, still suffering from a headache in their room. However, when they returned from the beach, Sarah saw her coming from the pool wearing a bathing costume and a filmy wrap, her hair wrapped in a bright turban.

She saw Sarah but didn't bother to wave, simply turning away to the annexe, a look of annoyance on her face. Sarah was glad they were all invited to a party that evening, because she would rather not have to see Nancy sulking all evening.

However, when Sarah came down for the evening, she saw that Nancy was already in the drawing room, dressed and ready for the party. She was laughing at something Pamela had said to her, and seemed in a much better frame of mind.

'Are you feeling better?'

'Yes, thank you,' Nancy said. She held her hand out for Sarah to see. 'Harvey just gave me this. He was saving it for our anniversary but decided not to wait. It is exactly like the one I lost in the burglary. I can't tell the difference.'

The ring was a magnificent solitaire and rivalled the one Miranda was wearing, which might have accounted for Nancy's pleasure.

'That is very special,' Sarah said, because she could see that it meant a lot to Nancy to have something that another woman might envy.

'Yes, I think so,' Nancy said, bestowing a rare smile on her. 'Did you enjoy your game of tennis this morning? Harvey says you are very good.'

'Oh, I'm not too bad. I'm looking forward to the party this evening.'

'Yes, I am too,' Nancy replied, her gaze moving away. 'Oh, Tommy, I have something to tell you . . .' She drifted across the room towards him, leaving Sarah temporarily alone.

'What happened to her?' Miranda drawled, as she came to stand next to Sarah.

'I think she is happy about something,' Sarah said but didn't enlighten her further. 'It looks as if everyone is ready to go.'

Miranda nodded, her eyes moving over Sarah. 'You look very nice this evening.'

Sarah murmured her thanks, moving in the wake of the others as they went outside to the cars. Everyone was deciding who was going with whom, and Sarah found that she had been elected to go in Tommy's car. When it came to it, she realized that she was his only passenger. He held the door for her to get into the front, smiling at her.

'Isn't this nice?' he asked. 'I've been hoping I might get you to myself for a while. The thing about these house parties is that there are always too many people for private conversations, don't you think?'

'I'm not sure,' Sarah said, glancing at him sideways. 'I suppose it is always possible if one wishes for it. Had you something in particular to say to me, Tommy?'

'Not really. I just hoped for a little time with you. Ashton has been monopolizing you ever since we arrived.'

'Has he?' Sarah was surprised. 'Because we played tennis this morning?'

'I've seen the way he looks at you. Be a little careful of him, Sarah. He doesn't flaunt it the way Giles did, but he likes women . . . and he isn't to be trusted.'

'You're talking about Giles Henderson,' Sarah said. 'He asked me out a couple of times, but I refused.'

'Yes, I know. I admire you for that, Sarah. You've got more pride than most of those little . . . the girls you work with on stage.'

Sarah frowned. 'I can't help wondering whether the police are any nearer to discovering who killed Giles . . .'

'It was a burglary gone wrong,' Tommy said. 'At least, that's what Pamela told me. I don't know much about it. Giles and I weren't really friends. He was a mere scribbler but he imagined his work compared to mine.'

Sarah decided to ignore that remark. 'I only knew him slightly. I didn't dislike him, but I wouldn't go out with him, because . . . well, I just wouldn't. Mr Ashton seems nice enough but you don't have to warn me about him. I would never think of anything like that with a married man.'

'Of course you wouldn't,' Tommy said and smiled at her. 'That's why I respect you, Sarah. I couldn't respect those other girls; they are nothing but sluts – but you are different.'

Sarah wasn't sure why but the back of her neck was tingling. She was very relieved when Tommy pulled the car to a halt in front of the villa where the party was to be held. There was something creepy about his manner . . . something that made her resolve not to be alone with him in future.

She forced herself to be natural as she walked to join Amelia and her hostess. They all went into the villa together. Sarah couldn't help feeling glad that there were so many people around.

It was a beautiful, warm night and the party had flowed out on to the patio at the back of the villa. Subdued lighting made the pool look intensely blue and there were lanterns strung from the trees, giving the scene a magical atmosphere. Music was playing somewhere and a man was singing a love song. Some of the guests were dancing, others standing around talking, drinking, simply enjoying themselves.

Sarah moved from group to group, making new friends and dancing occasionally. She danced once with Harvey Ashton, but when he asked again later, she refused, saying she was hungry. He insisted on accompanying her to the buffet and helping her to fill her plate with the delicious trifles on offer. Sarah found herself a seat at one of the tables and sat down to eat her supper, where Miranda and Amelia joined her. Harvey excused himself and went off. The music had stopped for a while and she glanced around the patio area. Some of the guests had disappeared, taking the chance to refresh themselves or explore the gardens, which opened out on to the wooded slope that led down to the beach.

'It would be lovely on the beach now,' Miranda said. 'Do you fancy a paddle, Sarah?'

'If I had my costume I would love to swim,' Sarah replied. 'Have you ever been swimming in the moonlight, Miranda?'

'No, I haven't – but I wouldn't mind a paddle on the beach . . .'

Sarah suspected that Miranda had drunk a little more champagne than perhaps she ought, but she rather liked the idea of going for a paddle.

'Yes, all right,' she said. 'Let's go together . . .'

They smiled at each other and got up, heading in the direction of the shrubbery. Sarah wondered if Miranda wanted to talk to her alone. She had been looking a bit pensive this evening, as though she had something on her mind, her mood of earlier elation seeming to have evaporated.

She glanced at her as they left the lights and noise of the party behind. The music had begun again but it was quieter as they walked down the slope towards the beach, and they could hear the sound of the sea lapping lazily against the shore.

'Did you want to tell me something?' Sarah asked. 'I'm happy to listen if you do and I shan't judge you.'

'What do you mean? What have you heard?'

'Nothing. It's just a feeling that you might have something on your mind.'

Miranda hesitated. 'I'm not sure. I thought it was all settled but . . .'

At that moment they heard screaming coming from just ahead of them, and then a woman rushed towards them from the direction of the beach. She was obviously terrified and would have gone straight by them if Sarah hadn't caught hold of her arm.

'What is it? What has happened? Did someone attack you?'

'Not me . . .' the woman said in a hysterical tone. 'Down there – on the beach. She's dead . . . murdered . . .'

'Who has been murdered? Are you sure she is dead?'

'Her face . . .' the woman gulped and Sarah recognized her as someone she had met earlier that evening. 'Nancy Ashton . . . she has been strangled . . .'

'Oh no!' Sarah exclaimed. 'Are you sure?' She looked at Miranda. 'I'm going down to the beach. You had better go back and fetch help. If Nancy has been attacked . . .'

'The murderer might still be out here,' Miranda said, turning a ghastly white. 'I'll take Mrs Baker back. I'm not going down there . . .' She put an arm about the shocked woman's waist, leading her towards the patio and the safety of other people. Sarah could hear the sound of her hysterical sobbing as she continued down the hill alone.

She shivered, feeling an icy chill trickle down her spine. Nancy Ashton wasn't her favourite person but she didn't deserve to be murdered. No one did! Glancing behind her several times, Sarah walked swiftly, almost running as she reached the beach and saw the slumped figure of a woman lying on the sand. Her heart was beating very fast as she went towards it, knowing what she was going to see and dreading it, and yet feeling compelled.

She hesitated as she approached, looking around her for signs of footsteps. There were three sets leading towards the spot where Nancy lay: presumably hers, the woman's who had found her – and the murderer's. The sand had been churned up all around her, indicating a struggle. Nancy had fought for her life. Looking closer, Sarah could see that one set of footsteps was obviously a man's; it didn't tell her much, but she knew that the tide was coming in and before long it would wash all the evidence away. At least she could tell the police that there had been three sets of footsteps, which probably meant that Nancy had been killed here and not carried here afterwards.

She approached, careful not to tread through the other imprints. Nancy was lying on her back, her eyes open and staring. She had been strangled with a blue scarf that she certainly hadn't been wearing that evening and her face had a strange purplish colour, her features contorted in an expression of horror. Sarah felt sick. She had been hoping against hope that Mrs Baker was wrong and there might be a chance of saving Nancy, but it was obvious that she was dead.

Her evening dress had been torn, exposing her breasts. Sarah looked at her hands, which were clenched like claws, and saw that Nancy's diamond ring had gone. It looked as if there might be blood beneath her nails. Had the motive been robbery? Sarah wondered. And yet there was something frenzied about the attack that suggested another motive.

'Sarah!' Looking over her shoulder, Sarah saw two men running towards her. One of them was Harvey Ashton, and the other was Ben.

Sarah felt a wave of relief. She had not expected Ben to call until the morning, but she was grateful that he hadn't waited. If she had ever needed him, it was now.

'Harvey . . .' she said in a choked voice. 'I am so sorry. Nancy has been attacked and killed – and her ring is missing.'

'Sarah!' Ben said as Harvey fell to his knees by his wife's side. 'What made you come down here alone? He might still be around.'

'I wanted to make sure there was no chance of saving her,' Sarah said. 'I hoped – but it was too late. There were three sets of footsteps in the sand before we all got here, Ben. Nancy's, Mrs Baker's – and a man's.' Ben looked and saw that Harvey had churned the sand up around his wife. There was no chance of examining a perfect print now. Harvey was gathering his wife into his arms, tears running down his face.

'Nancy . . . I'm sorry, so sorry,' he sobbed. 'Don't be dead . . . please, my darling, don't be dead . . . I don't want to lose you . . .'

'You were here first,' Ben said looking at Sarah. 'Was there anything else – anything dropped by either Mrs Ashton or her killer?'

'No, nothing,' Sarah said. 'I stood back and took a good look. Whoever it was killed her and then took the diamond ring Mr Ashton gave her earlier today. She had been showing it off all evening.'

'A reason for murder?'

'Perhaps . . .' Sarah glanced at Harvey Ashton. 'Should he be lifting her like that? Won't the police want to see where she was killed?'

'The tide is coming in,' Ben said. 'She can't be left here – besides, there is nothing much to find. Lady Avery was telephoning for the police when I left her. I'm not sure if I can do anything over here, Sarah. I'm ex-Scotland Yard and they aren't likely to take kindly to any interference from me.'

'No, I understand,' Sarah said. 'But we have to talk, Ben.'

Harvey had his wife in his arms. He was walking back across the beach, staring straight ahead of him, his face working with grief. He didn't look at Sarah or Ben, and she doubted he would have heard if they had spoken to him.

'We'll talk privately in the morning,' Ben said. 'We had better get back to the villa. The French police are going to want statements.'

'Miranda and I ate supper together. Harvey was there until twenty minutes or so before we decided to come down to the beach for a moonlit paddle. Mrs Baker found her and we met her on the way down. Miranda took her back to get help and I came down to make sure there wasn't a chance of her being alive. As far as the French police are concerned, that is all I know.'

'But it isn't, is it?'

'No, there are other things, but they are only my thoughts, Ben. I don't think I should tell the French police anything more – though it might help us in other cases . . .'

'Right, I get you,' Ben said. 'We'll talk tomorrow – but just be careful, Sarah. Especially where Tommy Rowe is concerned.'

'Yes,' Sarah said. 'I think we might both be on the same track . . . but we'll swap notes in the morning . . .'

Sarah found it difficult to sleep that night. A shadow had descended over the party after her return to the villa with Ben. The French police had come and asked for statements, which she, Miranda and Mrs Baker had given. They were told that they might be asked to make official statements and sign them and then be allowed to leave. Harvey Ashton had been detained, and he had gone with the police to make various statements and sign papers. Sarah wasn't sure if he had come in later that night or not.

She left her room just after eight o'clock the next morning and went for a swim in the pool. She didn't feel like going down to the beach after what had happened, because there was obviously a dangerous killer on the loose.

She was wearing a towelling robe and about to return to

her room when Tommy Rowe came out of the villa and walked to greet her.

'How are you, Sarah?' he asked solicitously. 'I hope you didn't have nightmares?'

'No, though I didn't sleep too well,' she told him. 'It was such a horrid thing to happen. Amelia and Lady Avery are very upset. Miranda was too when we heard about it last night.'

'She probably got what was coming to her,' Tommy said, a sharp note in his voice. 'She was a bitch to Ashton. I thought he would get tired of it one day.'

'Are you saying that Harvey murdered his wife?' Sarah stared at him. 'I don't understand. Why would he kill her – and why take her ring?'

'Was the ring missing?' Sarah nodded and he frowned.

'That is odd, because he only gave it to her yesterday – but who else would it be?'

'That is for the police to discover,' Sarah said. 'I don't know him well enough to know whether he is capable of murder – but he seemed genuinely distraught last night.'

'Grief is easy enough to fake. I warned you he wasn't to be trusted, Sarah.' His eyes glittered oddly, as if he were not quite himself that morning.

'Yes, you did,' she agreed. 'Thank you, Tommy. It is good of you to be concerned.' She shivered. 'I must go and change. I shall turn cold in these wet things.'

'I wouldn't want anything to happen to you, Sarah.'

Sarah walked away from him, wondering why that had sounded more like a threat than concern. She was thoughtful as she went up to her room, remembering something that Janey had told her before she left for Yarmouth. Tommy answered her description of the man Janey had seen outside the theatre perfectly. He knew Harvey Ashton well . . . and there had been something in his voice when he had called the other showgirls little sluts.

At least, he might have been going to say that, but had changed his mind. And his remarks about Giles had been disparaging.

It was just possible that he could be the murderer Ben was looking for. She knew that she had put two and two together and possibly made five. She had no proof, just a theory that wouldn't stand up in any court, especially here. The French police probably thought they had their man in Harvey Ashton, because jealousy and passion often caused crimes of this kind – and she had heard Nancy arguing with her husband. Nancy had been bad tempered and difficult, and her husband might have wanted her out of the way, especially if the money was hers. And yet Sarah felt that he had been genuinely distraught when Nancy's body was found. Of course, it was possible to fake grief . . .

Sarah found herself impatient for Ben's arrival, because she wanted to share her thoughts with him. He had hinted that Tommy Rowe wasn't to be trusted, and there had to be a reason why both he and Larch had decided to come here.

If Ben had found a connection to Tommy Rowe he would have been worried for her sake, and he had probably asked Larch to come and keep an eye on her. If Sarah's theory was correct, she wasn't in danger for the moment – but someone else might be. She had to have a word with Miranda before Ben arrived. She was fairly certain that Amelia's goddaughter had been about to tell her something the previous evening before they were interrupted, and it might be important.

Miranda was packing her things. She hadn't slept all night and she was frightened, because she thought that she might be the next victim of Nancy's murderer. Nancy's ring had been taken, which indicated that it might be a theft gone wrong – just like had happened to Giles. He had been shot but some of his things had been taken. Miranda shivered. She had valuable jewels with her. And the note she had found thrust under her door before she left for the party the previous evening had been menacing.

You think you're clever but the photos were your insurance. The emeralds will be the least of your worries if you don't pay up. I know what to do with a bitch like you, Miranda.

If Nancy's ring hadn't been taken, Miranda might have thought Harvey had killed his wife. She had been so awful to him and everyone else until she got her own way. Miranda wouldn't shed any tears for her, and she didn't want to stay around here to be murdered. She wasn't a witness and she was going home

on the first ship she could find. She frowned as someone
knocked at the door, holding her breath, hoping that whoever
it was would go away. She didn't want to talk to anyone. She
just wanted to get out of here as quickly as she could. All
thoughts of committing murder herself had fled. She was too
damned scared!

'Miranda, are you there?' She heard Sarah's voice and
almost changed her mind, then decided that it was too late.
She didn't want to confess that she had been blackmailed or
that she suspected she knew the name of her blackmailer –
and perhaps Nancy's killer.

Sarah went along the hall to Amelia's room. Her grandmother
invited her in when she knocked and she entered, feeling
concerned when she saw Amelia sitting up against a pile of
feather pillows.

'Are you all right, Gran?'

'Yes, dearest. I was a little upset last night, but Pamela's
housekeeper brought me a tisane and that helped me to sleep.
This is all rather shocking, Sarah. I thought we had put all
that behind us when we came here.'

'Yes, so did I,' Sarah said. She had no intention of telling
her grandmother her theory, because there was no way of
proving it and she didn't want to distress her even more. 'I
am so sorry that it happened. Nancy didn't deserve that . . .'

'No one does, my dear,' Amelia said. 'I feel so upset for
Pamela. She spent ages planning all this and now her party
is ruined. No one will want to stay here after this, will they?
And she had more guests coming next week.'

'I daresay most of us would rather go home,' Sarah said.
'We shall have to get permission from the French police, of
course, but hopefully they will give it in a day or so.'

'Yes, I suppose so,' Amelia said. 'I should like to leave
today, but I suppose we must wait – and it would be unkind
to leave Pamela so abruptly. Yet it has made things uncomfortable.'

'Don't worry, Gran. I don't think we are all going to be
murdered in our beds. I imagine the murderer had a good
reason for what he – or she – did.'

'Sarah! You can't think a woman did this?'

'It is possible, Gran. Tommy hinted that it might have been

Harvey Ashton, but he was distraught when we found her. He might have been faking it, but I don't think so.'

'You should never have gone down there, Sarah. Why didn't you come back with Miranda and Mrs Baker?'

'Because I thought there might be a chance that Nancy was still alive. I wanted to help her if I could.'

'He might have killed you as well!'

'I don't think I was in any danger,' Sarah said, looking thoughtful. 'At least, not last night. Whoever killed Nancy was angry. That person had no reason to be angry with me.'

'Sarah . . . please do not get involved in this affair!'

'Oh no, I shan't,' Sarah told her. 'I don't think the police would listen even if I talked to them . . .'

'Don't tell me you have more of your theories?'

'I might. Ben is coming today. He knows something, Gran.'

'Promise me that you won't go off on your own the way you did last time!'

'Larch is also coming today. I am quite sure he wouldn't allow it even if I wanted to, which I don't. Please don't be upset, Gran. I am just going to tell Ben my thoughts and that is all. I shan't accuse anyone of anything, and I shan't run any risks – knowingly.' She bent down to kiss Amelia's soft cheek. 'I promise you. I don't want to be involved in this any more than I have to.'

'Very well, my dear,' Amelia said. 'You were clever last time, solving the mystery, but you might have been killed – and I couldn't bear that, dearest.'

Sarah smiled but didn't say anything more. She had an uneasy feeling that she was already involved more than she knew.

Miranda waited until she was sure that Sarah had gone and then looked out into the hall. She was taking just her small suitcase with her, and her jewels were locked safely inside. Pamela would send the rest of her things on sometime, but they didn't matter. She just had to get away. She walked down the stairs, preparing to make a telephone call. She needed a taxi to take her to the railway station. From there she could get to Paris and she would stay at a decent hotel until she could make arrangements to get home.

'Where are you going, Miranda?'

Tommy's voice made her jump. She turned to look at him, her nerves jerking. Before Nancy was murdered she had been so angry that she had been prepared to kill him to save her marriage, but now she was terrified.

'I'm leaving before I get murdered too.'

'Don't be ridiculous,' Tommy said. 'Take that case back to your room, Miranda. You can't leave without permission from the French police – none of us can.'

'I don't care what they say,' Miranda said. 'I'm leaving now . . .'

Tommy reached out and took hold of her wrist, his eyes cold, menacing. 'Don't be a fool, Miranda. They would arrest you before you could get on a ship and you would end up in a French prison for weeks before the mess got sorted out.'

'You want me to stay because you think you can frighten me into giving you the emeralds!' she cried, forgetting caution as anger overcame the fear. 'Your dirty little blackmail didn't work. I've got my photographs back and I'm not paying you a penny . . .'

Tommy's eyes darkened with anger. 'Are you off your head? Stupid bitch! I have no idea what you're talking about.'

'I don't believe you. You've been telephoning me for ages, threatening to tell Peter . . . and I found the pictures in your room.'

His fingers tightened about her wrist, hurting her. 'I hope you haven't been in my room, Miranda, because I can be very unpleasant when people upset me – but I don't know anything about any photographs.' His expression was terrifying. 'You aren't going anywhere. Pamela is already upset over this business. If you run out on her she will be devastated. If you know what is good for you, you will do as I say!'

Miranda stared at him for a moment, then turned and ran back up the stairs. As she headed towards her room she almost bumped into Sarah leaving Amelia's bedchamber. She was on the verge of tears and rushed past her without speaking, going into her bedroom. Sarah followed her in.

'Go away!' she cried. 'I can't talk to you now! Can't you see I'm upset?'

'Yes, of course I can,' Sarah said. 'You need to talk, Miranda. You've had something on your mind for a while now. If you

talk to me I may be able to help you. It concerns Giles
Henderson – and Tommy Rowe, doesn't it?'

Miranda stared at her, eyes opening wide. 'How did you
know?'

'I don't know, but I'm guessing. You thought I might know
something about you and Giles, didn't you? That is why you
came down to Amelia's.'

'I had an affair with him but it was over ages ago.'

'I knew that and your secret is safe with me. But there's
more, isn't there?'

'There were some photographs I wouldn't want Peter to
see. Someone blackmailed me for weeks, demanding the emeralds Peter gave me. I didn't know what to do. I couldn't sell
them or have copies made, because Peter might have found
out . . .' Miranda smothered a sob. 'I've suspected Tommy for
a while, because of something in Giles's address book . . .'

'You took it?' Miranda nodded guiltily. 'Ben was right. He
came to the flat while you were there but you had taken the
address book he was looking for – so what did you find that
made you think the blackmailer might be Tommy?'

'Giles had changed "the Honourable Tommy Rowe" into
"Dishonourable",' Miranda said. 'That and the fact that it had
to be someone who had seen me wearing the emeralds at a
charity affair – and then I found the photographs in the drawer
of his dressing chest yesterday afternoon.'

'You found the photographs?'

'Yes, so that proves it was him – but he says he knows
nothing about it. He wouldn't let me leave, because he said
it would upset Pamela – and the French police would arrest
me if I went without permission.'

'Yes, they might,' Sarah agreed. 'It sounds as if Tommy
might have been blackmailing you, but finding the pictures
in his dressing chest isn't proof positive – someone could have
put them there.'

'Why would they do that? I don't understand. If he was
using them to blackmail me, why put them in someone else's
room?'

'I don't know. Unless . . .' Sarah shook her head. 'I don't
trust him, Miranda. He certainly has something to hide – and
someone killed Nancy.'

'Do you think it was Tommy? I thought it might be Harvey.'

Miranda had calmed down now. Talking to Sarah was the best thing she could have done. She put a hand to her throat. 'I don't want to end up like her.'

'No, I shouldn't think so, either,' Sarah said and smiled at her. 'I have a friend coming here this morning. He used to be a Scotland Yard inspector and he helped us clear up some murders in Beecham Thorny last year. I think you should tell him what you've told me, Miranda. Ben won't betray your secret and he already has some clues that seem to indicate Tommy. If we put them all together he might be able to arrange for the English police to come out here and arrest him.'

'You promise me Peter doesn't have to know any of this?'

'If you were involved in a murder I couldn't promise, but as you are a victim of blackmail I feel certain that your name can be kept out of it. If Tommy is what I think he may be, he will be charged with something far more serious than blackmail, terrible as that is . . .'

Miranda turned pale. 'Are you saying that he . . .'

'I'm not saying anything until Ben gets here,' Sarah said, 'and nor should you. Powder your face, Miranda. We'll go downstairs together and we'll stick together until Ben gets here – right?'

'Yes.' Miranda gave her a nervous smile. 'I'll feel better sticking with you, Sarah.'

'It's better for both of us at the moment,' Sarah said, 'because there is a dangerous man out there . . .'

They were sitting in basket chairs by the pool when Ben arrived half an hour later. Larch was with him and Sarah gave a cry of relief, getting up and running to greet him as he approached.

'I'm so glad you've come, Larch,' she said, and hugged his arm. 'It has all turned a little bit nasty . . .'

'That is an understatement,' he said, looking grim. 'What on earth did you mean by going down to the beach alone?'

'I was hoping she might still be alive. Don't be cross with me, Larch, please.'

'I'm not cross, just terrified that one of these days you'll get yourself killed.'

Sarah shook her head. 'He wasn't after me. I'm safe for

the moment, because he likes me. Whoever killed Nancy was angry.'

'Yes, I think Sarah is right,' Ben said and glanced around. 'Can we talk privately?'

'No one can hear us out here – and Miranda has something to tell you, Ben. She has been blackmailed. She thinks it was Tommy Rowe, though naturally he denies it. It may be him, but if I'm right he killed Esther and perhaps others. He may even have killed Nancy, though I don't know why . . . and perhaps Giles. But I'll let Miranda tell you her story and then you'll understand.'

'I know he sent you flowers from the florist that delivered to Esther that night,' Ben said. 'As soon as Gareth told me they had a lead I asked Larch to come out and contacted you myself. If he is Esther's killer he may well have killed Nancy Ashton, though like you I have no idea why. She wasn't the type he usually picks on.'

'She was saying something to him earlier in the evening,' Sarah said, looking thoughtful. 'Nancy had a habit of upsetting people and she might . . . though she was in a much better mood because her husband had bought her a diamond ring to replace one she lost in a burglary before they moved to the manor. She said it was exactly like the one she lost and that she couldn't tell the difference. She was a very particular lady . . .'

'What are you saying, Sarah?'

'I don't know . . . but it is all tied up with a diamond necklace that was copied. Giles knew where to get things like that made . . .' Sarah shook her head. 'Don't take any notice of that, Ben. I'm going off at a tangent, and it may have nothing to do with any of this.'

'And then again it may,' Ben said. 'I'll bear it in mind. I think we should listen to Miranda's story and then I might have enough evidence to make a couple of telephone calls . . .'

'You want to bring the English police in officially – get someone to come out and arrest him for Esther's murder?'

'For starters,' Ben said, 'I think Mr Rowe is going to have a lot of questions to answer.'

'Yes, well, I think we have enough clues to at least start questioning Mr Rowe,' Ben said when Miranda finished her tale.

'I don't intend to use the blackmail angle, Lady Bellingham, so please don't be alarmed – but the fact that he had the pictures ties him to Giles Henderson's murder, and that's the one we shall go with for a start. He may have murdered others and once the police have him in custody he will be questioned about all of it.'

'As long as Peter doesn't have to know about those pictures.'

'Yes, well, I think perhaps you should have this.' Ben reached into his jacket pocket. 'I found this on the floor at Mr Henderson's flat the day you were there. It is a pity you took the address book, because I might have got there a lot faster if I'd found it – but I believe this is your property.'

Miranda opened the envelope and looked inside. Her cheeks went pink and she closed it again, slipping it into her pocket. 'I thought I had burned all of them . . .' She stared at Sarah for a moment. 'I thought they were all there when I took them from Tommy's drawer and burned them, but there might be more . . .'

'Yes, it is possible,' Sarah said. 'We can't be sure that he was the blackmailer, Ben. Someone could have put the pictures there to be found . . . perhaps to incriminate Tommy.'

'You don't really think that?' Larch said.

'No, I don't. I think he is a blackmailer and a killer, but I am pointing out that we can't be sure – the fact that he had the pictures doesn't mean he blackmailed Miranda or killed Giles.'

'But we think he did,' Ben said. 'And we think he may have killed Esther – and the only way to make him confess is to arrest him.'

'Yes, I expect so,' Sarah agreed. 'We know he sent flowers that night – and I believe the person who sent those flowers murdered Esther because she wasn't me.'

'So that's why you thought you were safe!' Larch stared at her. 'Because he likes you . . .'

'He told me he admired me because I didn't go out with Giles.'

'Good God!' Larch looked furious. 'If he dares to think . . .'

'He hasn't asked me out to my face,' Sarah said. 'And I wouldn't go if he did – he gives me the shivers.'

'Sensible girl,' Ben said, but Larch was still glowering at her.

At that moment they saw Harvey Ashton walking towards them. He looked as if he might have been up all night. Sarah stood up and went to greet him, feeling sympathy as she saw how grey-faced he looked.

'How are you? I was so sorry, Harvey. Have the police told you anything?'

'No. They say I am eliminated from their enquires, because I was with you and other people – so they are just going to have to wait and see if anything turns up. There were no clues and anything they might have found was taken by the tide.'

'I know. I saw three sets of footsteps – two women's and a man's – but they would definitely have been gone by the time the French police arrived. Don't worry, Harvey. The culprit might be unmasked sooner than you think . . .'

'What do you mean?' He stared at her. 'If I knew who had done it I would kill him!'

'The police will sort things out – the English police, not the French – and Ben Marshall. Come and meet him. He is ex-Scotland Yard and we think we may know who the killer is, though we can't tell you just yet.'

Ben and Larch had stood up. They shook hands with Harvey, though Ben gave Sarah an odd look, as if questioning why she had told him as much as she had. Sarah smiled and shook her head.

'Why don't you go down to the village and start things rolling, Ben?' she asked. 'Come back and have lunch with us – unless you have promised to meet Cathy?'

'My wife is a very understanding woman,' Ben said. 'She told me that she was going to do some sightseeing and she went off on a bus this morning. She will expect me at the hotel for dinner, but until then . . .'

'Oh, poor Cathy,' Sarah said and laughed. 'You are very lucky, Ben. I am not sure you deserve her.'

'Nor am I,' Ben told her with a smile. 'I'll come for lunch if that is all right. You stay here, Larch. Keep an eye on Sarah and Miranda. It was nice to meet you, Mr Ashton. I am sorry about what happened to your wife. I hope to find justice for her and for you.'

'Thank you,' Harvey said, a break in his voice. 'Nancy was difficult at times but I loved her. If I knew who had killed her

I would . . . but that's foolish talk. I would prefer that the law took its course.'

'It will,' Ben said. 'Sometimes the law is an ass, and sometimes it takes a long time for justice to be served – but it usually is in the end.'

Twelve

'I am very pleased you could come,' Lady Avery said when Larch went into the house with Sarah and Miranda a little later. 'And I shall be glad to have Mr Marshall to lunch. We've met at various cat shows, you know. Indeed, I would be happy if both he and his wife joined us, because I am feeling very uneasy over what happened to poor Nancy.'

'I was pleased to come,' Larch said, with a lazy smile that hid his true feelings. 'I had decided to come out and visit Sarah, as you know – and now I am glad I am here. I think you need as many men about as possible until the murderer is caught.'

'Yes . . .' Pamela shuddered. 'It is horrible. Quite awful! Nancy might have been a little difficult but she certainly didn't deserve to be murdered.'

'No, you are right about that,' Larch said. He turned to Sarah, brows raised. 'I daresay you feel a bit uneasy since the murder. Would you and Miranda like to go sightseeing this afternoon? I have the car I hired and we could take Ben back to his hotel first . . .'

'Yes, that would be lovely,' Sarah said, thinking of all the pretty villages they had driven through on their way to the villa. 'I should like to look round a chateau if we could – perhaps taste some wine?'

'I'm sure we could manage that,' Larch said, smiling at her. She was looking a bit subdued and he wanted to get her away. If it had been possible he would have swept her off home straight away, but he knew things had to be cleared through the proper channels. He was glad Ben was bringing the English police in, because they would liaise with their French counterparts and maybe then he could get Sarah home. 'What about you, Lady Bellingham?'

'Oh, do call me Miranda,' she said. 'Yes, I'll come with

you – anything to get away from here.' She saw Lady Avery's expression and blushed. 'I'm sorry, Pamela, but I'm nervous.'

'Yes, of course. We all are,' Pamela said. 'Has anyone seen Tommy? He said he was going down to the village earlier to post a letter but I haven't seen him since.'

Sarah glanced at Larch, knowing he was thinking the same thing. Had Tommy got wind that they were on to him and done a bunk?

'I'm going up to my room,' Miranda said. 'I want to change before lunch. Are you coming, Sarah?'

'Yes, I might as well,' Sarah said, guessing that Miranda wanted to talk. They went upstairs and she followed her into her room. 'Something worrying you?'

'What will Mr Marshall do if Tommy has run off?'

'I expect they will put a police alert out for him. Don't worry, Miranda. I can't think that he knows we suspect him.'

'I hope not,' she said and shuddered. 'I shall keep looking over my shoulder until he has been caught.'

'Yes,' Sarah agreed. 'I feel much the same, but I'm sure he will turn up before long.'

There was still no sign of Tommy when they went downstairs for lunch. Pamela was upset because her brother had gone off without saying anything to her, adding to her problems. She tried to play the perfect hostess, but it wasn't easy for her, because her guests were all rather subdued.

Harvey went off on his own after lunch, so Ben, Larch, Miranda and Sarah got into the car Larch had hired.

'Well,' Ben said, on the way to his hotel, 'it looks as if Mr Rowe might have decided to make himself scarce, but don't worry, ladies, the police will pick him up soon enough. He won't be able to clear through the ports or the airport without showing his papers, which means he can't leave France. And even if he does somehow manage it, he will soon be found.'

'I hope you're right.' Miranda looked pale.

'Ben is right,' Sarah told her. 'Now, we are not going to talk about this again. Larch is taking us out for the afternoon and we shall have a lovely time.'

It was almost seven o'clock when Larch drew the car to a halt in the drive at the front of the villa, opening the door for his passengers to get out. They were all smiling, having tasted some gorgeous wine at the chateau they had visited, and the two women were giggling as they walked up to the house. However, the door opened before they could get there and Ben came out to them, the expression on his face sending shivers down Sarah's spine.

'What has happened?' she asked, feeling sick. 'Please tell me there hasn't been another murder!'

'I'm afraid there has been another death,' Ben told her sombrely. 'Lady Avery is lying down in her room and Mrs Beaufort is very upset. I'm afraid that when Lady Avery went to her brother's room this afternoon, she discovered him lying there. He had shot himself in the head. Amelia rang me at the hotel and we've had the police here for a couple of hours. They left just a few minutes ago, and they've said they will be back tomorrow – but they seem to think that it clears up Nancy's murder. You see, Tommy left a note.'

'He left a suicide note?'

'Just one word,' Ben said. 'Apparently he had written "Sorry" on a piece of Lady Avery's notepaper . . .'

'I feel faint . . .' Miranda said, and swooned. Larch caught her. He and Ben helped her into the house and sat her down in a comfortable chair. She sat there for some minutes, staring into space, as if it were all too much for her. Larch went off to fetch her a glass of water.

Sarah moved away and Ben followed her. 'Do you think he knew we were on to him?'

'Perhaps,' Ben said, and frowned. 'The police searched his room and found Nancy Ashton's ring. It was in the top drawer of his dressing chest . . .'

'The same place as Miranda found the photographs, just waiting to be discovered . . .'

'Yes.' Ben raised his brows at her. 'Very convenient.'

'If we hadn't agreed that he was a blackmailer and a murderer I would think it was too convenient,' Sarah said. 'But it all points his way, doesn't it? Janey saw him outside the theatre and he asked for me. He sent those flowers – at least he sent me flowers, but I had two baskets myself that evening, as well as the ones that went to Esther . . .'

'Are you saying that we were on the wrong track?'

'I don't know,' Sarah admitted. 'Things he said to me . . . the way he looked when he spoke about the showgirls and his respect for me, I was one hundred per cent certain that he was our murderer, Ben.'

'But now you have doubts?'

'Yes and no,' Sarah told him. 'What are you thinking?'

'I think that I am glad the French police have cleared this case up, Sarah. It means you will be allowed to go home when you are ready – and if I want to poke around a bit more when I get home I can.'

'Yes, I see,' Sarah said. 'Is there any way of finding out if the gun that killed Tommy is the same one that was used to murder Giles?'

'Valid point,' Ben said, giving her an admiring look. 'I can't do anything from this end, but I'll have a word with Gareth and see what he can come up with, Sarah.'

'Yes, that is a good idea, and now I had better go and see Amelia. I think she will want to go home as soon as it can be arranged.'

'I am very sure she will,' Ben said. 'And I have to get back to the hotel. Cathy isn't going to be too pleased with me as it is!'

Larch had returned with the water for Miranda, who took it gratefully. Sarah went in search of her grandmother and found her sitting out on the back patio. She looked very upset and got to her feet as soon as she saw Sarah.

'Thank goodness you are back, my dearest! The police are saying that Tommy killed Nancy and then shot himself. It is so very shocking! I can hardly believe it. Poor Pamela is distraught.'

'Yes, of course,' Sarah said. 'It is awful for her. First one of her guests is killed and then her brother . . . I imagine she doesn't know what to think.'

'She had hysterics. Mr Ashton slapped her and she burst into tears. He was wonderful, Sarah. He called the French police and a doctor. Pamela was given a sedative and went to bed before the police got here. They are coming back tomorrow to take statements, but after that we are free to leave.'

'I'll see to the arrangements for you,' Larch said, coming out to them at that moment. 'Miranda has gone to her room. She is shocked but seems to think it is for the best after all.'

'What do you mean?' Amelia asked.

Larch glanced at Sarah, who shook her head. 'Well, if he

killed Nancy . . . a trial would have caused such a scandal. I
know it is still a shock for Lady Avery, but she may realize
that it would have been even worse if the police had arrested
him.'

'Yes, I suppose you are right,' Amelia said. 'Poor Pamela.
I don't know how she will cope. Her brother committing
suicide like that . . . it will be a shadow over her for the rest
of her life. And I think she was very fond of him.'

'Yes, it will,' Sarah agreed. 'It is a horrid thing, Gran. But
if he did murder Nancy, it may be the best way out for him
– and Lady Avery.'

'Oh, I suppose so,' Amelia said. 'At the moment I can't see
it that way, but I know you are right. To be honest, my dear,
I just want to go home. And yet it seems awful to desert
Pamela . . .'

'Miranda said that she would stay with her for a couple of
days,' Larch said. 'They can travel back together.'

'Oh, well, in that case, I really should like to go home,'
Amelia said, 'if you would arrange it, Larch my dear?'

'That is why I am here, to look after you and Sarah,' he
said with a smile. 'You don't have to worry about anything,
either of you. I shall clear it with the French authorities in
the morning, and book a passage on the first available liner.'

'It is such a comfort to have you here,' Amelia told him.
'Isn't it, Sarah?'

'Yes, it is,' Sarah said, smiling at her. 'If you will excuse
me I shall go up and change, though I'm not sure what we
ought to do if Lady Avery is in bed.'

'I am sure we just carry on as best we can,' Amelia said.
'One always does, Sarah. One always does . . .'

Sarah was thoughtful as she changed for dinner that evening.
Ben's message had been clear enough. It was very convenient all round that Tommy Rowe had chosen to take his
own life, and she wasn't sure what to make of it. She had
always suspected that Madeline Lewis-Brown had been
murdered rather than committed suicide, but the murders
at Beecham Thorny were very different from what was
happening now.

She had been almost certain that Tommy had killed Esther,
and it seemed obvious that he had also blackmailed Miranda

– but something was wrong somewhere. She couldn't put her finger on it, and yet she knew it didn't quite make sense.

Why would Tommy have killed Nancy and taken her ring if he intended to take his own life? Had he somehow guessed that he had been found out? Was the suicide a panic measure, because he was afraid of being hanged?

It was all so neatly packaged, tied up in pink ribbon and handed out as a gift. And there were lots of loose ends . . . things that couldn't be explained no matter how much Sarah tried.

Ben seemed to think it was best to let the French police get on with it. Sarah agreed, because she couldn't face trying to explain her thoughts to anyone other than Ben. He was the only one who understood her. Even Larch didn't think in quite the same way, though she knew his main concern was for her safety.

Sarah appreciated his care of her, and yet it hampered her a little, because she wasn't afraid to follow her hunches. Yet this was a messy business and she would leave it to Ben to sort out, because she didn't want to be involved. When they got home she would concentrate on helping Larch with his exhibitions and forget all this unpleasantness.

If Tommy was the killer it was all over and if by some chance he had been murdered to make it look that way . . . well, that wasn't her affair. She would stay well clear of it!

It was a subdued group that met for dinner that evening. Harvey Ashton was very quiet, though polite and concerned for the ladies. He told Sarah after dinner that he had never been more shocked in his life.

'I still can't believe it,' he said as they walked out to the pool. It was a pleasant night, the air soft and balmy. 'First Nancy and then Tommy . . . I just don't understand why he did it. I mean . . . for a ring? It was valuable but not worth a woman's life. And why did he kill himself?'

'Perhaps he was overcome with remorse,' Sarah said. 'It is all quite horrid. I am very sorry about Nancy. You must be devastated.'

'I am. Thank you. You are so very kind, Sarah. I shan't come back to the manor for a few weeks. I am not sure what I want to do for the future, but perhaps I can come and see you when I feel better?'

'Yes, of course. Amelia will always be pleased to see you, even if I am not there.'

'Are you going away?'

'I'm not sure. I've promised to help Larch with the exhibitions for his paintings. After that, well, I might get a part in another musical show in London.'

'I hope you do. You were wonderful in the last one.'

Sarah stared at him. 'I didn't know you came to the show, Harvey?'

'Oh no, I didn't,' he said. 'I've just heard people say – and you sang delightfully for us on our first evening here.'

'Thank you,' she said. 'Of course you will be welcome if you come to the show.'

'Then I shall – and I might ask you out to dinner afterwards, but perhaps you don't accept invitations from admirers?'

'I don't as a rule, unless it is with friends. If you were to invite others as well, make it a little party, I would be happy to come.' Sarah gave him a sweet smile. 'And now, if you will excuse me I shall go in. We are leaving tomorrow and I need to do some packing.'

Sarah left him standing by the pool. She said goodnight to Amelia and Larch. Amelia said that she wanted to go up too and so they left together. She kissed her grandmother goodnight.

'I hope you get some sleep, Gran. We shall soon be home and this will all be over.'

'Yes, dearest,' Amelia said. 'I do hope so.'

Sarah was thoughtful as she went into her room. She hoped it was over too but she wasn't at all sure that they were out of the woods just yet.

Pamela Avery was ready to greet her guests in the morning. It was obvious that she was making an effort but seemed determined to put a brave face on it all. She kissed Sarah and told her that she hoped they would meet again soon under happier circumstances, and she thanked Amelia for being a comfort to her when she first made the discovery of her brother's suicide.

'I can hardly believe what they are saying about my brother,' she told her with a sob in her voice. 'I know Tommy did things . . . things I couldn't approve of, but – murder . . . No, I just do not believe it.'

'Well, I daresay it will get sorted out,' Amelia said. 'What do you mean by saying there were things you didn't approve of?'

'Oh, he used opium, you know – and . . .' she shook her head. 'No, I shan't say any more because I've never been sure that he took it . . .'

Amelia sensed that she was hiding something but she wasn't prepared to push it. Lady Avery was far too upset over her brother. Besides, she had no intention of repeating the conversation to Sarah, because she would only get ideas again, and it might set her off on a dangerous path. If the occasion arose she might mention it to Mr Marshall – on the other hand it was probably best to forget all about it. Pamela Avery had nothing whatsoever to do with any of this deplorable business.

Amelia sighed with relief as she got into Larch's car. They had a long journey in front of them, but she was going home.

'You were very quiet all the way home,' Larch said to Sarah when Amelia was safely ensconced in the Dower House and they were saying goodbye outside. 'Is something worrying you?'

'No, not really,' Sarah replied and smiled. 'I was concerned about Gran, but she will be all right now that she is home with Millie and Andrews to cosset her. Even if I did have some thoughts about what went on out there, I would rather not get involved, Larch. I just want to help you as much as I can and enjoy life.'

'Sensible girl,' he approved. 'Put it all behind you, Sarah. I think Tommy Rowe was a bit of a bounder. Someone told me that he smoked opium, and he may have done worse. We shall never be certain, unless Ben comes up with the answers – but it doesn't matter. You are safe and I'm looking forward to the summer and being with you.'

'Yes, it is going to be fun. When shall we start?'

'I'll call for you in the morning. We'll have a look at some of my stuff and then I'll take you to lunch.'

'Oh yes, that sounds lovely. I'm going in to see if Gran is all right, and then I shall walk down and visit Rosalind afterwards.'

'I'll see you tomorrow then.' Larch turned and got into his roadster, reversing in the drive and then setting off down the hill.

Sarah watched for a few minutes and then went into the house. She felt a bit guilty about allowing Larch to believe that she had put all the events of the past weeks behind her. That was almost impossible, because there were so many loose threads, and her mind kept returning to them, trying to weave them into the pattern. So far she hadn't managed to do it. She thought perhaps she ought to start another notebook, the way she had for the murders at Beecham Thorny.

Yes, she would go down to the village and buy an exercise book, and on her way back she would call in on Rosalind.

'You are back so soon,' Mrs Roberts said when Sarah went into the village shop. 'I hope Mrs Beaufort wasn't taken ill out there? I couldn't face the thought of all that fancy food myself.'

'Lady Avery gave us very nice food,' Sarah said. 'Gran is very well, thank you, but there was an unpleasant accident out there so we came home.' Mrs Roberts looked at her curiously but Sarah didn't enlighten her. It was best forgotten now that she was home.

Sarah bought her notebook, some sweets, a bar of chocolate and two sticky buns. She tried to think about something other than the murders as she walked back towards the woods and Rosalind's cottage. It really wasn't up to her to solve them after all, and Ben was still in France. He owed it to his wife to make it as much of a holiday as possible.

As she approached the cottage, she saw that Ronnie Miller was standing in the lane, looking towards the woods. He turned just as she reached the cottage gate, looking at her with his blank eyes for a moment before recognition came.

'You're nice, you are,' he said and looked at her expectantly. Sarah smiled inwardly and handed him the paper bag.

'How are you, Ronnie? Have you been busy in Mrs Darby's garden?'

'She ain't there,' he said. 'I ain't had me tea and cake. She's gone to the woods with them dogs.'

'Oh, I see,' Sarah said, feeling vaguely disappointed. 'Never mind, Ronnie. You've got some buns now. Mrs Darby will give you cake another day.'

'Come tomorrow,' he said and his gaze darkened. 'Don't go in them woods, miss. You're nice. Ronnie likes you. If they put you in the earth I'll dig you up.'

Sarah nodded but didn't say anything. It was obvious that he didn't understand what death meant, and yet there had been something about him at that moment that sent shivers down her spine.

'You shouldn't have bothered to come out,' Ben said to his friend. 'I rang to tell you that the French police have it all sewn up.'

'Wouldn't trust them as far as the end of my nose,' Gareth said pessimistically. 'If Rowe was our man I want to know more about it, tidy the loose ends. Got any ideas for me?'

'I've been told he smoked opium,' Ben said. 'Don't know how true it is, but it might explain his fixation with showgirls – or sluts, as he thought of them.'

'How do you know he felt that way about showgirls?'

'Something he said to Sarah. She was convinced about him being the murderer.' Ben decided not to muddy the waters with Miranda's troubles. He had promised to keep her name out of it if he could. 'However, she isn't convinced that it was suicide or that he killed Nancy Ashton and took her ring. The French police consider that finding the ring clears the case up, but I have my doubts. It doesn't fit the pattern . . . she was sharp-tongued by all accounts, but she was a respectable married woman.'

'Unless he knew more,' Gareth said thoughtfully. 'So what is your theory – or Sarah's?'

'Sarah hasn't told me anything yet. I think she has decided to stay out of this – had enough of it, I daresay. I can't make up my mind whether Harvey Ashton had anything to do with it. He was out of his mind with grief when we found his wife. If he thought Tommy Rowe had killed her . . .'

'You think he might have set it up to look like suicide?'

'Well, that might be the case. Sarah wondered if the gun that killed him was the same one used to murder Giles Henderson.'

'How did she make that jump?' Gareth thought about it for the moment. 'She's a bright girl this friend of yours, Ben. Yes, I can see where she is coming from. If it is, he might be Henderson's murderer.'

'Or a victim of the same killer.'

Gareth stared at him. 'One of your hunches?'

'Yes. I think there is a lot more going on here than we yet know, Gareth. On the face of it we have Tommy Rowe, a man who smokes opium and has probably killed more than once. But he specifically goes for a certain type of woman. Somehow I don't see him as the type to use a gun.' Ben frowned. 'I found a notebook written in code in Henderson's flat. I gave it to someone to decode for me. He hasn't come up with anything yet, but before we left he told me he thought he was on the verge of a breakthrough.'

'Yes, I see.' Gareth nodded. 'What else have you got up your sleeve?'

'Don't know for sure. Talk to the French police, Gareth. See what you can find out about the gun – and the ring they found in his dressing chest drawer.'

'What about the ring? It belonged to Nancy Ashton, didn't it?'

'Yes. I want to know if it was a fake.'

'Good grief!' Gareth's eyes gleamed with sudden excitement. 'Are you telling me that this has something to do with the jewel thefts?'

'At the moment I am not telling you anything for certain,' Ben said. 'But if the gun is the one that killed Giles, and if the ring was a good fake, I think you can safely say that there is a link to these people.'

'I'll certainly have a word,' Gareth said. 'I shall tell them we think Rowe had killed repeatedly and I daresay they will let me look at the ring and the gun – though I shan't be allowed to take them home. It would be like trying to get blood out of a stone. I could get my boss to try but only if we have concrete proof that the gun was used in a murder in England.'

'Well, I can't give you that proof yet,' Ben said. 'I've got another week out here and I must take Cathy wherever she wants to go. She's been sightseeing on her own, but that wasn't what I planned. I'll be in touch when I get back, but I need to talk to Sarah first.'

'Fine.' Gareth grinned at him. 'You will have to introduce me to this young lady one day, Ben. We interviewed her briefly, but I didn't speak to her myself. She sounds very interesting.'

'Yes, she is,' Ben said. 'I don't like involving her, but I think she knows something I don't – even if she hasn't realized it yet.'

'Oh, I love those pictures,' Sarah said as Larch showed her some work he had done in Italy. 'You really have made huge strides in your painting, though I still love your pictures of Norfolk. There is something haunting about those skies and lonely beaches.'

'You have a good eye,' Larch said. 'So you approve of my choice for the showing in Norwich then?'

'Oh yes, very much so. I am really looking forward to it.' Sarah picked up the poster he had roughed out. 'The artwork is very good, Larch, but you're too modest. You should put your name larger, and you should add a few words to boost your reputation.'

'Like what?' He was amused. 'I haven't done anything before, Sarah. I've never sold a painting, though I've given them to friends who admired them.'

'That is because you are too modest. You wait until you see the price the gallery puts on them. You are a very talented artist.'

'Thank you, Sarah,' he said and smiled at her. 'It means a lot when you say that, because I respect your judgement and . . .' he broke off, shaking his head. 'I think that is probably enough for this morning. Shall we go and have our lunch?'

'Yes, please,' Sarah said. 'I don't want to go to the Chestnuts, just a nice little pub where we can have something home cooked and light.'

'You know, you are the easiest girl in the world to treat,' Larch said with a warm smile. 'I'd like to spoil you but you won't let me. Not many girls I've known would turn down a lunch at the Chestnuts.'

'Have you known many?' Sarah's eyes twinkled at him.

'Yes, a few. Especially before the war,' he said. 'I haven't bothered much since then. I've concentrated on my painting. I think it helped me through a bad time, Sarah.'

'Yes, I know. Are you over it now, Larch?'

'Yes, I think so. I hope so.'

She tucked her arm through his. 'I hope so too. You're my

favourite person, Larch. I love Amelia and Daddy, of course, but you're the one I like to be with the best.'

Larch smiled at her, leaning forward to kiss her cheek. 'Do you know, that is exactly how I feel about you. You're the most honest, nicest girl I know, Sarah – that is why I get angry when you're reckless. I don't think I could bear it if anything happened to you.'

Sarah heard the passion in his voice and looked at him in surprise. She hadn't truly realized how much he cared.

'Don't worry, Larch. I've finished with all that stuff. I'm perfectly safe. Why should anyone want to kill me?

Thirteen

'Sarah?' Rosalind's voice came over the telephone. 'I heard you were back. I was hoping you might pop down and see me one day, perhaps have tea? I never did read your fortune, did I?'

'I did come the first day we were back but you were out,' Sarah told her. 'I'm sorry I didn't get back to you before this, but we have been so busy getting ready for Larch's first exhibition. It opens in Norwich tomorrow, and I'm going to be in the gallery talking to people. You must come and see it, Rosalind.'

'Yes, I shall,' Rosalind said. 'I am glad you've been busy and happy, my dear – but do come and see me when you can, won't you?'

'Yes, of course.' Sarah hesitated. 'How are you getting on with Ronnie?'

'Oh, he is fine. It was my fault for leaving the whisky out like that but it seems nothing happened. I saw Mrs Miller and she didn't say anything about it. I give her a few shillings every week for him now, and he has his tea and cake, which seems to keep him happy.'

'Good,' Sarah said. 'Well, take care of yourself. I might walk down later this afternoon. Larch said he would call me, but if he doesn't ring before three I'll come down and he can pick me up there if he wants. I think everything is ready for the show, but he wanted to complete another painting. He might ask me if I think it should be included.'

'He is a very nice young man, Sarah. You could do worse than to marry him, my dear.'

'Well, perhaps I might if he asks me,' Sarah said and laughed. 'I may see you later, Rosalind.' She hung up and went through to the front parlour, where Amelia was sitting reading a newspaper.

'Was that Rosalind?'

'Yes.' Sarah looked at Amelia curiously. 'She asked me to tea. Did you want to speak to her?'

'No. I thought she would telephone today, that's all.'

'Is something on your mind, Gran?'

'Rosalind asked about you when we went to our bridge club the other day. I think she has something on her mind, Sarah. She seemed anxious about you until she knew you were with Larch.'

'Oh . . .' Sarah felt a cold sensation at the nape of her neck. 'I wonder why?'

'She didn't say, but then she wouldn't tell me, because she knows I worry. I'm not sure about those dreams of hers, Sarah. I shouldn't take too much notice of them if I were you.'

'No, of course not, dearest Gran,' Sarah said. 'Was that the post boy?'

'Yes, I think so,' Amelia said. 'Are you expecting anything, Sarah?'

'No, not really. I just thought Janey might have written to tell me how she is getting on with the show.'

'Yes, that is a little odd,' Amelia said. 'Perhaps she has been too busy.'

'I expect so,' Sarah replied, feeling a bit disappointed. 'New show, new friends. I am sure it is all very exciting for her.'

'Yes, of course,' Amelia nodded. 'Our holiday didn't turn out too well, did it, my love? It was such a shame, because you had been working so hard.'

'I'll fetch the letters,' Sarah said and got up. She saw a small pile lying on the mat. Picking them up, she discovered that most were for her grandmother, but there was one for her from America. She was frowning over it as she took it back into the parlour. 'I think this must be from my mother. She doesn't often write, but I did tell her that I was coming to stay with you after the show closed.' She ripped open the thin envelope and scanned the brief letter. 'She says she has been ill and she would like me to go for a visit when I can . . .'

'Oh . . .' Amelia stared at her uncertainly. 'How do you feel about that? She hasn't asked you before, has she?'

'No, she hasn't,' Sarah agreed. 'If I'm honest, Gran, I don't know how I feel. I have more or less forgiven her for going off the way she did and leaving Father – but I don't think he has. I couldn't go without talking it over with him.'

'No, of course not,' Amelia said. 'He would be upset if you did, but I am sure he will want you to do as you wish, my dear.'

'Yes, perhaps – but that only makes it more difficult,' Sarah told her. 'I am not sure what I want . . .'

'Well, take your time over making a decision.'

'Yes, I shall. I can't go to stay with Daddy until Larch's show is over, but I may do then, just for a few days . . .'

'I'm so glad you could come,' Rosalind said when they were settling down over tea that afternoon. 'I didn't want to say anything on the telephone, but I've had a most unpleasant dream a couple of times . . .'

'The same as before?' Sarah asked, thinking that Rosalind looked tired.

'No, much worse.' Rosalind hesitated, then, 'I want you to let me read your tealeaves, Sarah. I know you were against it, but I have a good reason for wanting to do it.'

'Well, if you really want to,' Sarah said. 'What do I have to do?'

'Finish your tea down to the last drop, then swirl it round the cup and give it to me.'

Sarah did as she was told, handing Rosalind the cup. She turned it upside down on the saucer, waited a moment and then looked inside. Sarah watched as she studied it for some minutes and then gave an audible sigh of relief.

'Oh, thank goodness,' Rosalind said. 'I thought it might be you, but it isn't. You have a long and happy life ahead of you, Sarah – but there is something. Some sort of danger . . . but you come through it.'

'I am very glad to hear it,' Sarah said. 'So what did you see that worried you, Rosalind?'

'I saw a death,' Rosalind replied. 'I know what happened in France – but that isn't connected with my dreams. This is something near here, in the woods I think or a wooded area. I saw a girl being attacked by someone. He was strangling her and I thought it was you, but it wasn't. I do feel so much better now!'

Sarah felt a chill at the back of her neck. 'That is awful

for you, Rosalind. Do you think it is all to do with Esther's death? Should you talk to anyone about it?'

'If you think that I am brooding unhealthily I assure you it isn't so,' Rosalind said, looking a little bit upset. 'I don't ask for these dreams, Sarah. They just come and I can't stop them.'

'I am sorry if I have offended you. I didn't mean to – I just feel it is so awful for you.'

'Yes, it is. But I have learned to live with it. You must find it equally awful to be caught up in all the unpleasant incidents that have happened to you recently?'

'Yes, I do,' Sarah agreed. 'But they just seem to happen around me. I have felt so guilty about what happened to Esther, because those flowers were meant for me.'

'Yes, I knew you were upset,' Rosalind said. 'I'm glad it wasn't you in my vision, Sarah, but I can't help thinking it is someone I know . . . and I don't mean Nancy . . .'

Sarah went out to dinner with Larch that evening. She tried very hard to put Rosalind's vision out of her mind, but it was difficult – especially as she had started to worry about Janey. It was very odd that her friend hadn't written or telephoned, and she couldn't help wondering if she was all right. If she hadn't been caught up with Larch's exhibition, she might have gone down to Yarmouth to visit her friend.

'You're a bit quiet this evening,' Larch said after the waiter had served them with their wine. 'Something on your mind?'

'No, not really. I suppose with all the things that have happened recently, it is hard to put them completely from your mind. I haven't heard from Janey and I can't help wondering if she is all right.'

'I am sure she is. Once the exhibition is over we could go and see her on stage, go out for a meal together afterwards if you like?'

'Yes, I should like that,' Sarah agreed. 'I am sure she is fine, just busy, as we are. I am sure your show is going to be a great success, Larch. I'm really looking forward to it.'

'I dread it,' Larch said and pulled a wry face. 'I'm sure the critics are going to say my work is awful.'

'No! How could they?' Sarah shook her head at him. 'I think you will be surprised at how much people will love your work. The trouble is you will have the gallery owners plaguing you for more, and knowing how difficult you found it to come up with enough pictures that satisfied you for this show, you may hate your own success.'

'That is exactly what I fear, Sarah. I've painted for my own satisfaction, never expecting any of this. I'm not sure I actually want to sell anything, though of course I owe it the gallery owners to at least make it worth their while.'

Sarah laughed softly, shaking her head at him. 'I don't think anything could change you, Larch. I am sure you will do exactly as you wish whatever happens.'

'Do you want me to change?' He looked at her anxiously.

'No, of course not. I like you as you are, my very best friend.'

'Your best friend?' Larch reached across the table to take her hand. 'I've thought that perhaps we might be more than that – when you are ready?'

'Yes, perhaps,' Sarah agreed. 'I've had a letter from my mother. She wants me to visit her. I might but not before I've asked Daddy how he feels about it.'

'I know that you aren't quite ready yet, Sarah,' Larch said softly. 'I'm in no hurry, my dearest Sarah.'

Her heart gave a little jump as she looked into his eyes. 'Perhaps when I come back from America – if I go?'

'Yes, perhaps.' Larch gave her a look that warmed her right through. 'I wanted you to know that I care about you, Sarah, and if I get cross sometimes it is because I worry about you.'

'Well, you don't need to worry any more, because I've made up my mind that I'm not going to get involved in anything like this again . . .' She lifted her wineglass. 'To success, Larch. I just know everyone is going to come tomorrow.'

Sarah glanced around her. The response to their posters had surprised even her, because the gallery was crowded and had been since they opened. Somehow Larch's reputation had spread, perhaps from the few pictures he had given away to friends, perhaps because it was a dull day and people wanted somewhere to go to get out of the chill wind. However, if that were the case, they were buying an awful lot of pictures!

Already three of her favourites had been snapped up, and

several people had said they were interested in others. In fact she could see a woman coming back now, who had expressed a desire to buy one of the Norfolk landscapes.

'I've made up my mind,' she said to Sarah and laughed. 'I've overspent my allowance this month and my husband may grumble – but I think it is an investment. I am sure the price will shoot up once the reviews get into the newspapers.'

'I doubt if Captain Meadows will put his prices up just for that,' Sarah said. 'But the gallery owners may, of course. You will have a rarity value, because I don't think the market will be flooded. The artist is too particular about his work.'

'Well, that has just confirmed what I thought,' the woman told her with a pleased look. 'I am going to buy it.'

'I'll fetch Mr Pearson. He owns the gallery and will see to the sale for you.'

Sarah handed her on to the gallery owner, and wandered round the gallery, talking to various people who were admiring the pictures. She head the bell go a couple of times but didn't look round until a voice spoke from behind her.

'Sarah! I thought you might be here . . .'

Sarah turned and found herself looking at Harvey Ashton. She smiled politely, because she wasn't sure how she felt about him but couldn't be rude.

'Mr Ashton – Harvey. Are you back at the manor now?'

'Yes, just for a while,' he said. 'I am going to put it back on the market. I don't think it would suit me to live there alone. I may go back to London. I prefer living in town. It was Nancy who wanted to come this way – her parents were from Norfolk originally. Did I tell you that?'

'I thought you were both American?'

'Yes, we are – first generation. Our parents moved there from England.'

'I see.' Sarah hesitated. Perhaps that was why she had noticed that his American accent seemed to have become very less marked recently, especially when he was under stress. 'Well, it was nice to see you, but I must circulate.'

'Perhaps we shall see each other soon,' Harvey said, 'when you have more time? I would like your advice about something. I don't suppose you would have coffee with me one day?'

'Perhaps,' Sarah said. 'Are you interested in art?'

'I sure am,' Harvey said and the strong twang was back in his voice. 'I think some of these paintings are kinda cute.'

Sarah moved away. It had been on her mind for a while – the way Harvey sometimes forgot to be the cuddly, innocent American abroad. Of course if he had lived here for a while . . . but she suspected it was an act. She suspected that he wasn't truly the genial, nice guy he appeared to be, but she wasn't sure where that fitted into the mystery.

She didn't believe that he had murdered Esther or those other poor girls, but he was hiding something. The tiny hairs were standing up at the back of her neck and she was certain that he had a secret he needed to protect.

Miranda was putting her jewels away when she heard a noise behind her and turned to see her husband. Her face lit up with a smile of welcome, as he came towards her, taking her into his arms.

'When did you get back?' she asked.

'Just a few minutes ago,' he said. 'Did you miss me?'

'Yes, very much,' Miranda said. 'It was all so horrible, Peter.'

'I heard about Tommy Rowe. It's a pity you went there. I should stay away from that crowd in future if I were you, Miranda.'

'Yes, I shall. I would much rather have been with you.'

'I wish you had been,' he said. 'Never mind, darling. We'll take a little trip to Paris soon, and I'll buy you some nice things.'

Miranda took a deep breath. 'Peter, there's something I ought to tell you. It was before we were married . . .'

He stared at her for a moment. 'If you mean your affair with Henderson, I know, and I'm not interested, Miranda. That was over before we married. Just don't give me cause to be jealous in future, my darling – because I might not be so forgiving then.'

'I promise I will never be unfaithful,' Miranda said, a sob in her voice. 'Are you sure you can forgive me?'

'I knew before we were married,' he said. 'I suggest you forget all about it, Miranda. Get dressed up, we're going out tonight . . .'

*   *   *

'Sarah, there is a telephone call for you,' Amelia called upstairs to her that evening. 'It is Mr Marshall. Shall I ask him to ring back later?'

'I'm ready now,' Sarah said, coming to the head of the stairs in a rather grand brocade dressing gown. 'I'll take it, Gran.' She ran down the stairs and accepted the receiver from Amelia. 'Ben, how lovely to hear from you! Did you have a wonderful time on holiday?'

'Yes, we did,' Ben said. 'We didn't stop in one hotel all the time, just went touring and stayed at some lovely places. We had one night in a chateau, Sarah. You would have loved it.'

'Yes, I should,' Sarah agreed. 'Larch has been doing very well at his exhibition. We sold six paintings today, and he is going through all his stuff to see if we can fill any empty spaces, but he is very particular about what he shows.'

'Exactly what I would expect of him,' Ben said, a smile in his voice. 'An excellent young man, Sarah.' He hesitated, then, 'Do you think I could come and see you one day?'

'We have another show tomorrow. Could you come down on Sunday and bring Cathy for lunch? Amelia would be pleased to see you I know.'

'Are you sure that isn't too much trouble? We could have lunch out somewhere.'

'Gran would love to have you both, and so should I.'

'That's settled then,' Ben said and sounded pleased. 'Lunch on Sunday it is.'

'I shall look forward to it,' Sarah said. 'I have made a few notes, though they may not make sense.'

'Good girl. I was hoping you might. I shall see you on Sunday.'

Sarah hung up. She frowned as she glanced at herself in the hall mirror. She had promised Larch she wouldn't get involved again, but she wasn't sure that she would be allowed to keep her promise. It would be best to tell Ben what she was thinking and then she might be able to let it go. Whether it would let her go was another matter.

If anything the show on Saturday was even more successful than on the first day. They sold seven paintings, but the gallery owner was asked for more Norfolk scenes. The pictures Larch had painted while abroad were admired, but only one was purchased; all the others were his trademark – the stark, lonely beaches and marshes of the Norfolk coast.

'They are going to haunt me,' one art critic told Sarah after he had spent half an hour staring at one picture. 'The artist's soul is in this seascape. It gives me goose pimples all over.'

'It is rather wonderful,' Sarah agreed. 'I think it is my favourite. I should like to buy it myself, but not before the show is over. If it hasn't gone by then I shall. My father would love it and it is his birthday soon.'

'Not everyone could live with that,' the critic said. 'But it beats all those pretty Norfolk cottages that were popping up everywhere a year or so ago.'

'Yes. Very different,' Sarah agreed and couldn't prevent a shiver down her spine, because she knew that some of those pictures he was talking about would have been painted by Madeline Lewis-Brown.

When they had a few minutes alone together, Larch suggested going out to dinner that evening. Sarah said she would rather give it a miss.

'I have a few things to do at home – but you could come over for coffee in the morning if you like?'

'Yes, of course, Sarah. I have a meeting after we close so it would have been late anyway. I hope you're not too tired?' He looked at her anxiously.

'No, of course not.' Sarah smiled but didn't tell him that she wanted to go through her notes for Ben, because he would not have approved.

After the gallery closed, Sarah went outside to wait for Andrews. He had rung earlier to say that he had to come in on an errand to Norwich for her grandmother and offered to pick her up. She had agreed, because she knew Larch had business to finish that might keep him at the gallery until later. As she was standing on the pavement waiting, a car pulled up to the kerb. She turned her head to look and saw that it was Harvey Ashton.

'Can I give you a lift, Sarah?'

'No, thank you. Andrews is picking me up . . . he is here now.' She felt pleased to see her grandmother's Rolls-Royce pull up to the kerb just behind Harvey's car.

'Don't forget our date,' Harvey said. 'I need your advice,

Sarah. It's about some of Nancy's things. I thought I might donate them to charity, but I would like you to take a look. If you could come to the house one day?'

'Perhaps. I'll think about it,' Sarah said. 'I mustn't keep Andrews waiting. We shall block the traffic.'

She moved away, getting into the front of the car with her grandmother's chauffeur. 'Thank you for being so prompt.'

'Something wrong, Miss Beaufort?'

'I'm not sure. There might be.' Sarah frowned. 'I shall probably know after tomorrow.'

'You're not going to do anything reckless, miss?'

'Oh, no,' Sarah said. 'I promise you I shan't but . . .' She shook her head. Her feeling about Harvey Ashton was growing stronger. Why did he want to get her alone? Did he think she knew something she didn't – or did she know something but just hadn't realized it? When she got home she was going to look through her notes again.

Sarah had dinner with her grandmother that evening, and then played a game of chess with her, because Amelia had set the board out and was obviously looking forward to it. She went to bed at half past ten and sat for an hour reading her notes through and adding bits that came to her. Gradually, something began to take shape, and she nodded to herself. Of course! She might be putting two and two together to make five, but something Nancy had said to her that evening before they left for the party had given her an idea.

It made sense of all the things that had puzzled her about Harvey Ashton and Tommy Rowe. She hadn't solved the murders, though she knew that Ben was fairly certain Tommy had sent the bouquet to Esther. She believed that she understood what lay behind much of what had been going on. And she thought she knew why Giles Henderson had been killed.

Miranda had thought it might be because of the blackmail letters, but it wasn't at all. If Sarah was right, it was for a very different reason. There was one way to find out a bit more, but it was risky. She ought not to do it and yet . . .

Sarah closed her book and reached for the light switch. She would sleep on it and decide in the morning.

* * *

'What are you going to do today?' Amelia asked Sarah when she joined her at the breakfast table. 'Ben and Cathy are coming to lunch so you won't want to go far, my dear.'

'No, of course not,' Sarah said. 'Larch is coming for coffee at about ten. I thought I might just have time to pop down and see Rosalind. I want to ask her a favour.'

'What kind of favour?'

'Oh, Harvey Ashton asked me if I would look through some of Nancy's things that he wants to give to a charity. I was going to ask if Rosalind would come with me. I don't particularly want to go there alone.'

'He hasn't made any unpleasant advances I hope?'

'Oh no, he is always very polite to me,' Sarah said. 'I just think it would be best if Rosalind came with me.'

'Very sensible, my dear,' Amelia said with a nod of approval. 'You get off when you are ready and if Larch arrives before you get back, I'll tell him where you are.'

'Thanks, Gran.' Sarah kissed her cheek. She went out into the hall and picked up a long, straight cardigan that was just right for a cool morning. The weather was typical of an English summer: one day warm the next overcast.

She walked quickly down the hill. Just as she got to Rosalind's gate, Harvey Ashton's car passed her heading towards the village. He waved to her and she waved back, because she couldn't be sure she was right, and there was no point in letting him see that she was wary of him.

Rosalind opened the door before she got there, looking pleased.

'I thought you might come this morning, Sarah. It is lovely having you so close. I shall miss you when you leave.'

'I am going to visit my father for a few days, and then I'll come back – until I go to America, if I go . . .'

'Yes? You want to ask me something, don't you?'

'I wondered if you would come with me tomorrow morning? Harvey Ashton has asked me to go to the manor and help him decide about Nancy's things – he wants to give some of them to a charity.'

'You don't want to go there alone?'

'No, I don't, for various reasons.'

'I don't think you should. But you do want to go – may I ask why?'

'It's just a feeling. He is trying to get me alone. He has

something on his mind. I need to speak to him to discover what it is, but I don't want to be alone with him.'

'Yes, I understand. Certainly I'll come with you. He may not like it, of course, but I wouldn't advise you to be alone with him, Sarah.'

'I have no intention of it.'

'Good. I've never been sure of him, though he seemed very pleasant – but that may be a façade.'

'I think it almost certainly is,' Sarah agreed. 'I can't tell you anything more just yet. I have to talk to Ben first.'

Rosalind had got up to put the kettle on the gas ring. She looked through the window. 'Ronnie is here again this morning. I don't know what he finds to do. A lot of the time he simply sits there sharpening his spade. I should imagine that thing could be a lethal weapon.'

'Yes, I suppose it could,' Sarah agreed. 'In the wrong hands it could kill – but I don't think Ronnie is a killer, do you?'

'I wouldn't have said so,' Rosalind said. 'I think he could be violent if provoked, and he is very strong . . . but I doubt that he has the mind of a killer.'

'No, I'm sure he hasn't. He is always fine with me.'

'Vera Hayes was here yesterday, wanting items for her latest bazaar,' Rosalind said. 'If Mr Ashton genuinely wants to give his wife's things away I am sure she would be glad to have them.'

'Yes, I am sure she would be glad of clothes, shoes and bags, and I daresay there were a lot of them.'

The conversation turned to clothes and village affairs, and it was half an hour before Sarah got up to leave. Ronnie was in the front garden as she went out. She smiled at him, and his eyes followed her as she went up the hill. Sarah didn't look back so she had no idea that Ronnie was at the gate watching her.

What she was aware of was the car that stopped beside her. Turning her head, she saw Harvey Ashton. He wound his window down and called to her. Reluctantly, Sarah stopped and waited as he got out of the car and came towards her. She kept her distance, her nerves tingling. He was smiling but something in his manner wasn't right.

'Have you been avoiding me, Sarah? I thought you were coming to have coffee with me and help me with Nancy's things?'

'Yes, I will tomorrow morning.'

'Why not come now? Hop in the car. It won't take long, I promise.'

'I am sorry. I am meeting someone at Gran's . . .'

'You're not very friendly, Sarah. I thought we were friends?' His tone was genial but with a hint of underlying menace.

'Yes, of course, but I don't think it would be a good idea for me to come to the manor alone. It might set people talking . . .'

Harvey moved closer to her. 'What does it matter about a few gossips, Sarah? You know I like you. We could be friends.'

'I am not sure I want to be your friend.' Suddenly the words were there in her head and she couldn't stop them. 'Why did you take Nancy's ring, Harvey? Were you afraid that someone might discover it was her original ring – that it had never really been stolen at all?'

Harvey's eyes glittered. 'The stupid bitch! I knew she had told you something. And you're too clever for your own good, Sarah. You've worked it all out, haven't you?'

'Some of it,' Sarah admitted, noting that his American accent had disappeared. 'You were seen arguing with Tommy Rowe in the woods here – something about getting your share or he would be sorry. He didn't take you seriously, did he? He should have known that you meant every word.'

'Very clever,' Harvey said. 'It was my idea, of course. Tommy didn't have the brains to be a jewel thief, but he gave me the information – who was going to be at a certain charity event and where they lived – and I arranged the rest.'

'But you thought Giles Henderson knew something, didn't you?' Sarah nodded as the details became clearer in her mind. 'Tommy took his sister's diamond necklace, but he didn't share it with you, did he? He couldn't, because it was a fake. Pamela asked Giles to get a copy made for her, because she'd sold it to give her brother money, but she didn't tell Tommy and he took it hoping to sell it himself.

'When it was stolen she was afraid it might be recovered and her husband would find out . . . but Giles discovered something about the whereabouts of the stolen necklace. He started nosing around and probably discovered that Tommy had tried to sell it. It made him suspicious about what was going on – so you arranged for Nancy's jewellery to be stolen to put him off the scent. When it didn't, you killed him. You bought Nancy some other stuff to replace hers but she wasn't satisfied so you gave her back her own ring that night – and she told everyone that she couldn't tell the difference.'

'The stupid bitch couldn't keep her mouth shut,' Harvey said, eyes glittering. 'I knew she would land me in trouble and . . .'

'You killed her . . .' Sarah gasped, because she hadn't been sure of that bit. 'And when I told you that the murderer would be found sooner than you might think, you panicked. You killed Tommy and I am pretty sure the police will discover that it was the same gun that was used to kill Giles. You wrote the suicide note and put the ring in Tommy's dressing chest – so that he would be blamed for Nancy's murder. You wanted him dead, because it was too dangerous to let him live. He knew too much and you thought you had planned the perfect murder.'

'Worked it all out very neatly, haven't you?' Harvey said, his gaze narrowing. 'I thought you might, which is why I can't let you tell anyone else.' He made a grab for her arm, his fingers digging into her flesh as he dragged her towards the woods. Sarah fought him for all she was worth, kicking, screaming and scratching at his face, but his strength was gradually overpowering her. 'You're a bright girl, Sarah, but you made a mistake. You let me see that you knew too much . . .'

Sarah screamed again and again. She struggled desperately, kicking out at him as he tried to drag her further into the woods, because she knew he was going to kill her. He thrust her back against a tree trunk, his hands about her throat. She could feel them squeezing, her breath being forced from her body and everything was going black around her. She didn't hear the man shout. She didn't see him come running and she didn't see him bring his spade down hard on the back of Harvey's head. She opened her eyes just in time to see Ronnie standing over his victim. He had grasped the spade handle in both hands, lifting it high above Harvey as if intending to bring it down on his throat.

'No, Ronnie!' she screamed. 'You mustn't. Please, don't do it . . .'

Now she was aware that someone else was there. She could see Larch behind Ronnie and she shook her head at him, reaching out to touch Ronnie's arm gently.

'No, Ronnie. It is all right now. He didn't hurt me, you saved me. I am all right. Please don't do it.'

Ronnie's eyes blazed at her for a moment, then they glazed over and he giggled. 'He was going to put you in the earth, like they done to her. Ronnie didn't like that. Ronnie likes you . . . you give him cake . . .'

'Yes, I give you sticky buns,' Sarah said. 'You helped me, Ronnie. I'll give you some more tomorrow, but you mustn't do anything else. You should go home now.'

'You're nice,' Ronnie said and looked down at Harvey, who was unconscious from the blow to his head. 'He tried to hurt you. Jethro said we should kill him because he hurt Morna . . . his head came off . . .'

Sarah felt a little sick, but she kept her smile in place. 'You should go home now, Ronnie. I'll bring you some buns tomorrow.'

Ronnie looked at her for a moment, then put his spade over his shoulder and walked back the way he had come, down the hill. Larch was bending over Harvey, feeling for a pulse.

'He's still alive, but he's lucky. If it hadn't been for you Ronnie would have cut through his neck with that damned spade.'

'Do you think . . .' Sarah turned pale. 'Simon Beecham . . .?'

'Yes, I do,' Larch said. His gaze was intent as he saw her face pale. 'Are you all right? I saw Ashton's car and stopped and then I heard a scream. What happened?'

'He dragged me in here to kill me, the way he killed Nancy. He killed Tommy too and he was involved in those jewel thefts. Both he and Tommy . . .' She saw the way he was looking at her. 'No, don't look at me that way, Larch. I didn't do anything . . . well, when he tried to make me get into his car I came out with it, but it would have happened anyway. Maybe it was a good thing it happened now, because Ronnie saw it and he must have run here as fast as he could. He just banged Harvey over the head with his spade and . . . you saw the rest.'

'Yes, I did,' Larch said grimly. 'We'll talk about this later. Go back to the house and telephone my father, Sarah. Harvey

Ashton is going to need hospital treatment. I'll stay with him until the ambulance gets here.'

'Yes, of course,' Sarah said. 'But what about Ronnie?'

'He is probably a murderer, Sarah.'

'I know . . .' She sighed and turned away. 'I'll be as quick as I can, Larch. Come up to the house as soon as you can please.'

'Go on, Sarah. Leave this to me . . .'

Sarah walked away. She was feeling shaken and distressed but this wasn't the time to break down in tears. Larch couldn't leave Harvey, even if it wasn't likely that he would come to his senses. She wondered what would happen if he didn't . . . Would Ronnie be charged with his murder?

He had come to her rescue and she would always be grateful to him for that, but he didn't understand what he had done. He was a strong, sometimes violent man with a child's mind – and that made him dangerous. She didn't know whether he had killed Simon Beecham, but he had certainly been there, and if she hadn't stopped him, he would have killed Harvey in the same fashion.

It was a horrible, horrible thought and she couldn't stop shivering as she ran back to the house. She went straight to the telephone and rang Sir William's house, feeling relieved when he answered himself.

Sarah explained what had happened. Sir William told her not to worry.

'I shall telephone for an ambulance at once, and the police must be informed. You need not worry about anything else, my dear. Just go and sit down and have a nice cup of tea.'

'Thank you . . .' Sarah's hands shook as she hung up. She went through to the sitting room, her legs giving way as she half fell on to the sofa. Amelia looked at her, suddenly aware that she was distressed.

'What is it, my dearest? Something has happened! I knew you were up to something!'

'No, I promise you.' The reaction had set in and Sarah was shaking uncontrollably. 'It wasn't my fault. He stopped the car and tried to force me to get in and then I told him what I knew . . . and he tried to strangle me, and then Ronnie came and hit him with his spade . . .' She was babbling, close to hysteria as it suddenly hit her.

'Sarah!' Amelia was on her feet. 'You need some brandy!' She went to the sideboard and poured brandy from the decanter standing on a silver tray, bringing it back to her granddaughter. 'Drink this and then tell me slowly.'

Sarah held the glass with two hands. She was still shaking as she gulped the brandy down, feeling it warm her. It took her a minute or two to finish it, because it stung her throat, and by then she had stopped shaking.

'Thank you,' she said. 'Ronnie Miller saved my life, Gran. He hit Harvey Ashton from behind with his spade, but then . . . then he looked as if he was going to . . . chop down on his throat. I talked to him and he stopped. He likes me, you see. He went off home when I told him to.'

'Where was this?'

'As I was walking home from Rosalind's. Larch was coming up the hill. He saw Harvey's car and stopped – and then he heard me scream. He saw what happened and he told me to come here and phone his father. It is all under control, Gran.'

'And that makes it all right?' Amelia put her arm about her shoulders, feeling angry. 'What was Larch thinking of to send you home alone? He should have left that man and looked after you!'

'No, Gran, he couldn't do that,' Sarah said. 'Mr Ashton may have killed his wife and Tommy Rowe, but that doesn't mean that Larch should just leave him there to die. He did what he had to do – and he knew I was capable of making that call.'

'But he didn't see you like this . . .'

'No, and I don't want him to know, Gran. No one else is to know. It was just a little silliness, that is all. I think because of Ronnie . . .'

'You think he killed Simon Beecham, don't you?' Amelia nodded. 'That wouldn't surprise me – and I understand why you are upset. But you know he can't be allowed to remain free, don't you?'

'Yes. Larch says we'll talk about it later, but he has to tell the police. He doesn't want to any more than I want to, Gran, but he has to – doesn't he?'

'Yes, my darling, I am afraid he does,' Amelia said. 'Now why don't you go and have a little lie down until our guests arrive?'

'No, I am all right now,' Sarah said. She lifted her head and smiled, holding her hands out in front of her. 'I'm fine. Look, I'm not shaking now. It really is all over, Gran. Harvey Ashton was the final piece in the puzzle. I just hope that he survives and confesses to the police . . .'

Fourteen

'I had it all wrong,' Ben told Sarah later that day, 'though I arrived at the same conclusion. I knew Giles had had Lady Avery's necklace copied and I thought the ring might be a fake. But then Giles's code was broken and I was able to decipher something in his book. He suspected that Tommy Rowe was involved in the jewel thefts. I haven't decoded everything, but I daresay I shall discover that he also suspected Harvey Ashton of being involved.'

'Yes, I am sure he did. It was actually the same ring, and Nancy kept telling everyone she didn't know the difference. I think Harvey got nervous and they may have had a row. I'm not sure he intended to kill her, but once he had he saw a way to get rid of Tommy and put the blame on him. They had fallen out over Lady Avery's necklace. Tommy took it but discovered it was a fake when he tried to sell it. Out of a perverted sense of loyalty to his sister, he kept quiet about it, but Giles discovered that he had tried to sell it. I don't know all the details, but Harvey confessed to the murders in anger and then tried to kill me.'

'I thought it might have been him, but I was working on the idea that he had asked Giles to have the ring copied and that they had somehow fallen out over it.'

'No, it was the original ring. Harvey thought he could give it to Nancy and she wouldn't know, but I think she started to get suspicious, because it was so like her own. Perhaps it had some tiny defect that only she knew of . . .' Sarah shook her head. 'Lady Avery was the one who asked Giles to have her necklace copied for her because she didn't want her husband to find out it had been stolen. It puzzled me as to why she would do that for a long time, and then I realized that she was protecting someone. Janey gave me a big clue when she told me that she had heard Harvey arguing with someone. Especially when I realized that the description matched Tommy's. It was all too much of a coincidence. I heard Pamela exchanging sharp words with her brother at the villa, and then it came to me. She knew Tommy had taken her necklace – but he didn't pass it on to Harvey to get rid of. He tried to sell it himself and refused to give Harvey anything when he realized it was a fake.'

Ben nodded. 'It was a case of thieves falling out I expect. Ashton killed Nancy in a temper and then saw his chance to make Tommy the scapegoat.'

'What I am not sure of is whether Tommy killed Esther. I had a strong feeling that it was him, but I don't have proof.'

'Nor do the police,' Ben told her. 'Gareth has been through all the evidence and he is convinced he was the killer of at least three women, but proving it is another thing. The florist spotted his photograph and that gave Gareth a name. There are other things – descriptions of a man seen at the previous crime scenes, which resemble Tommy Rowe. The police were prepared to arrest him and try for a confession, but without that they can't wrap the case up finally. However, Gareth says he isn't looking for anyone else at the moment.'

'So we think Tommy committed those awful showgirl murders,' Sarah said. 'So in a way justice has been served, hasn't it?'

'Yes, in a manner of speaking,' Ben agreed. 'I would have preferred to have it all sewn up, case closed and tidy – but it was Gareth's case, not mine. I am hoping that Ashton will recover and we can finally tell Major Henderson why his son was murdered.'

'I am pretty sure of that bit. Giles discovered what was going on between Tommy Rowe and Harvey Ashton. He realized that they were behind the jewel thefts, which were happening when people were out at charity affairs. He had worked it out that Lady Avery was involved with all the charity events, and since he didn't believe that she had anything to do with it, he guessed that it must be Tommy. I think that when he discovered Miranda's photographs had gone he rang Tommy and accused him of taking them – and he mentioned what he suspected. Tommy probably passed the message on to Harvey and he—'

'He decided to make sure Giles couldn't tell what he knew.'

'Do you think Harvey had any idea that Tommy had killed those women?'

'I doubt it. No one else did, so why should he? Tommy kept that side of his life very secret. His sister knew that he smoked opium sometimes, and she either suspected or knew that he had stolen her necklace, but she had no idea of his other life. After all, on the surface he seemed a perfect gentleman – a bit of a snob and a scrounger at times, but harmless. It isn't easy to read the mind of a killer – especially one who kills for pleasure.'

'Harvey Ashton is a different kind of killer,' Sarah said and frowned. 'He killed in anger or to cover up his crimes. Tommy killed because . . . he could. I think he liked the power it gave him.'

'That is very deep,' Ben said. He smiled at her. 'Gareth has told me he would like to meet you one day. He knows how much you've helped me with these crimes – and those last year.'

'I just told you what I thought. To be honest, I wouldn't have known about Harvey if he had simply left me alone, but he kept wanting to get me on my own, and it set a tingling sensation off at the nape of my neck. I knew he had a reason, and I wrote everything down that I had learned. Suddenly it all clicked into place. I had suspected him of being involved in the jewel thefts almost from the beginning, but I thought it was my imagination playing games. Taking Nancy's ring was a mistake. If he hadn't done that I would never have seen it.' Sarah frowned. 'I doubt if he is really an American. If the police dig deep enough I think they will discover that it was a false identity. Nancy probably didn't know the truth – but he let his mask slip a few times when he was angry.'

'Murderers usually make mistakes,' Ben told her grimly. 'If they didn't we should never catch them.'

'Well, I'm glad it is all over,' Sarah said. 'Only it isn't quite, because there's still Ronnie . . .' She looked at her watch and then at the mantel clock. 'I thought Larch would have been here by now. I feel so awful about this, because if Ronnie hadn't hit Harvey I might be dead – but his intention was so clear. He would have brought that spade down on Harvey's throat if I hadn't stopped him. Larch is right to say that he has to tell the police. I know that but . . .'

'It feels uncomfortable,' Ben said. 'Sometimes it is hard to punish the guilty, especially when the crime was one of passion – and if Ronnie killed Simon Beecham, it was because he was incited to it.'

'And because he cared about Morna. He may be a bit simple, but that doesn't mean he can't feel things . . .'

'No, of course it doesn't,' Ben said. 'He'll never stand trial, Sarah – but he does need to be shut away in a secure institution. He is a danger to himself and the rest of us . . .'

Ronnie trudged down the hill, his eyes staring fixedly in front of him. He was trying not to let the bad thoughts through, but he could not stop them. It was because he had hit that man – the one who was hurting the nice girl who gave him sticky buns. He liked her. She was pretty, like Morna – and it was remembering Morna that brought the bad thoughts.

Someone had hurt Morna. Jethro said they had put her in the earth, but Ronnie remembered seeing her lying on the ground in the wood. Her face had looked funny and she had been cold. He had touched her and it had frightened him so he ran away, and then the police had come. Afterwards, when he was home again, Jethro had given him some of the good stuff and said they should kill the man who had hurt Morna.

Ronnie had agreed with him. He had wanted to punish the man who had put Morna in the earth. He didn't like her being there. He wanted to dig her up but Jethro said he couldn't. He'd said they should kill the man who had put her there.

Ronnie tried hard to shut out the bad thoughts. He needed some of the good stuff and he still had half the whisky he had taken from Mrs Darby's cottage in his shed at home. He needed to drink it so that he wouldn't remember . . . but the pictures were in his head and he couldn't get them out.

They had gone to the nursery where Simon Beecham lived, and they had waited for him to come out.

'Hit him, Ronnie,' Jethro had urged. 'Hit him with your spade!'

Ronnie had obeyed blindly, felling him from behind with one massive blow, just as he had today when that man was trying to hurt the nice girl who gave him buns. He had dropped his spade then and . . . Ronnie's eyes suddenly glittered as he remembered. Jethro had picked up the spade and . . .

Ronnie stopped at the side of the road and was violently
sick. Jethro had brought the spade down hard on the man's
neck, and it had cut almost all the way through . . . just like
the cats.

Ronnie had killed two cats that way. He hated cats, because
they always stuck their claws in him, and he'd swung his
spade at them, cutting their heads off. He had almost done
the same thing to that man today, because Ronnie never forgot
when he learned something. Jethro had laughed and said it
served the bugger right, but Ronnie had been terrified and
he'd run away. Afterwards, he'd looked for his spade but he
couldn't find it. He looked for Jethro to ask if he knew where
it was, but Jethro had gone too – and then the police had
come. He'd run away and when he woke up he was in hospital
– and they had sent him away to that place.

Ronnie didn't want to go back there. They let him do the
garden, but he wasn't allowed to go where he liked, and sometimes he was shut in. He hated being shut in, but he knew he
had done bad things and he was afraid that someone would
come and take him away again. Tears began to run down his
cheeks, because he didn't know what to do. All he could think
of was the good stuff in his shed. If he drank enough of that
all the bad thoughts would go away.

'I am so sorry, Mrs Miller,' Larch said. He stood up, preparing
to leave the cottage. 'What Ronnie did today probably saved
Sarah's life, but if she hadn't stopped him he might have
killed. I am afraid that I am going to have to tell the police.
He could be dangerous.'

'Yes, I know,' Mrs Miller said. She dashed a tear away with
her hand. 'I do understand, Captain Meadows, and I am grateful
that you came to me first. It was good of you to let me know.'

'As I said, it is the last thing I want to do. I didn't believe
Ronnie was capable of anything like that . . . and I'm sure he
didn't know what he was doing. I think Jethro Scaffrey was
with him, and that he put him up to it – but the fact remains
that he may be a killer.'

'It was that gypsy got him into bad ways,' Mrs Miller said.
'He was just a big daft lad until he got in with him, sir. But
he changed. I know he has done wrong and I can't control him
any more. I suppose he should be put away before he . . .' She

shook her head, tears slipping down her cheeks. 'I just can't think of my lad as a killer, Captain Meadows.'

'It is difficult,' Larch agreed. 'But there may be two sides to him – the soft, likeable lad and . . .' He shook his head. 'I saw what he did, Mrs Miller. If Sarah hadn't coaxed him to stop he would have killed.'

'And yet he is a hero in his way, isn't he? He saved Miss Beaufort's life.'

'Yes, he did, and I am grateful to him for that,' Larch agreed. 'I'll speak up for him, see if I can arrange for him to go back where he was . . .'

'I doubt if they will allow that, sir,' Mrs Miller said. 'It will be a secure institution now.'

'Yes, perhaps.'

'Would you do one thing for me, sir?'

'Certainly, if I can.'

'Will you give me one last day with him? Tell the police tomorrow?'

'I'm not sure. If you are thinking that you could take him away . . .'

'Oh no, sir. He will be here when they come. I promise you that.'

'Very well,' Larch said. 'But you must promise to keep him here if he comes back.'

'He is in the shed now,' Mrs Miller said. 'I saw him go in as we were talking. Just give me a few hours with him, sir.'

Larch looked at her and then nodded. After all, Ronnie had saved Sarah's life and it was still only conjecture, because he couldn't be certain that Ronnie had killed Simon Beecham. It seemed very likely, but that was not a matter for him. He must tell the police of his suspicions but then it was up to them.

'I'll give you the rest of today,' he said. 'And once again, I am very sorry to give you this news.'

'It isn't your fault, sir,' Mrs Miller said and smiled oddly. 'I suppose I've known this day was coming for a long time. Goodbye now, and thank you for coming to me first.'

She took her visitor to the door and stood waiting as he drove away, and then she went back into the house and started baking. She set the table with the results of her work and fetched the bottle of whisky she had been keeping in case she

needed it; she hesitated and then took a packet of tablets from
her apron pocket. She placed most of them between two sheets
of paper and crumbled them with her rolling pin, adding them
to the bottle of whisky and giving it a good shake. Then she
went out to the shed.

'Ronnie,' she said, smiling kindly at her son. 'Come in and
have some cake, love. I've baked your favourite.'

Ronnie looked at her, his eyes glazed. He was holding an
empty whisky bottle. 'I want some of the good stuff . . .' he
said, his voice blurred. 'Bad thoughts, Ma . . . bad thoughts
won't go away . . .'

'Come into the house, Ronnie. I've got a bottle of the good
stuff especially for you. You can drink as much as you like.'

Sarah was sitting in the parlour reading a magazine when
she heard a car draw up outside the house. She jumped up
and looked out of the window, pleased to see that Larch had
arrived at last. She went out into the hall as Millie answered
the door.

'Sarah.' Larch looked at her anxiously. 'I am so sorry that
I've been so long. I had to go to the hospital with Ashton. He
was still unconscious when I left, and then I had a difficult
hour with Mrs Miller.'

'You told her about Ronnie?'

'Yes, I did,' Larch said. 'I wanted to prepare her. She asked
me not to talk to the police until tomorrow, so I agreed. I
phoned and made an appointment for the morning.'

'Poor Ronnie,' Sarah said. 'I know you have no choice,
Larch. You have to tell them what you saw – and they will
draw their own conclusions, but it seems so cruel. Especially
after he saved my life.'

'Don't you think I feel that too?' Larch shuddered. He
moved towards Sarah, drawing her into his arms, holding her
pressed against his chest. 'If Ronnie hadn't been there I might
have been too late. If I'd seen that devil trying to strangle you
I might have killed him myself. I couldn't bear it if . . .'

Sarah looked up at him, smiling. 'I'm glad you came when
you did, Larch. I was terrified. Ronnie might have killed him
and who knows what might have happened then? I don't blame
you for saying that you have to tell the police. But it doesn't
stop me feeling sorry for him and his mother.'

'She took it very well,' Larch said. 'I think she must have known something. Or perhaps she just realized that Ronnie was becoming a menace.'

'Yes, perhaps,' Sarah agreed. She smiled and moved away from him. 'Now let's forget about it, Larch. Ben and Cathy have just gone. He said he would telephone you. I think he would like to meet, just to talk things through with you.'

'It really isn't anything to do with me,' Larch said. 'Father says he wouldn't have got involved with any of it if he had realized that it might put you in danger.'

'Nothing your father did affected me at all,' Sarah said. 'Actually, it was probably a good thing he brought Ben in, Larch, because I was involved anyway. Tommy liked me. He had been sending me flowers. I think Harvey may have visited the show too, though he denied it. Esther got the flowers meant for me, which means I was involved from the beginning. If Ben hadn't been investigating Giles Henderson's murder we might never have solved this mystery – and Tommy might still be alive, free to carry on killing women he thought of as sluts. If I had done something to displease him—'

'God forbid!' Larch stared at her. 'If that is the case it is as well that Ben became involved – but I think you should give up singing, Sarah. If being on the stage attracts nutters like that . . .'

'Please don't overreact, Larch,' Sarah begged. 'I promise you it isn't always like that – and I've had a telephone call from Janey. She is fine and enjoying herself with her friends. What happened was terrible and it upset me. I shan't deny that, but it will never happen again.'

'How can you be sure?' Larch asked. 'I'm beginning to agree with your father, Sarah. I don't like the idea of you living alone in London and being on stage. It makes you vulnerable – and Tommy Rowe isn't the only villain out there with ideas about women.'

'I am quite safe, because I don't go out with men who send me flowers,' Sarah said. 'When I do accept an invitation it is with a group of friends from the show. Please don't be like this, Larch. I get enough of it from Daddy. I thought you understood.'

'I do understand.' Larch ran his fingers through his hair. 'I've encouraged it, because I knew how much you wanted to do this, Sarah – but I didn't think being on the London stage would put you in danger. If I'd known I would never have—' He broke off, because he'd said too much. 'Haven't you had enough yet? I thought you might like to get married and—'

'You wouldn't have what?' Sarah had picked up on the very thing Larch hadn't meant to say. 'What did you do, Larch?' Her gaze narrowed, because it suddenly came to her. 'You didn't! Oh, Larch, please tell me you aren't our angel?' He was silent, obviously guilty. 'You are, aren't you? You backed that show just so that I got a job singing on stage at a London theatre. Larch! How could you do that to me? How could you?'

'What do you mean?' Larch asked, but he understood perfectly, because he knew that he had hurt her pride. 'You got the job on merit, I promise. I did give them a hint but I didn't make it a condition . . .'

'I thought I had got the job on my own,' Sarah told him. Her throat was stinging and she felt bitterly disappointed. 'Do you realize how humiliating that is for me? To know that I was given a spot in the show because you paid for it? I wish you hadn't, Larch. I really wish you hadn't.'

'I'm sorry, Sarah. I was going to tell you, but you were such a success that I thought it didn't matter. I made them promise not to tell anyone.'

'Yes, but they knew,' Sarah said. 'You've ruined everything! I'm right back at the start, because I have no idea whether I would have ever got anywhere or not without your help. You had no right to do it, Larch. No right!'

'I am very sorry. I didn't mean to upset you . . .'

'How did you think I would feel if I found out? I keep wondering if anyone knew, if they thought I was being favoured. I wanted to do it on merit, Larch.'

'I don't know what to say. You were out of a job and I knew you were worried. I just wanted to make things better.'

Sarah blinked back her tears. 'Please leave now, Larch. I'm sorry but I can't talk to you now. I just want to be alone.'

She walked away from him, and then ran up the stairs, leaving Larch to stare after her in dismay. If he had been in any doubt about wanting to marry her, knowing that Ashton had tried to kill her had cured him. He was in love with Sarah and he wanted her for his wife – but he knew that he had hurt her badly. By paying for her to get into that show, he had ruined the trust between them and he wasn't sure it would ever come back.

Sarah sat staring out at the moonlight. She had cried for a long time, but now she was calm. She felt drained, a little numbed, as if she had been ill. It wasn't just discovering that Larch had arranged for her to get the job in London, though that was the bit that hurt most. She was still upset about Ronnie Miller, because his was a cruel fate – to be shut away for the rest of his life.

She had given way to the shudders when she got home, something she had never done before. It had been a horrible experience in the woods, and she thought it would take her a while to forget.

Getting up to go to bed, Sarah had made up her mind. She would visit her father for a few days, and explain why she was going to accept her mother's invitation to visit her in America. She needed to get right away, give herself a chance to clear her mind completely. It had upset her that Larch had done something that humiliated her, and she wasn't sure how she felt about him anymore.

If he could do something like that, how could she trust him again?

'Telephone for you, Larch,' Sir William said as his son came downstairs the next morning. 'It's Mrs Miller . . .'

'Oh . . .' Larch frowned as he took the receiver. He hoped Ronnie hadn't run off again, because the police wouldn't be too pleased if they had to search for him. 'Mrs, Miller – what can I do for you?'

'I just wanted to tell you that everything is all right now, Captain Meadows. Ronnie won't be a danger to anyone ever again.'

'What do you mean?' Larch felt chilled. 'What has happened?'

'Ronnie passed away peacefully in the night,' Mrs Miller said. 'When he was a lad they told me it could happen at any time. He had a little problem with his heart when he was born, you see. Last night he just went to sleep and he didn't wake up. I've called you and then I shall call the doctor – but it is all over.'

'Ronnie had a heart condition?'

'Yes, as a child. He seemed to outgrow it, but it must have been getting worse, because he died last night. I wanted to let you know.'

'What did you do, Mrs Miller?'

Larch stared at the receiver as the phone went dead. He turned to look at his father, his face ashen.

'Ronnie Miller went to sleep last night and didn't wake up – at least that is what his mother says . . .'

'Good thing,' Sir William said. 'Better than shutting the poor devil up in a lunatic asylum, wouldn't you say?'

Larch felt cold all over. 'Yes, I suppose so but . . . I think she put him to sleep. I don't know how, but . . . What a damned fool! She asked me to give her until today before contacting the police and I agreed. I never dreamed she would do something like this . . .'

'Are you sure?' his father asked, frowning. 'Can't go around making accusations like that without proof – what did she say?'

'She said Ronnie had a weak heart as a child . . . the doctors told her he could die at any time.'

'It might be true,' Sir William said. 'And even if it isn't, it's not your business, Larch. I should say it's the kindest way out for the poor devil. Even if he did kill Simon Beecham it wasn't his fault. We all know who put him up to it. No, I think it would have been cruel beyond belief to shut the lad up in a lunatic asylum. If you ask me, justice has been served. No need to do anything more about it.'

'No, perhaps you are right,' Larch said. 'I shall simply tell the police what happened in the woods – how he saved Sarah's life. Leave it to them.'

'Yes, I agree,' Sir William said. 'You're showing some sense now, Larch. Why don't you do something even more sensible and ask Sarah Beaufort to marry you?'

'I'm not sure she would have me,' Larch said. 'We had a bit of an argument . . .'

'Lovers' tiff,' his father snorted. 'Go and apologize, Larch – and get your hair cut first! Make yourself presentable and you might stand more of a chance.'

'Yes, Father,' Larch said. 'I shall but I had better go and talk to the police first . . .'

'Have a good time with your father,' Amelia said. 'And don't let him bully you. I know it upset him when your mother left him for that American – but he has no right to stop you seeing your mother, my dear.'

'Oh no, I am sure he wouldn't try,' Sarah said and kissed her cheek. 'I just want to tell him and talk it over, because I don't want to hurt him. I know we've had words over me going on stage, but I still love him – and I know he loves me.'

'Yes, of course, dearest,' Amelia said. 'Write to me and come and see me when you get back.'

'Yes, I will,' Sarah promised. 'Goodbye now. Tell Rosalind I shall send her some postcards and I'll visit when I get back.'

'Yes, my love. Off you go now.'

Amelia went to the door to wave her off, Mr Tibbs weaving his way around her legs, purring loudly. She picked him up, stroking him thoughtfully as she watched Andrews driving the car away. Sarah was deeply upset about something, though she wasn't saying anything. If she were any judge, it had something to do with Larch. She would be giving that young man a piece of her mind when she next saw him!

'Sarah has gone to stay with her father,' Amelia said when Larch called on her later that day. 'Her mother has invited her to stay with her in America, and she wanted to tell him first.'

'Yes, she did say she was going to visit,' Larch said, frowning. 'I didn't realize she intended to go just yet.'

'I doubt if she did,' Amelia said. 'What did you do to upset her? You did upset her, didn't you? I know Sarah, and she is deeply hurt over something.'

'Yes, I think that is my fault,' Larch admitted. 'She guessed that I funded the London show she was in—'

'You did what?' Amelia stared at him in astonishment. 'What a very stupid thing to do! Surely you understood that this whole business of the singing comes down to Sarah's need to prove herself? Yes, I know she loves to sing, but I doubt she would ever have done it if her father hadn't told her she was a fool to try. He tried to bully her into giving up the idea and that made her more determined to prove that she could. Sarah is very stubborn, though the sweetest of girls – but you have to coax rather than bully. She had always been spoiled, given everything she wanted on a silver plate – singing was her way to prove that she could do something herself.'

'She couldn't get a job. I just wanted to make her happy . . . but I've made a mess of things, haven't I?'

'Yes, I rather think you have,' Amelia said. 'She will feel betrayed, because she thought you understood – believed in her talent.'

'I did – do,' Larch said. 'She was a brilliant success. The director wanted to give her a much bigger billing next time – and that wasn't down to me. She had earned it.'

'I know how good she was,' Amelia said. 'But you've hurt her pride, Larch, and that takes a little time to get over.'

'You don't think I should drive down to Hampshire – apologize?'

'No, I don't,' Amelia said. 'Write to her if you wish. Tell her why you did it and what the director said, and leave it to her to come back to you when she is ready.'

'I wanted to tell her about Ronnie Miller, too. He died in his sleep last night and the police have decided to let things lie.' He kept his suspicions to himself, because surely Mrs Miller had suffered enough.

'How odd,' Amelia said. 'He seemed such a strong young lad, but it is for the best no doubt. Have you heard anything about Mr Ashton?'

'Apparently, he is still unconscious,' Larch said. 'The police have put a constant guard on his room, but they seem to think he may have brain damage if he lives. So that may be another case that remains open, though unofficially closed.'

'Ben is hoping he will recover. He is very keen to get this business finished, though I understand he is going to visit Major Henderson and tell him what he believes happened.'

'At least he will know that Giles wasn't mixed up in any of it,' Larch said, looking at her doubtfully. 'So you think just a letter . . .'

'For the time being,' Amelia confirmed. 'Let Sarah have some time to herself, Larch. She has been through a lot lately.'

'Yes, she has,' Larch agreed. 'And I've gone and spoiled the best bit for her . . .'

'I think you can be pretty sure that Giles was killed because he stumbled on the truth about those jewel thefts,' Ben said. 'They were very nasty people, Major Henderson, and Giles was unfortunate. He got involved in something unpleasant – but he was not in any way to blame.'

'Thank you for telling me that,' Major Henderson said. 'I am resigned to the fact of his death, but this makes it easier to accept. I can move forward now. Will there be a trial?'

'Perhaps, if Ashton recovers his senses, but he hasn't yet and the doctors seem to think he may not. It is possible that he could remain in a coma for a long time and then die.'

'Well, it would have been nice to see him brought to justice,' Major Henderson said, 'but perhaps this is best in a way. You said the young lad who stopped him murdering Sarah has died in his sleep?'

'Yes, that seems to be the official view,' Ben said. 'Mrs Miller's doctor confirmed that he did have a heart problem when he was born, though he was thought to have grown out of it . . . something about a hole in the heart at birth. I don't know much about the condition but I understand it often clears up during childhood. Whatever, the authorities have accepted it and he was buried yesterday, I understand.'

'Well, that puts an end to his part in it,' Major Henderson said. 'Thank you for clearing up this mystery for me, Mr Marshall. What do I owe you?'

'Nothing. It was a favour for a friend,' Ben said. 'Glad to have been of help – but I couldn't have done it without Sarah. She was the one who finally worked it out – got there ahead of me again, though I had come to the same conclusion.'

'She sounds a very interesting young lady.'

'Oh, she is. I have hopes that she will marry a friend of mine very soon. He will keep her out of danger.'

'Surely nothing like this is likely to happen again, is it?'

'No, probably not,' Ben agreed and frowned. 'I hope not, anyway. She had a nasty experience this time – but knowing Sarah it won't stop her if she does get a whiff of another mystery . . .'

*   *   *

'I think that is an excellent idea,' Mr Beaufort said as they sat together over a glass of wine that evening. 'Yes, why don't you go and see your mother, Sarah love? I'll give you some money to pay your expenses.'

'Mother said she would repay my fare when I got there,' Sarah said. 'But I shan't say no if you want to give it to me, Daddy. I am a little short of money.'

'Why don't you let me restore your allowance, Sarah? You've proved your point, shown me you can do it – and I was a damned idiot to say those things to you in the first place.'

'But I haven't,' Sarah said and her voice wavered. 'I didn't know, but Larch backed that show in London. He made them promise not to tell anyone and he didn't make it a condition that I got a part – but it certainly made them anxious to please him.'

'Damned fool!' Mr Beaufort growled. 'But it doesn't matter, Sarah – the fact remains that you were a success. A big success – and deservedly so, my dear. I came to watch you several times, and I thought you were wonderful. I was very proud of my little girl.'

'Daddy! Why didn't you tell me you were there?'

'Because I didn't want you to think I was spying on you.' He smiled at her. 'You've won hands down, my darling. I take back everything I said, and if you want to return to the stage when you come back from your visit to America, I shall be with you all the way. I shan't go behind your back and put up the money for a show, Sarah – but if you will let me give you your allowance back, it will enable you to wait for the right show to come along.'

'It might not . . .'

'I don't believe that,' her father said. He was still an attractive man, rich, generous and very fond of his only child. 'You are too good to give up for a silly reason like that, Sarah. Larch made a mistake, but he did it for the right reasons, because he cares about you. He is the sort of young man I would like to see you marry one day – but not until you are ready. I want you to be happy, and if singing is what makes you happy, I am with you.'

'Oh, Daddy!' Sarah cried and hugged him. 'Thank you so much! I was feeling awful, but you've made me see that it doesn't really matter. I was a success. I truly was. Larch gave me the opportunity, but I proved that I could do it, didn't I?'

'Yes, my darling, you did,' he agreed. 'And now that you've agreed to let me give you your allowance . . .'

'Half of it,' Sarah said, and smiled as he pulled a face. 'You know you always gave me too much. You spoil me.'

'Because I love you,' he said. 'Half of it into your bank – and half of it into a trust for when you need it then.'

'All right.' Sarah smiled at him. 'Thank you very much. I must admit it was hard giving up all the things I had been used to – especially my car.'

'Well, it is still here when you want it. Come and see me again when you get home, Sarah?'

'Of course I shall. I'm not sure what I shall do then, Daddy – but I will certainly stay with you sometimes.'

'Then go with my blessing, my dearest.'

'Thank you,' Sarah said and hugged him.

She was thoughtful as she went upstairs to her room to begin her packing. She could take some of her good clothes and jewellery with her now that she had made it up with her father. She was feeling very much better about herself, and what had happened. She had proved herself on stage and perhaps it didn't matter so much that Larch had used his money to back the show, though she wished he hadn't done it.

As for the rest of it, she had come to terms with her near escape from death. Ronnie had saved her. She was grateful to him, and she hoped that the authorities would treat him kindly. Even if he had killed Simon he wasn't really a killer – not the way Tommy Rowe and Harvey Ashton were, cold-blooded and ruthless. He hadn't understood what he was doing and she knew she owed her life to him. He might have taken a life but he had also saved one.

She felt that all the mysteries were finally closed. Now she could pack her suitcase and look forward to her holiday. If a little voice at the back of her mind kept asking where Larch was and why he hadn't come to see her while she was staying with her father, she ruthlessly crushed it.

It could wait until she returned. Time would ease the hurt inside her and while she was away she would learn to forgive. In the meantime she was going to enjoy herself on a nice cruise to America. She hadn't seen her mother for a long time. She felt a little nervous about meeting her mother's new family but it was something she had secretly wanted to do – and it would certainly take her mind away from those horrible murders . . .